SUN
LIGHT

OTHER TITLES BY DEVNEY PERRY

Haven River Ranch Series

Crossroads

Sunlight

The Edens Series

Indigo Ridge

Juniper Hill

Garnet Flats

Jasper Vale

Crimson River

Sable Peak

Christmas in Quincy (prequel)

The Edens: A Legacy Story

Treasure State Wildcats Series

Coach

Blitz

Rally

Clifton Forge Series

Steel King

Riven Knight

Stone Princess

Noble Prince

Fallen Jester

Tin Queen

Calamity Montana Series

The Bribe

The Bluff

The Brazen

The Bully

The Brawl

The Brood

Jamison Valley Series

The Coppersmith Farmhouse

The Clover Chapel

The Lucky Heart

The Outpost

The Bitterroot Inn

The Candle Palace

Maysen Jar Series

The Birthday List

Letters to Molly

The Dandelion Diary

Lark Cove Series

Tattered

Timid

Tragic

Tinsel

Timeless

Runaway Series

Runaway Road

Wild Highway

Quarter Miles

Forsaken Trail

Dotted Lines

Holiday Brothers Series

The Naughty, The Nice and The Nanny

Three Bells, Two Bows and One Brother's Best Friend

A Partridge and a Pregnancy

Stand-Alone Novels

Clarence Manor

Rifts and Refrains

A Little Too Wild

SUN LIGHT

DEVNEY PERRY

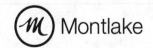

Text copyright © 2024 by Devney Perry
All rights reserved.

Published by Montlake, Seattle

www.apub.com

Amazon, the Amazon logo, and Montlake are trademarks of Amazon.com, Inc., or its affiliates.

ISBN-13: 9781662518973 (paperback)
ISBN-13: 9781662518966 (digital)

Cover design by Sarah Hansen, Okay Creations
Cover image: © Angyalosi Beata, © SpicyTruffel, © Oksana_Schmidt, © Teemu Tretjakov, © isciuceodor, © Wirestock Creators / Shutterstock

Printed in the United States of America

SUN
LIGHT

Chapter 1
JAX

The growl that echoed across the IGA's parking lot sounded more animal than human. "I'm calling the cops."

What the hell? The grocery store's double doors slid closed behind me just as I spotted Carla, the owner, facing off with another woman. Both clutched opposite ends of a shopping cart teeming with paper bags.

"I'm not stealing." The other woman gave the cart a tug. "I swear. Please. I just need to borrow this. I will bring it back."

Carla huffed. "You expect me to believe that bullshit?"

My truck was parked on the other end of the lot, but rather than head home, I walked toward the commotion instead.

"Give. This. Back." Carla jerked on the cart with each word, yanking so hard that the woman was nearly pulled off her feet.

"Please. These are my groceries. I just bought them. I only need to take them home." She flung out an arm. "It's three blocks. I'll be there and back in less than fifteen minutes."

"You're not stealing my cart."

"I'm not stealing—"

"Ladies." The tug-of-war stopped the instant I put my hand on the cart's metal basket. "Everything all right?"

"No, it's not all right." Carla's face was flushed as she whipped her attention in my direction. Her cheeks were as red as her fiery hair. "She's stealing my cart."

The other woman opened her mouth, then clamped it shut, taking a breath as she composed herself. Then she looked up to me, and my heart skipped.

Beautiful brown eyes. Long, straight hair in the same rich chocolate shade, the strands so sleek they reflected the bright afternoon sun. A heart-shaped face with delicate features and a dusting of freckles across her cute nose.

Damn. Who was she? Definitely not someone I'd seen around town before. Hers was a face I would have remembered.

"I walked from my house to the store." She enunciated every word with a calm, smooth voice. Every syllable worked to defuse the tension.

Any other person and she probably would have succeeded. Except Carla was . . . Carla. Rationality was not on her strengths list.

"I assumed the bags would be plastic," the woman said.

Ah. There was the mistake. Carla hated plastic.

"I hate plastic." Carla seethed. "It's bad for the environment."

The woman held up one hand while the other kept a firm grasp on the cart's handle. "I'm not arguing. I just assumed the bags would be plastic, and I could carry more than one at a time to my house three blocks away. I cannot carry all of these paper bags."

The cart had at least six plus a gallon of milk.

"You checked me out," the woman said, her pretty gaze pleading with Carla. "I bought ice cream to celebrate moving. I just want to get it home and in the freezer before it melts."

Carla pursed her lips.

"Okay." I dug out my wallet and plucked out a hundred-dollar bill. "Carla, how much are these carts?"

"Two hundred and seventy dollars plus shipping."

Of course, she had the price memorized. Carla might not be exactly levelheaded, but she ran her business with an iron fist.

"Take this." I took out two more hundreds and held up the money. "It's a deposit. I'll escort the cart to this woman's house and back. If I never return, you'll have enough to buy a new cart."

"Fine." Carla snatched the bills so quickly that she almost gave me a paper cut. Then she shot the woman a lethal glare before storming away.

"Oh my God." The woman let go of the cart, finally, lifting both hands to rub her temples. "I don't know if I should be furious or mortified."

I chuckled. "Carla gets a little worked up at times."

"Wow." She blew out a long breath. "Should I expect this every time I come to the store?"

"Nah. The only other time I've seen her this fired up was when she caught her son shoplifting condoms when we were teenagers. She still likes to throw that in his face, but it's only been fifteen years."

"Only fifteen?" The corner of her pink mouth turned up. God, she was pretty.

"Eventually Carla will let this go. It might take a couple decades, but I wouldn't give up hope."

She dropped her gaze to the cart, that faint smile still on her lips. "Thank you."

"Welcome."

"You don't need to escort the cart to my house. I promise to return it."

"Carla is, without a doubt, watching from the window. I'm not taking a chance that I'll land on her bad side, so you can either let me drive you or we can walk the three blocks. Just know that if you choose the ride, I'll immediately dive into a lecture about getting into vehicles with strangers."

"No lecture needed. I'll walk, thanks. But I'm not sure I want a stranger who I met in the grocery store's parking lot to know where I live either."

"Fair point." I chuckled. "I can produce references. The sheriff is a good friend. We can give him a call to come down and attest to my character. Though, chances are, your ice cream won't survive the wait."

"Then I guess for the sake of my cookies and cream, the walk is a risk I'll have to take." She gripped the cart's handle and started for the sidewalk. "Sorry about this. I'm keeping you from your own shopping."

"It's all good. My shopping is done." I dug the scratch tickets I'd bought inside from my jeans pocket, holding them up before tucking them away again. "I have a deal with my grandpa. Every week, I buy him lottery tickets from the two gas stations in town and the grocery store. In exchange, my grandma cooks me dinner once or twice a week."

"So your grandfather has the chance to win money, and you get free meals. What about your grandma? Seems like she's getting shortchanged."

"Well . . . I do give her hugs when I go over for dinner."

She raised two perfectly arched eyebrows.

I leaned in closer. "I'm *really* good at hugs."

Her eyes sparkled as she let out a quiet laugh. She settled into a swift, natural pace.

The cart's wheels were a rattle along the concrete, drowning out the muffled thud of my cowboy boots as the first block disappeared too quickly.

"I'm not sure I've ever met someone who walks as fast as you." Normally, I'd shorten my stride to walk beside a woman, but not this one. "I'm guessing it has nothing to do with the ice cream, does it?"

"I walk fast." She shrugged as we reached the first corner, each of us checking both ways before crossing the intersection. Then we were on the sidewalk again, already barreling down block number two.

Except I wasn't ready for this walk to be over quite yet. Not quite so fast.

"Tell me a lie."

She slowed—mission accomplished—and her eyebrows knit together. "Huh?"

"A lie. Tell me one."

"Why?"

"Why not? A lie seems more interesting than small talk."

"No one has ever asked me to tell them a lie before." A ghost of a smile tugged at her lips. "All right. I love grilled cheese."

"What?" I came to a dead stop. "You don't like grilled cheese?"

"Not even a little bit."

I smacked a hand to my heart. "That's one of two things I can actually cook."

"What's the other one?"

"Breakfast for dinner. I'm really good at hugs and pancakes." And delivering orgasms, but that was something I preferred to show women, not tell.

"I've never had breakfast for dinner," she said.

"Excuse me?" My jaw nearly hit the concrete sidewalk. "You've never had breakfast for dinner. That's . . . a travesty."

"Sorry to disappoint." She smiled, wider this time, and continued walking.

"Tell me a secret."

"Secrets and lies? This might be the weirdest conversation I've ever had with a stranger."

Weird. But, hopefully, unforgettable.

She pondered it for a few moments, then said, "I don't like cats."

"You're a monster." I feigned horror, slapping a hand to my heart again. "Carla was right. You were going to steal this cart, weren't you?"

She laughed, and it transformed her, like she'd turned on a light and it radiated through her face. Those brown eyes dazzled, revealing flecks of gold and cinnamon. Her straight white teeth flashed as pink colored her cheeks.

Well, fuck.

Now I was in trouble.

"In my defense, I'm allergic," she said. "But I'd rather have a pet spider than a cat, and I'm also terrified of spiders. Not that I'm scared of cats. I just don't like them. They're too independent."

"What about kittens?"

"They're cute. But not as cute as puppies."

5

"So you're into dogs. Thoughts on horses?"

"I've never been around them before."

Never had breakfast for dinner. Never been around horses. Both were problems I wanted to solve.

Except before I could invite her out to the ranch for a ride and dinner, she pointed to a duplex building ahead with tan siding. Somehow, blocks two and three had gone faster than the first. "That's my place."

It was an older home, but the yard looked freshly mowed, and other than the junk car in the neighbor's driveway, the street seemed quiet. Across the road, her other neighbor had crammed their yard with inflatable Halloween decorations.

"I'll just run these inside quickly," she said, stopping at the mouth of the walkway that led to her front door.

"Want some help?"

"No, that's okay."

"All right." Maybe someday she'd invite me inside. But until the day I wasn't a stranger, I wasn't going to push.

She took two trips with the bags, rushing them inside, until everything was unloaded, and she rejoined me on the sidewalk.

"I can take this back," I told her, turning the cart.

"Mind if I tag along? At this point, my honor is at stake."

Hell yes. "Who am I to deny you your honor?" I grinned as she fell into step at my side, letting me push the cart on the return trip.

"Your turn. Tell me a lie," she said.

"I never lie."

"Is that the lie? Or are you saying you can't tell me a lie because you never lie?"

I winked.

"That's not an answer." She rolled her eyes. "Fine. How about a secret?"

"I have no secrets."

"Everyone has secrets."

"Not me." Certainly not in my small hometown. Around here, everyone's dirty laundry hung out on the line, side by side, mine included.

She studied my profile as we walked. "You're really not going to spill?"

"I told you. I can't lie, and I've got no secrets." I kept my gaze straight ahead, fighting a smirk.

When was the last time I'd flirted with a woman like this? College, maybe? The girls around town were sweet, but flirting wasn't exactly required. My good looks were usually all it took to get a woman in bed. That, or my last name.

But damn, this was fun. Refreshing. There was something different about this woman. She'd challenge me, wouldn't she?

At the moment, I couldn't think of anything else I'd rather do than work for it. Hell, I didn't even know her name.

"You're having ice cream tonight. How about dinner first?" I asked. "They don't have pancakes, but the Thirsty Turtle makes great burgers."

She stayed silent and kept walking.

With every step, my heart ratcheted higher and higher toward my throat. My nerves spiked. Was she thinking about how to turn me down? For the first time in a long damn time, I was about to get rejected, wasn't I?

She made me wait, my dinner invitation hanging between us as we crossed the last intersection and walked all the way into the IGA's parking lot.

"You're risking your reputation by being affiliated with a suspected thief," she finally said.

Fuck yeah. That was a yes. I was taking it as a yes.

"A risk I'm willing to accept." I held out my hand. "I'm Jax Haven."

"Haven." Something like panic flashed across her expression, her eyes flaring wide. "As in Haven River Ranch?"

"Yes," I drawled. Most of the time my last name worked in my favor. So why was the color leaching from her face?

"Oh. Um." She worried her bottom lip between her teeth as she took a step away, then another. "Thanks. But I think I'd better stick to my ice cream. Nice to meet you."

Wait. What? Before I could ask for an explanation, she turned and walked away.

I stood with my hand latched on the shopping cart, my jaw slackened, until she disappeared from view. "What the actual fuck?"

No. She'd told me no?

Had I read that wrong? We'd been flirting, right? What the hell was happening right now?

My good mood turned to shit as I pushed that cart back to the rack and stalked inside, then held out my hand for Carla to return my money. The moment she slapped it into my palm, I left without a word, stomping to my truck.

I drove to the ranch, bruised ego riding shotgun. Then I made myself pancakes for dinner and did my best not to think about the dark-haired beauty who should have been sharing them with me.

~

"How long is this going to take?" I asked West.

"I don't know. Ten minutes."

I sighed. "Why am I even here?"

"Because you're an owner of this resort." He gave me a sideways glance. "What's wrong with you today?"

"Nothing," I lied.

My brother frowned. "Then stop being so damn grumpy."

"Now you sound like Dad," I muttered.

I loved West, but the problem with me being nine years younger was that there were times when he treated me more like his son than his brother.

We were standing in the lodge's lobby beneath the glowing antler chandelier. Smiling guests were milling around, sipping coffee and hot cider. A family of four was at the desk, luggage waiting at their feet as they checked out.

Everyone was so damn happy this morning. Everyone, except me.

"Let's just get this meeting over with." Then I'd disappear to the stables to saddle my horse and go for a long, hard ride. Maybe a day spent outside, enjoying the crisp fall air, would help me forget about the woman I'd met yesterday at the store.

Her rejection gnawed deeper this morning, somehow worse than it had last night as I'd tossed and turned, replaying every minute of that walk. I couldn't even cuss her name because I didn't fucking know her name.

Yet she knew mine. And clearly, it was reason enough to run in the other direction.

Was she friends with a woman I'd hooked up with before? Maybe she knew I had a preference for one-night stands, and she'd wanted to steer clear. But how? She was new to town, right? Unless I was more infamous in the single-female circuit than I'd realized.

"Stop." West smacked my arm.

"What?" I barked.

"Stop scowling. Plaster on a smile, for fuck's sake. This is important to Indya."

I showed him all my teeth.

"Shithead," he muttered.

Relaxing my lips, I did my best to soften the frown that I'd been wearing since yesterday. "I don't know why we needed to hire a manager. I told you that I'd take over while Indya was on maternity leave."

"You've got plenty on your plate. And I've got plenty on mine. We need help at the rate we're growing. Having someone who can be here to manage the lodge and resort will make all our lives easier."

"Fine." I crossed my arms over my chest. "He or she better not boss me around."

"She. And I'm sure she won't."

"Indya bosses me around."

He chuckled. "Me too."

The only woman in the world West would gladly take orders from was his wife. And maybe their daughter, once she was born.

Voices drifted from the hallway that led toward the executive offices, and West turned, a smile stretching across his mouth as Indya's curly blonde hair came into view.

Normally, I'd tease him for being such a goddamn sap when his wife was in the room.

Except it was impossible to form words with my jaw on the floor.

Beside Indya walked Grocery Store Girl.

Beautiful. Striking. As perfect as yesterday.

Fuck me sideways.

Indya's smile brightened as she came to stand by West's side. "Guys, I'd like you to meet Sasha Vaughn, our new manager. Sasha, this is my husband, West, and my brother-in-law, Jax. Together, the three of us own the ranch and resort."

Together was generous. I owned a mere fraction of this place compared to West and Indya. But those details didn't really matter today. Not when I was staring at stunning brown eyes and that splash of freckles across smooth skin.

Sasha. Her name was Sasha.

"Nice to meet you." West shook her hand. "Glad you're here."

"So am I, Mr. Haven."

"West. Just West," he corrected.

"West." Sasha gave me a polite smile as she faced me next. There wasn't a flicker of surprise or familiarity on her face. Not that there would be. She knew who she'd be meeting this morning. Me?

Totally fucking clueless.

"It's nice to meet you." She extended a hand in my direction.

So that's how she wanted to play this, huh? To pretend like yesterday hadn't happened?

Fine. I'd play that game. For now.

"Nice to meet you too." The moment our hands touched, tingles raced beneath my skin. The widening of her eyes said she felt it too. I smirked as I held her delicate fingers for a moment too long, then let her go. "Welcome to Haven River Ranch, *Sasha*."

Chapter 2
SASHA

Three months later . . .

A clunk echoed through my shower. A clunk that lingered, like it was making its way through a maze of pipes.

My hands were in my hair. My fingers were covered in shampoo suds. Lukewarm water cascaded down my naked body.

Until it didn't.

"No. No, no, no."

The water slowed to a trickle.

"Oh my God." I still needed to rinse.

"Come on." I twisted the knob, turning it back and forth. "Please."

Off. On. Off. On. Nothing.

The only water left rushed down the drain with a gurgle.

I groaned, dropping my forehead to the wall. "You've got to be kidding me. How is this my life?"

I hated this shower. I hated this rental.

I hated Montana.

Goose bumps spread over my skin as the air turned cold. I hurried out of the shower, wrapping my body in a towel. Then I squeezed out as much soap and water as I could from my hair before rushing to my closet to pull on a pair of warm sweats.

Maybe the water would come back on soon, but if I waited too long, I'd be late for work. And at the moment, work was the only positive thing in my life. I couldn't be late.

That, and there was a shower in the women's locker room guaranteed to have hot water.

So I quickly collected clothes, a brush, my hair dryer, and my makeup case, then stepped into a pair of snow boots before heading out the door.

The cold air was startling. One breath and my lungs froze. Before I even made it to my car, my wet hair began to turn white with icicles.

I slid behind the wheel of my Mazda, my body shaking with the chill that seeped into my bones. It took me two attempts to get the key into the ignition. The engine made a wheezing sound, protesting the start, but finally turned over. When I cranked the heat, it just blew frigid air into my face, so I shut it off.

As the dash illuminated, the thermometer read negative ten.

"What am I doing here?" I rubbed my hands together, then cupped them to my mouth as I blew hot air into my palms.

Teeth chattering, I waited a few minutes as the car warmed up, and when the windshield was finally defrosted enough for me to see, I eased onto the snow-covered street, shooting a glare at the duplex attached to mine.

The neighbors were probably still asleep. They'd spent their night having loud, wild sex and making sure their headboard banged against our adjoining wall as many times as possible. *Assholes.* It had gone on until three in the morning. I'd climbed into the shower around five.

God, I needed to move.

Somewhere warm. Somewhere quiet.

Somewhere with hot running water.

Except for now, I was stuck in Montana. I was stuck in a shitty house. I was stuck with the below-zero temperatures. I was just stuck.

Stuck in so many ways, I'd stopped keeping track.

But at least I was stuck with a good job.

I took Big Timber's side streets slowly as I made my way to the highway. Driving on snow was a skill I had yet to master, and my two-wheel-drive car handled ice about as gracefully as a giraffe would roller skates.

It made for a harrowing forty-five-minute trip to the Haven River Ranch. Every day, I looked forward to this drive less and less.

When I'd moved here three months ago, I'd enjoyed the drive from home to work. I'd liked the time alone on an open road. I'd soaked in the scenery, the sprawling fields stretched between rugged mountain ranges.

But then the first winter storm had blown in, and the commute had become pure stress. I actually missed California's rush-hour traffic, not something I'd ever thought I'd admit.

My knuckles were white by the time I turned off the highway and onto a frozen gravel road. But I didn't truly breathe until I passed beneath the resort's archway. "Made it."

This trip might be the only victory for today. One I needed to repeat on the drive home.

I forced my shoulders away from my ears as I inched my body back from the steering wheel. Then I tapped the brake to slow for the last bend in the road.

One moment, I was aimed straight down the gravel lane. The next, my rear tires skidded to the side.

"Oh shit." I turned the wheel, frantically trying to correct.

It only caused the front wheels to start skidding too.

"Stop. No." I gasped as the car moved closer and closer to the ditch. "Please stop."

I stomped on the brake.

The car just kept on sliding. Straight into the ditch, where it stopped with a muffled thump.

"Damn it." I pressed the gas. The engine revved, but the car didn't so much as budge.

This wasn't happening. Not today.

I was so close. I could see the red tin roof of a guest cabin ahead. I could practically smell the bacon and eggs cooking in the lodge's dining hall.

"Ugh." I dropped my forehead to the wheel. A lock of wet hair fell from my tie and smacked me in the cheek. "I hate Montana."

Maybe if I was an outdoors person, I wouldn't mind trekking through the glittering morning snow. Maybe if I'd slept for more than two hours, I wouldn't have snoozed my alarm and my shower wouldn't have been cut short. Maybe if I had made better decisions over the past ten years, I wouldn't be in Montana in the first place.

Yet here I was, collecting my tote crammed with toiletries from the passenger seat. Because like it or not, I'd be walking to work.

The car was tilted sideways, and when I attempted to open the door, it just slammed closed on my arm. So I twisted, using my feet to push hard enough to shove it wide. Then, with my tote looped over a shoulder, I wiggled out, instantly sinking into knee-deep snow.

Icy clumps filled my boots. "You suck, winter."

Like Mother Nature heard me, a gust of wind whipped ice crystals into my face.

Bitch.

I trudged forward, practically clawing my way out of the ditch and onto the road. Then I brushed as much snow as I could off my sweats before slogging toward the lodge.

My breath billowed around my face in a white cloud. My hair regrew those icicles before I'd even made it fifty feet. The sting of cold in my nostrils was so sharp it brought tears to my eyes.

People chose to live here. Permanently. People came to visit here. For. Fun. Seriously?

I was not that kind of person.

But I was the kind of person who needed a paycheck, and this one was the best.

An engine rumbled in the distance. "Please be West. Please."

Indya's husband would rescue my car and not make a production out of it. He wouldn't ridicule me for the rest of my life for driving into the ditch.

It wasn't West's truck that appeared from around the bend. Of course it wasn't. My luck showed no signs of improving today.

The gray Silverado that came into view belonged to the last person on earth I wanted to see this morning.

Jax Haven.

He wasn't alone. Of course he wasn't alone.

Mindi, one of my front desk clerks, was riding in his passenger seat.

Which meant by noon, everyone on the resort would know I'd gotten stuck.

"What am I doing here?" I muttered. "This is not my day."

Jax slowed to a stop, rolling down his window to flash me an arrogant smile as white as the snow. "Morning, Sasha. Stuck?"

"No, I just thought I'd test out a new area for employee parking," I deadpanned. "Of course I'm stuck."

Very, very, very stuck.

His sky blue eyes crinkled at the sides as he looked me up and down, his grin turning into a lopsided smirk.

That freaking smirk. It was just so cocky, like whatever retort went through his head was infinitely amusing. On any other man, it would have looked condescending, but somehow, it worked on his gorgeous face—which made it all the more aggravating.

Did he smirk at everyone? Or was I just the unlucky recipient? In the past three months, I couldn't think of an encounter with Jax when that smirk hadn't been an obnoxious intruder.

Well, there'd been the grocery store. He hadn't smirked at me then. But I did my best not to think about that day. About how differently that day might have gone if Jax wasn't technically my boss.

"Hey, Sasha." Mindi leaned forward and gave me a finger wave. Her smirk *was* condescending.

"Hi, Mindi."

"Your hair is freezing." Mindi excelled at stating the obvious. "You should dry it on cold mornings like this."

"Great advice," I muttered, then shifted my attention back to Jax, who was fighting a laugh.

"Hop in." He jerked his chin to the back seat. "I'll run you to the lodge, then we'll get your car out."

"Thank you." I climbed in the truck, sighing at the warmth and scent.

Cedar and spice and citrus, like he'd peeled an orange this morning and the smell lingered on his fingers.

He'd probably peeled that orange for Mindi.

She was wearing a hoodie that was massive on her petite frame. She'd probably stolen it from Jax's closet. She'd been flirting with him for weeks, and apparently, all that effort had finally paid off.

Well, I hoped she didn't get too comfortable in that seat. Since I'd moved to Montana, I'd heard from more than one woman that Jax was a brazen playboy and flirt.

Considering how we'd met, it wasn't hard to believe.

"I was just telling Jax this weather is, like, really cold," Mindi said.

"Yep." I popped the *p*. "It's cold."

I hated small talk. I really hated small talk about the weather.

Jax's eyes met mine through the rearview mirror as he turned us around for the lodge. "Mindi, Sasha hates talking about the weather."

"She does?"

"She does," Jax and I said in unison.

Wait. How did he know that? "How did you know that?"

"Your lip curls whenever it comes up."

It did? *Huh.* And he'd noticed. Why?

"It's just the weather." Mindi giggled. "Everyone talks about the weather."

My lip curled automatically.

This time, Mindi noticed it, too, and held up her hands. "Fine, no weather. Jeez."

"I just . . ." I massaged my temples, the headache blooming in my skull. "It's been a morning, and I just want to wash the shampoo out of my hair. I'm not good company at the moment."

Not that I was particularly chatty with Mindi on a normal day. We hadn't exactly hit it off in the three months I'd been working at the Haven River Ranch. I was her boss and was perfectly fine maintaining a professional relationship.

That rule extended to Jax too. Besides, cowboys weren't my thing.

"Figured you'd take the weekend off," Jax said.

"There's a lot happening. I want to get in as much time as possible before Indya goes on maternity leave."

"Even on a Saturday?"

"Even on a Saturday. Not everyone can gallivant around on the weekends."

He scoffed and glanced to Mindi. "I don't gallivant. Do I gallivant?"

"No." She batted her eyelashes as she giggled.

When Jax chuckled, I eyed the door's handle. For the first time in my life, I considered a tuck-and-roll exit.

Had I already become the laughingstock? During my first week here, I'd been talking to a guest who lived in Big Timber. He'd brought his wife out for their anniversary weekend, a short getaway to enjoy our spa and chef's cuisine. When I'd told him I was from Sacramento, he'd joked that most Californians only endured one Montana winter.

Maybe he was right.

What the hell was I doing here?

I didn't belong. Everyone in this truck, everyone on this ranch, knew I didn't belong.

But my job as the resort manager paid nearly double my previous salary. And sure, I'd run out of water this morning, and my neighbors were amateur porn stars, but the rent was dirt cheap.

Right now, I needed every penny.

So Jax and Mindi could laugh. They weren't wrong. I didn't belong.

But I wasn't leaving. Not yet.

I breathed as Jax pulled up to the employee entrance at the lodge. At least he wouldn't make me walk through the lobby with frozen, soapy hair and sweats that had seen much, much better days. I wasn't even wearing a bra yet.

"Thanks." I jumped out, about to make my escape, when Jax rolled down his window again and held out a hand. Was that for like a high five or something? "What?"

"Keys."

"Oh." Subzero temperatures, yet my face flamed around this man. Damn it. That really, *really* needed to stop.

"Um . . . thanks." I fished the keys from my purse and handed them over. Then, as I backed away, I curtsied.

In a parking lot, wearing ratty sweats, I curtsied like I was greeting the queen of England. My tote slipped off a shoulder, nearly throwing me off balance before I straightened.

What was that? I didn't curtsy. Ever. Not once in my life had I curtsied. Why the fuck was I curtsying? This was a nightmare. This was like those moments when a waiter said "Enjoy your food," and I replied with "Thanks, you too." What was wrong with me today?

Jax, as expected, smirked.

Before he rolled up his window to drive away, I raced for the door.

The employee locker rooms weren't spacious, but thankfully, they were empty. And after a long, hot shower—dressed in a pair of jeans and my warmest sweater—I tracked down a cup of scalding coffee and retreated to my office.

"A curtsy?" I cringed as I sat behind my desk.

Someday, when I was far, far away from Montana, I'd probably think back to that moment and laugh. But not today. Today, I fought the urge to curl into a ball beneath my desk and hide for all eternity.

Since that wasn't an option, either, I spent the next few hours buried in work, doing everything in my power to forget about the morning. To get Jax's smirk out of my mind.

Three months I'd been on the receiving end of that smirk. The first had come the day after we'd met, my first morning as manager of the Haven River Ranch. The morning I'd pretended I'd never met Jax before.

He'd smirked, and I'd been seeing it ever since. And after three months, everything about him set me on edge.

That man took nothing seriously, and any time that we had a management meeting, he acted more like an employee than an owner. He was so cavalier. So carefree. So ridiculously attractive it made me irrationally angry.

Why did he have to be so hot? Why did he have to be the grocery store guy? Why couldn't he work *anywhere* else?

"Hi, Sasha." Indya knocked on my open office door and stepped inside. Her curly blonde hair cascaded around her shoulders, a section draping into her face as she dug through her purse, retrieving my keys to set them on the desk. "West parked your car in its usual spot."

"Thanks." I blew out a long breath. "I feel like such an idiot."

"Don't." She waved it off. "People get stuck around here all the time. No one cares."

"I'll tell him when I see him next, but would you pass along my thanks to West?"

"Sure." She moved to a guest chair, not so much sitting as leaning back far enough to finally recline in the seat, her hands automatically splaying across her pregnant belly.

Indya, along with West and Jax, owned Haven River Ranch. They had more wealth than I could ever dream of amassing—not unlike most of our guests at the resort. We catered to a rich clientele across America. But despite her riches, Indya was sweet, down to earth, and . . . normal. Working for her these past three months had been a dream.

In another life, I would have wanted to be her friend.

In this life, I'd settle for being her employee.

"It's beautiful out today." Her eyes drifted past me to the windows overlooking the patio.

I pivoted my chair, following her gaze.

The sun sparkled off the snow. The sky was a cloudless blue. Steam billowed from the outdoor hot tub. It was a winter paradise. At least, that's what we pitched to our guests.

Yes, it was beautiful. But why did it have to be so cold?

"You don't like winter, do you?" Indya asked.

"I'm partial to summer."

"Do you like it here? In Montana?" The look on her face was so hopeful I almost lied.

"It's, um, different. I'm not really the outdoorsy type, so it's been . . ." *Awful.* "An adjustment. My rental isn't exactly dreamy either. The neighbors are, um, loud. And there's been a couple maintenance problems."

Indya's eyes bulged. "Do you hate it here?"

This time, I did lie. "No, I don't hate it."

She studied my face for a long moment. "Sasha, be honest. Do you like this job?"

"Yes." It was the truth. "I'm just struggling with winter. It's not my favorite."

"Are you miserable? I don't want you to be miserable."

"Not miserable." I wasn't happy, but I wasn't miserable either.

"Please don't quit," she whispered, panic lacing her voice.

"I'm not going to quit."

"Are you sure?"

"Yes, I'm sure."

"What can I do?" Indya held out her hands like she could magically bind me to this chair. "What can I do?"

"Nothing. It's fine. Really." More lies. Nothing about me being in Montana was fine. But it was necessary. For now.

"Can I ask a favor? If you decide to leave, please come and talk to me first."

I nodded. "I'm not going to leave. But if that changes, yes, I'll talk to you first."

Her shoulders sagged. "I'm spending the afternoon catching up in my office on emails if you need anything. West is bringing the boys over later for the Saturday campfire."

It was a tradition at Haven River. Every Saturday, they built a fire outside on the patio where kids could cook hot dogs and roast s'mores. Guests would enjoy burgers grilled over the open flame. Before the snow, there'd been yard games and activities on the lawn. Sometimes, Indya hired a local musician to sing and play guitar.

The Havens made sure to attend every Saturday. Usually, West and Indya were here. Though Jax often came too. I made it a point to be available as well to support the staff and mingle with guests.

The smell of campfire smoke always stuck in my hair. It usually wasn't a problem because I'd go home and shower before bed. But tonight, there were no guarantees I'd have water.

"Do you mind if I miss tonight's campfire?"

"Not at all," Indya said. "It's always optional."

"Thanks. I can be sure to attend after the baby is born."

"Jax promised to be here too. Maybe you two can coordinate."

"Of course." I stifled a groan.

Whether I liked it or not, Jax was unavoidable. And with every smirk he sent my way, it was a silent reminder of the day we'd met. How I'd been shouting over a shopping cart. How I'd shamelessly flirted while my ice cream had melted in a paper grocery bag.

I was a mess. I'd been a mess for ten years.

Fake it until it breaks you. That was my motto. I worked hard to hide the disaster that was my life. But Jax had seen the real me. He'd seen the disaster that was Sasha Vaughn.

Was it really a wonder that he smirked?

At least we didn't work together on a daily basis. Unless he was in the lodge to visit with Indya, our paths didn't cross often. West spent most of his time doing work for the ranch and cattle operation. Jax managed the guest excursions and worked primarily out of his office in the stables.

"Before I have this baby," Indya said, stroking her belly, "I'd like to have you start coordinating with Jax on guest excursions. He manages most of it, but we usually meet once a week to sync up."

"I doubt he'll need my input." Ugh. My lip curled before I could stop it.

And Indya, sharp as a tack, definitely noticed. "Is Jax a problem? Did he do something?"

"No. It's . . . I just don't think I'll have anything to offer. That's his area of expertise. I don't think he'll appreciate me getting in his way. We're not exactly, um, friends."

"So he is a problem."

"No." I waved it off. "It's fine. He's fine. Everything is fine."

Indya stared at me so long I began to squirm. She didn't want me to quit. Thank God. But I definitely couldn't afford to get fired. Especially if she thought I had a beef with Jax.

"I'm happy to meet with him," I assured her. "No problem. Coffee? I'm going to get more coffee. Can I get you anything? Water. Tea. Cookie."

"No, thanks." She narrowed her gaze. "Sasha, are you okay?"

"Great!" I lied, swiping my empty mug from the desk as I shot to my feet. "Probably too much coffee. I'm a little jittery. I'd better switch to water."

She was still in my office, still in the chair, looking at me like I'd sprouted wings, as I breezed for the door, then vanished down the hallway.

"Shit." Freaking Jax.

This was his fault. He'd flustered me this morning, and now I was frazzled. Or maybe it was the shower. Maybe it was the car. Maybe it was the lack of sleep.

This was not my day.

I refilled my coffee in the lobby, desperate for the caffeine, then retreated to my office. Indya had moved to her own. The moment I sat behind my desk, my phone rang.

Micah.

I scrambled to answer. "Hey. Hi. Thanks for returning my call."

"Hey, Sasha."

"How is he? Is he okay?"

"It's, uh, been an adjustment."

I almost laughed at his word choice. But as far as adjustments went, mine was minor compared to Eddie's. "But is he . . ." I couldn't even finish the question.

Alive. Was he alive?

How bad was it that I simply wanted him to be alive? How had we gotten here?

"He's all right," Micah said. "Like I told you last time, there's not much I can tell you."

"Can I talk to him?"

Micah hesitated, and it was answer enough. "Not yet."

Was that Micah's decision? Or had Eddie point-blank told him he didn't want to speak to me? I wasn't sure which hurt worse.

"Keep writing him letters," he said. "He's reading them."

Did those even count as letters? So far everything I'd written had been short. "I don't know what to say to him. They're just notes at this point."

"That's all right. Say anything. They don't need to be long or profound. Sometimes less is more. He just needs to know you're there."

"I am here," I whispered past the lump in my throat. "Thanks for checking in."

"No problem. We'll talk soon."

"Bye." I ended the call and squeezed my eyes shut.

Not to keep tears at bay. There were no tears.

I'd cried myself dry a long time ago.

Sometimes, it felt like a bad dream, and if I closed my eyes tight enough, if I blocked out every sound and sight, when I opened my eyes, I'd wake up and it would all be okay.

Except when I opened my eyes, it was to that blinding white winter beyond my windows. I gave it my back and went to work. Lunch—two granola bars I dug out of a drawer—was spent at my desk.

Afternoon was bleeding to evening as I finally took a break to return my empty mug to the kitchen. The room was bustling with activity as the staff prepped for tonight's campfire meal. I slipped in and out, not stopping to say hello to Reid, the resort's chef.

A yawn tugged at my mouth on the way back to my desk. Voices drifted from Indya's office, and I veered toward her open door, hoping to say thanks to West for rescuing my car.

I stopped short as Indya pointed her finger in Jax's face. "You have to be nice to Sasha."

"What?" Jax scoffed. "I am nice to Sasha."

"Then why does she hate you?"

Hate was a strong word. I never said *hate*.

"Did she actually use the word *hate*?" Jax asked.

"No. But she's not your biggest fan." Indya clasped her hands together. "I'm begging you. Be nice. I need her to stay until after my maternity leave."

"I am nice."

"Then be *nicer*," she said.

"Fine," he grumbled. "Did you have to hire someone so . . . uptight?"

Uptight. Uptight? I was not uptight.

Before I could stop it, a growl clawed its way free from my throat. West, Indya, and Jax all whirled at the sound.

But I was already gone, storming to my office. My hand gripped the door's edge, ready to slam it shut. Yet I held back the rage, easing the latch closed with a soft click. Then I sat down and wrote Eddie a letter.

Voices drifted from the outside patio as I fixed a stamp on the envelope. Guests bundled in coats, hats, and gloves stood beneath propane heaters, every person wearing a smile with their winter gear. A group of men waved as West and Jax joined them around the campfire.

I gathered my things, pushed my chair into my desk, and turned off the lights before I retreated to my car in the lot. The drive home was as harrowing as it had been earlier.

There was a note tucked into my door from my landlord, apologizing about the water. He'd fixed part of the issue, so the cold worked, but I'd be without hot showers until Monday.

It should have been a relief. Coming home after a stressful day should have felt good. But as I crawled into my bed, I just felt numb.

The moment I closed my eyes, the shouting started. If the neighbors weren't screwing, they were fighting.

I squeezed my eyes shut so tight it made me dizzy. "What am I doing here?"

Even a pillow over my head didn't muffle the noise from next door. Finally, after an hour, they stopped screaming. I heard a door slam, then an engine roar to life. Then silence. Blissful, incredible silence.

I was asleep in seconds.

The sound of howling wind woke me with a jerk. It rattled the windows and screamed through the night.

"Seriously?" I grumbled and climbed out of bed, then shuffled to the bathroom. I flipped on the light and went to the sink—except the reason I hadn't washed the makeup from my face was because I had no hot water.

Cold would have to do.

I turned on the faucet and squirted a glob of soap onto my fingertips. One moment, I was grimacing at the dark circles beneath my eyes. The next, the house went pitch black.

What. The. Hell?

The wind seemed to laugh, taking pride in knocking out my power.

"I hate Montana."

Dear Eddie,

It was so cold this morning that when I went outside, my wet hair froze into icicles. It was like a blast into the future to see what I'll look like with white hair. I've never felt cold like this before. I'm not sure I'm made for winter.

Are you warm? Do you like the snow? I think about you every hour of every day.

Someone at work called me uptight today. I was angry at first. It hurt my feelings. But he was right. I am uptight. I'm not sure I know how to relax and slow down. I pushed you too hard, didn't I? I was so busy trying to stay busy that I didn't realize things were bad until they were so far gone we couldn't recover.

Stay warm, okay? I miss you.

S

Chapter 3
JAX

Be nice. Indya had ordered me to be nice to Sasha.

Damn it, I was nice. I'd been the epitome of nice since the day we'd met at the grocery store. Did anyone on the ranch know about the shopping cart fiasco? No. Because I'd kept my mouth shut. Since she'd started working at the resort, hadn't I been civil? Hell yes, I'd been civil, despite the fact that she barely acknowledged my existence. Who'd hauled her car out of the ditch on Saturday? Me.

That was me being nice.

But all of the niceness wasn't doing a damn thing to win favor with Sasha. All I'd gotten in three months was a frosty stare and some snarky comments. Saturday, she'd added a mocking curtsy to her repertoire.

A smarter man would probably give up. Move on. Every encounter with Sasha was brutal for my ego.

Except I couldn't get her out of my head. I liked her snarky comments. That mocking curtsy had been cute. There was no reason her frosty stare should be attractive, but damn if it didn't turn me on. Maybe because I knew, down to my bones, that the vibrant woman I'd met in the grocery store parking lot was in there somewhere. She *had* to be in there somewhere.

It had been three months. Three fucking months, and she still wouldn't admit we'd met before her first day at the lodge. Why?

The reason she'd turned me down for dinner that day had to be because of her job at the resort. It was understandable. Granted, she could have just told me she was coming to work at the ranch, but whatever. Maybe she'd been embarrassed. I wasn't her boss, but as an owner, I wasn't *not* her boss, and those lines were blurry.

But was friendship out of the question? At this point, I'd settle for being an acquaintance. I'd take anything other than her cold shoulder. Three months, and Sasha still hadn't thawed.

She was so damn uptight—probably shouldn't have said that out loud Saturday, but it was true. And whether she liked it or not, we were going to have to work together. While Indya was on maternity leave, Sasha and I would need to spend more time together.

I refused to spend those weeks working with an ice queen.

It was time to clear the air. For good. Maybe then I could get Sasha Vaughn and her pretty brown eyes out of my head.

I stomped my boots outside the lodge's front door, kicking off the last bit of snow before stepping inside. A blast of warmth greeted me in the lobby. The scents of bacon and brown sugar filled the air. The clink of utensils on plates and the murmur of conversation sounded from the dining room. The antler chandelier hanging from the rafters cast a golden glow through the room.

Indya had changed a lot about the resort in the past seven years. She'd expanded the lodge, adding a spa, fitness center, and locker rooms for our staff. She'd turned our old barn into an event venue for weddings and parties. She'd renovated cabins and guest rooms. She'd transformed our family's small business into a premier Montana resort. We were booked solid for the next two years, and the waiting list was a mile long.

But even though there had been countless changes, Indya had also stayed true to our family's roots. The sentimental areas had been left mostly untouched.

Other than some additional lighting, the lobby looked just like it had when I was a kid. Rustic, wooden walls. Oak floors my grandfather had installed himself. And that antler chandelier my grandmother had commissioned specifically for this space.

This was one of my favorite places on the ranch. The energy from guests. The nostalgia. The food and hot coffee. Every time I visited, it felt like home.

The lodge used to be a regular stop in my daily routine. I'd swing in to refill my thermos or grab an employee sack lunch from the kitchen. On days when I wasn't slammed, I'd bullshit with Indya in her office or talk to guests milling about.

But I'd been avoiding the lodge lately.

Because of Sasha.

No more. This had to stop. We didn't need to be friends, but I was sick and tired of seeing her frown whenever I walked into a room.

"Morning," I told Mindi as I crossed the lobby.

"Hey, Jax." She fluttered her fingers at me from the reception desk.

"Is Sasha here?"

Mindi nodded. "She's in her office."

"Great." I started for the hall, but before I could disappear, Mindi stepped out from behind the desk, blocking my path.

"Thanks again for the ride on Saturday," she said.

"No problem. I was going into town anyway." Grandpa needed his scratch tickets.

Mindi had hitched a ride to the ranch on Saturday morning for her shift. The friend who'd dropped her off had left for the day, planning on coming back to pick her up that evening. Except Mindi wasn't working on Saturday. She'd gotten her schedule mixed up.

So I'd offered to give her a lift home so she wouldn't have to sit around the lodge all day.

I moved to sidestep Mindi, but she put her hand on my arm and inched closer. Too close.

Well, shit. Mindi was nice enough, but I wasn't interested in anything romantic. Not even a little. Now things were going to get awkward.

"Do you want to get a drink or something after work?" She batted her eyelashes as she asked the question.

Why did women bat their eyelashes? It didn't do a damn thing for me, but it happened a lot.

Wait. Had she actually gotten her shift wrong on Saturday? Or had it been some sort of ploy?

"Look, Mindi. I appreciate the offer, but no, we can't get a drink or something after work."

"Oh." She pouted.

I hated pouting.

"It's because I work here, isn't it? Since you're, like, my boss's boss." She glanced over her shoulder, making sure we were alone before she lowered her voice. "I could quit."

What the actual fuck? She'd quit her job for a date? I did not understand women. "Don't quit your job."

"Are you sure? I don't love working for Sasha. She's very . . ."

Professional. Composed. Organized.

"Bossy," Mindi said.

"She *is* your boss."

"Yeah, but you know what I mean."

No. I really didn't. "Don't quit your job, Mindi. Okay?"

Another pout.

Time for this conversation to be over. I tugged my arm loose from her grip. Part of me wanted to leave it at that and just walk away. But I wasn't sure Mindi was the type to read between the lines. So I made sure my message was perfectly clear.

"Even if you weren't working here, I don't think us dating is a good idea."

Her eyes blew wide. "What? Why not?"

Once upon a time, I'd make up some ridiculous nonsense, like how I was afraid of commitment or how I had too much personal baggage for a relationship. But more often than not, any time I'd shown my red flags, it'd lured women closer rather than sending them running.

Apparently, they saw me as a challenge. A guy they could fix.

"I like someone else," I told her. And it was the truth.

"Oh. Then why were you flirting with me on Saturday?"

Seriously? She thought me talking with her about her dog was flirting?

"Well, I'm late for a meeting with Sasha." I stepped around her, successfully this time. "See ya around."

She harrumphed. "Yeah. I guess."

Yep, awkward. Fantastic. That was exactly how I *didn't* want to start my Monday.

I raked a hand through my hair as I made my way down the hall. Then I smoothed down the front of my coat and took a fortifying breath before I reached Sasha's office. My heart was racing as I stepped across the threshold.

What was it about Sasha Vaughn that was so damn frazzling? No woman had ever unnerved me this way. That meant something, right?

I cleared my throat and knocked on her open door.

Her pretty eyes shifted away from her monitor. For the briefest moment, they widened and her mouth parted, like her breath hitched. Then that unguarded surprise was gone, replaced by the cool stare and blank expression.

Grrr. It was infuriating and annoying and . . . gorgeous. There was no reason for a woman that irritated by my presence to be so hot.

"Come in," she said, her voice flat.

I stood in the doorway and crossed my arms over my chest. Today, I didn't really feel like taking her orders.

"Or not," she muttered, smoothing the hair at her temple. She'd slicked it into a bun above her nape. Uptight.

And stunning. As stunning as the winter paradise beyond the windows at her back.

Other than Saturday, when her hair had been wet and frozen, I rarely saw her with it loose and long like she'd worn it at the grocery store.

Like most days, it was smoothed to perfection. Not a strand out of place.

God, what I wouldn't give to tug free that hair. To unravel this woman with my hands and watch her come apart beneath my touch.

But since that wasn't likely to happen, it was time to do what I'd come here to do. Starting with an apology.

"I'm sorry I called you uptight."

"Oh." She blinked, clearly expecting me to continue with something else. Her guard dropped, for just a moment, her shoulders sagging. But as quickly as they'd fallen, they snapped into place, her spine stiff and her voice impassive. "I am uptight. No need to apologize for stating the truth. It's fine."

Was it fine? She didn't sound fine. "You're also smart. And hardworking. And beautiful."

A flush of pink colored her cheeks as she looked anywhere else but at the door.

For once, it was nice not to be the only one frazzled here. I shoved off the door's frame and walked into the office. Sasha's eyes snapped to mine.

"According to West, I take next to nothing seriously," I said. "Maybe being a little uptight isn't a bad thing."

She watched me cautiously as I sank into one of the chairs in front of her desk, relaxing into the seat to kick up an ankle over my knee.

"Indya told me that we need to start coordinating on guest excursions."

"Yes." She cleared her throat.

"All right." I nodded. "What do you need?"

"I honestly don't know much about your side of the business."

"Then I'll give you an overview." Since Sasha had started as manager, her focus had mostly been on the lodge. Housekeeping. Maintenance. Dining. If it occurred under this roof, it fell under her umbrella.

In just three months, she seemed to have picked up a thorough understanding of all the resort's operations. It was incredible how quickly she'd picked it all up.

Indya hadn't wanted to overwhelm Sasha with the excursions, too, not when she'd just started. But now that Sasha was settled, there was more to learn.

"Maybe we could walk through how the scheduling works," she said. "That way I can answer questions from guests. Right now, I just send those questions to Indya."

"Sure. Would be good for you to take a few of these excursions too."

"Oh, uh . . ." She shook her head. "That's okay. Just the logistics will be fine."

"Not even a hayride?"

"Allergies." Her eyes flicked to the ceiling. It happened so fast I almost missed it. Almost.

Sasha wasn't allergic, was she?

"And horses? Allergic to those too?"

"No. But I'm not really a horse person."

"Yet you took a job at a Montana guest ranch where horseback riding is a main draw."

"For the guests."

"Why not you?"

She shrugged. "I'm not particularly interested."

"Ah." The corner of my mouth lifted. "Scared of horses?"

"No." That pretty gaze flicked skyward again.

Interesting. I'd seen that flicker before, but I hadn't realized until just now what it meant. Did she know that she looked up when she lied? It was a dead giveaway.

A smirk stretched across my mouth. It was going to be fun watching for her lies.

"Excited for the party on Saturday?" I asked, changing the subject.

"Not especially. I'm not really a party person."

This woman. No hayrides. No horses. No parties. Did she hate all fun things?

Saturday was the annual Haven River Ranch employee celebration. It was a tradition that Indya and West had started five winters ago. Rather than host a big Christmas party during a hectic time of year, we threw a party in January for the staff.

For one night only, we shut down nearly everything on the resort. We blocked out the day so there were as few reservations as possible. Often, staff members would rent rooms, so they didn't have to drive into town. We ran the lodge with a skeleton crew so that as many people as possible could participate.

There'd be a local band in the event space for dancing. We'd have food and drinks all night. We'd even run a shuttle to and from town for the folks who didn't spend the night, so no one would be tempted to drive home drunk.

"It's a fun night," I told Sasha. "Don't skip it."

"I wasn't planning on skipping." Another eye flicker. Another lie.

I grinned and shook my head, about to bust her for this one when the phone on her desk jingled.

She picked it up, glancing at the screen. "I have to take this."

"Find me later when you want to talk about scheduling."

"Okay." She glanced at the door, a clear *get out and be quick about it.*

I shoved to my feet and walked out as I heard her answer the call. "Hey, Micah."

Micah. Who was Micah?

If I asked, I'd probably just get another lie.

So I pulled her door closed, then retreated toward the lobby. That had gone about as expected. Not bad. Not great. But not bad.

Luck was on my side when I emerged from the hall. Mindi was on the phone with a guest, so I could skip another awkward moment. I lengthened my strides, wanting to duck out before she finished. I was nearly to the door, nearly free, when it opened, and Lily walked inside.

Damn. There'd be no avoiding awkward, not today.

35

"Jax. Oh, um, hi." She masked the surprise quickly as she stomped the last bit of snow from her shoes.

"Hey."

"Hi." She tucked a lock of dark hair behind her ear. There were more strands of gray than normal. I guessed she'd stopped getting it colored. "How's it going?"

"Fine," I clipped.

Was she going to move? Or just block the door forever? Definitely should have taken the employee side entrance today.

"I'm meeting West for some coffee and breakfast if you'd like to—"

"Can't." Join them? Absolutely not. I'd gladly have breakfast with my brother, but not Lily. I nodded to the door she was still blocking. "I've got to get to work. I'm taking out the hayride today."

Granted, it wasn't until three, and I didn't need more than an hour to prep. Something Lily knew. Unlike Mindi, Lily could read between the lines. And I'd rather muck stalls than share a breakfast table with her.

"Right." She winced as she shifted out of the way. "I'll let you get to it."

Without a goodbye, I opened the door and slipped past her outside. A gust of icy wind blasted me in the face, the cold doing little to cool my rising temper as I marched to the stables.

Lily had been coming to the resort more often these days. Too often for my liking. Every time, it was like a slap in the face.

She'd been married to Dad for years and used to manage the resort. As a kid, the hours I'd spent in this lobby had been at her side. But she was West's mother, not mine. Something she'd made abundantly clear.

So if she drove out here to see him, fine. This was his ranch. But she could leave me the hell alone.

I wasn't her son—that had been her choice, not mine.

Lily was the only mother I'd ever known. She'd changed my diapers. She'd rocked me to sleep. She'd sung me lullabies when I had bad dreams.

But she'd drawn a line. I was nothing more than the bastard child from Dad's one-night affair decades ago. Lily had drawn that line.

It would be great if she could fucking respect it and leave me the hell alone.

By the time I made it to the stables, the edge to my anger had dulled. I opened the door and breathed in the scent of hay and dirt and horses. There was only a handful of animals inside today. Most of the others were outside grazing the hay that we'd put out for them this morning.

This building was another one of Indya's upgrades. It was massive, with spacious stalls for the animals and plenty of room for storage. Next door was another new building—a shop where we kept our equipment and tools out of the weather. Both the stables and shop were set away from the lodge but close enough that guests could make the short walk for their excursions.

I walked down the long center aisle to my office, then opened the door and flipped on the light. While Sasha's office was organized and clean, mine was a disaster. Paperwork was scattered across the desk. The calendar on the wall was two months behind. The trash can was overflowing with wadded-up schedules and a few crushed beer cans.

If Sasha wanted to review the excursion process, it would be easier to do it out here than in the lodge. But I had a feeling that she'd take one look at my mess and run the opposite direction, so I snagged the trash and carried it out to the larger bin we kept by the stalls.

A horse nickered, the sound echoing through the wooden rafters, just as the door opened. The light from outside was a flash of white before it vanished as Dad stepped inside, closing out the cold behind him.

He stomped his boots and tugged off his leather gloves. "Hey."

"Hi."

"Figured you'd be out here. Just ran into Lily in the lodge."

She'd probably taken one look at him and changed her mind about breakfast altogether. Or maybe that was why he was here. He'd been the one to run away.

While I hadn't spoken much to Lily in years, not since our big fight before I left for college, we still acknowledged each other, even if those interactions were short and stunted.

But she hadn't spoken a word to Dad in years. Not a single word. She'd taken the silent treatment to a whole new level.

"What's up?" I asked Dad.

"Thought I'd see if you needed any help today."

"No, not really."

"You sure?"

"Yeah. I'm good. It's quiet today."

"Oh." Dad frowned. Was he bored or something? Dad wasn't great at being idle, and even though he'd been retired for over seven years, he was still adjusting to the slower pace.

Mondays in the winter were the quietest days for guest excursions. It was too cold for long trail rides. Most of my team had the day off, and while we offered private riding lessons, none of the current guests had signed up, giving me most of the day off too.

We had a handful of snowmobiles for tours around the ranch, but that particular excursion didn't run on Mondays. Today was the hayride with hot cocoa. So the stables were quiet. The spa, on the other hand, was slammed on Mondays.

"I could do the hayride," Dad offered.

"Really? It's freezing."

"I don't mind."

Then he must be desperate. The last time Dad had offered to lead an excursion had been, well . . . I couldn't remember when. Definitely not when the temperature was below zero.

It had been before Indya had bought the ranch. And before that, West and I had managed them all with the staff.

Dad sighed. "I'm just trying to help out. If I can."

"Ah." Was this offer to win favor with me? Or West?

There was a lot of tension between my father and older brother. Years ago, Dad had gone behind West's back and sold the ranch to Indya. It was before West and Indya had gotten together.

For me, that betrayal had faded with time. For West? I wasn't sure he'd ever really get over it. Everything had worked out in the end, but my brother's hard feelings had lingered.

While the sale had dented my relationship with Dad, it had nearly broken his with West.

"If you really want to do the hayride, I'm not going to stand in your way." There were a few projects waiting for me at home I wouldn't mind tackling.

"Great. I'd love to do it." He clapped me on the shoulder, then put on his gloves. "I'll be back this afternoon. Ride's at three?"

I nodded. "Yeah. Three o'clock. Guests can swing by the dining room to pick up their beverages. Then they'll walk over here to load up."

"Sounds good." He waved, then headed for the door.

Once he was gone, I spun in a slow circle, making sure there wasn't anything urgent for the day. Then I shut the lights off in my office and made my way to my truck parked outside to drive home.

The lane was nothing more than two narrow, beaten paths of tire tracks in the snow, but I didn't need much of a road. Not when I was the only person who came this way regularly. On occasion Dad or West or my grandparents would swing by my house, but for the most part, I didn't have many visitors. I had this quiet, secluded slice of the Haven River Ranch to myself.

Ages ago, my grandparents had built two cabins for full-time employee housing. They'd been used for a time when Dad was a kid, but that was long before I'd been born. Most of my life, they'd sat empty, suffering the Montana seasons year after year.

When I was a kid, the cabins had been my hideaway forts. As a teen, my friends and I had snuck out and thrown parties inside. Then after college, when I'd moved home to live on the ranch, I'd decided to take them over for myself, restoring them piece by piece.

It had taken years of sweat to turn them into homes. Most of the remodeling I'd done myself, stealing West's help when I'd needed extra hands. My house was finished now. I'd done a massive add-on a few years back, and it hardly resembled the small place it had once been.

The other cabin had been my most recent project. Since I wasn't living there, the updates had been slow, but after months and months, it was nearly finished too.

I owned the five hundred acres surrounding my houses. A gift from Indya and West I still wasn't sure I deserved.

While she and West owned the bulk of the acreage, my grandparents along with Dad and me each had a sizeable chunk too.

Mine was the prettiest spot on the whole property. West argued the plot where they'd built their house was better—my brother wasn't wrong often, but in this case, he was wrong.

The sprawling meadow that surrounded my house was blanketed in snow. The evergreens were kissed with frost, glittering beneath the morning sun. A plume of steam rose from the furnace vent in my roof.

I cut a path in the snow to the cabin beside my house and headed inside. The oak floors were new, and I wanted them to stay perfect for a little while longer, so I toed off my boots as I stepped inside, then made my way to the laundry room at the rear of the house.

It was the last space to be completed. Every other room was done and furnished. The stone tile was in place and needed grout. Then I'd finish up with some sealant and bring in a new washer and dryer.

Dad thought fixing up this place was a waste of money. He thought bulldozing it to the ground would have been a better use of my time. Maybe he was right. It was fifty yards from my own house, and I had no desire for a neighbor. But the idea of leveling one of Grandpa's creations didn't sit right.

Sure, it looked different than it had when he'd built it. But it was still standing. That counted for something, right?

I'd saved as many pieces as possible. On both houses, I'd kept the original wooden siding and used it for accents to the new board-and-batten. I'd refinished and rehung a few of the original doors, one to my pantry and the other to this laundry room. I'd even saved one of Grandma's old claw-foot tubs for my primary suite's bathroom.

With my supplies ready, I got to work, grouting the whole floor just as my stomach began to growl, hungry for lunch. I was at the kitchen sink, washing up, when the sound of an engine rumbled outside. I dried my hands and headed to the door, opening it just as West climbed out of his truck.

"Hey." I waved him inside.

"Hi." He shook my hand as he stepped inside, his boots joining mine. "This place looks great. You've done a lot since I was here last."

"Thanks. It's been keeping me busy since Christmas."

He walked deeper into the house, turning around in a slow circle. "You furnished it all?"

I shrugged. "I figured maybe this could be a guest house whenever we have company who don't want to stay at the lodge."

Not that we ever had much company. I certainly didn't. No aunts or uncles. My grandparents had their own house. Dad had his. My college buddies came from time to time, but it was rare.

Maybe I'd just sleep over here when I needed a different view.

West hummed, rubbing a hand over his stubbled jaw. "This might work."

"What might work?"

"I, uh, need a favor." He took another slow spin before facing me again. "I need you to let Sasha live here."

Not a chance I'd heard that right. "Say that again."

Chapter 4
SASHA

There was an email pulled up on my computer screen. The words blurred together into fuzzy gray smudges. This was my third attempt at reading the message. It was from a wedding planner in Phoenix. Her bride wanted . . . something. Every time I got to the second sentence, my mind wandered.

My brain was stuck on that call from Micah.

There'd been an incident with Eddie yesterday. An "altercation," according to Micah. Meaning another fight. They'd had to sequester him. Again.

Micah couldn't expand on the details. Eddie's program came with strict confidentiality protocols. But because there'd been a need for medical treatment, he hadn't wanted me to be surprised when I saw the added charge on my upcoming invoice.

I'd asked to speak with Eddie, but Micah had told me not yet.

Just keep writing letters.

Was that going to be Micah's answer for everything? Letters?

The last thing I wanted was to write another note. Every time I slipped one in the mailbox, it felt like sending a piece of my heart into the void, knowing I'd never get that piece back. But if that was all we had, then so be it. We'd get through this. *I'd* get through this. Even if it meant letters.

So after Micah had ended our call, I'd written a note to Eddie.

It wasn't much. My letters seemed to get shorter and shorter. Maybe when Eddie replied, when we developed a dialogue through these messages, I'd have more to write. Until then, short would have to do.

After the envelope was sealed and stowed in my tote, ready to be taken to the post office on my drive home, I refocused on my email. Reading it for the fourth time was the charm. The bride wanted to do pictures on horses for their wedding shoot, but not just any horses, two black horses. Did we do that? Did we have two black horses?

Replying to that email meant asking Jax.

I didn't want to talk to Jax, not again. Not twice in one day. If I wasn't thinking about that call with Micah, then I was replaying every second of Jax's visit this morning.

How good he'd looked in my office chair, his jaw stubbled and his hair unruly. Disheveled had never been my type until Jax.

He'd smelled so good too. He always smelled good, but there'd been a hint of soap, like he'd just showered. He'd been apologizing to me while I'd been picturing him naked. I bet he had great abs and a rock-hard ass. I bet he could curl a woman's toes with a single kiss. I bet sex with Jax was—

"Focus, damn it," I muttered. Stop thinking about sex with Jax.

"Sasha?"

My attention whipped to the doorway, where Indya was standing in the threshold. Heat bloomed across my face as I gulped. "Oh, hi."

"You okay?"

I forced a smile. "Great. How are you?"

"Good." She smoothed a hand over the oatmeal sweater that stretched over her belly. "I have something I wanted to show you. An idea."

"All right." I stood from my chair, grateful for anything that would get my mind off Jax Haven. "What's up?"

Indya walked to the rack in the corner and lifted off my coat. "You'll need this. And I'm going to need you to keep an open mind."

"Okay," I drawled. *Ugh*. Anytime I was told to keep an open mind, I hated the outcome.

"It's a good thing, I promise," she said as I put on my parka and followed her into the hall. "Do you trust me?"

"Of course," I lied. I wasn't sure I trusted anyone at the moment, not even Indya.

"Let me just grab my coat." She ducked into her office, quickly returning with a tan canvas Carhartt jacket that was so big on her frame it must have been West's. But it zipped up over her belly, even if the sleeves draped past her fingertips.

She covered her curly hair with a beanie, then led the way through the lodge and to the exit door that opened to the employee parking lot. Her SUV was running and ready.

"So where are we going?" I asked as we both climbed inside, the leather seats warm beneath my jeans.

"You'll see." She winked and pulled away from the lodge.

Rather than start down the road that would lead toward the highway, she turned past the stables and shop, weaving through the snow-covered lanes around the resort.

The road hadn't been plowed, and if not for the path of tire tracks, I wouldn't have even known this was a road. We were surrounded by a sea of white in every direction.

For a moment, I thought she'd take the path toward her home, but when we passed the turnoff, I glanced around, trying to figure out where we were going.

"You've never been out here, right?" she asked.

"I don't think so, but honestly, with the snow, I can't tell." I lifted a hand to shield my eyes. I should have grabbed my sunglasses before leaving the office.

The sun was shining in a cloudless blue sky, its rays catching the blinding white and reflecting it in all directions. If it wasn't so damn cold, I might have liked the snow. It was clean and crisp. But the temperature on the dash had a minus in front of the number.

I was withering with that minus.

Where were we going anyway? Surprises were not my favorite. At all. Part of me being *uptight*.

Indya had taken me on a ranch tour after I'd first started working at the resort, but those initial weeks had been a whirlwind. Maybe we'd come out here, but I couldn't remember now. There'd been so much crammed into my brain over the past three months that it had been impossible to retain it all.

"When I first moved to Montana and took over at the resort, West lived out here," she said. "We lived in his house until our place was built. A few years ago, there was a massive water leak, and because we didn't come out often, we didn't catch it soon enough. By the time we found it, the damage was so bad that we ended up just tearing the house down."

"Oh no. I'm sorry."

She gave me a sad smile. "Me too. It was one of the original homes on the ranch. Broke West's heart the day he had to demolish it."

I knew what it meant to say goodbye to an important house.

"Curtis lives out this way," Indya said, pointing straight ahead through the windshield. "Past his house is Alan and Sarah's place."

West and Jax's grandparents were regular visitors at the lodge. While I didn't know them well, they were always kind when we crossed paths.

Indya turned off the road and onto another. The tire tracks were thinner this way, the road narrower.

Was she planning on an expansion or something? Maybe another building out here for guests? She'd mentioned wanting more private cabins, but this seemed too far from the lodge. Our staff would have to trek out here to clean. And for anyone who arrived without a car, we'd have to provide transportation back and forth. It was too far to walk, especially as she kept driving.

But all of the reasons this wouldn't work vanished the moment we passed a grove of trees and two stunning homes came into view. They sat in the middle of a blanketed meadow, the forest and mountains their backdrop.

The exterior of both houses was a brown so dark it was nearly black. The barnwood planks used as accents were graying and worn, like those boards had weathered a hundred Montana winters.

The largest of the two had an attached garage and was bigger than any of the other private chalets. The smaller cabin was finished in the same style, with enough space between the two buildings that guests wouldn't be on top of each other.

While they had a rustic style, it was a bit different than those cabins by the lodge. These had a fresh, modern edge.

Indya drove to the smaller cabin and parked. "Come on."

I followed her inside, taking off my boots as she did the same. Then we padded in our socks around the cabin. "This is adorable."

"Isn't it?" She ran her hand across the back of an oversize leather chair. On a cold day like this, I'd love nothing more than to curl up under a blanket in that spot and read.

I couldn't remember the last time I'd read a book. I used to love to read. Maybe I'd take up reading again while Eddie and I were apart. How many books would it take to fill that void? Five? Twelve? Ninety-one?

"So this is my idea." Indya clapped. "Your current living situation, well . . . sucks."

I opened my mouth to argue but snapped it closed.

I'd hinted about enough problems with my rental that she knew she was right. Just this afternoon, after Jax had waltzed into my office and rattled my nerves, I'd told her about the water and power outages over the weekend.

"It's not the best," I admitted.

"There are still weeks of winter left. The drive back and forth to town is stressful this time of year. And while I'm on maternity leave, your hours could become unpredictable. I don't like the idea of you on icy roads in the dead of night. So my suggestion is that you should move in here."

"Here. Here?" I pointed to the floor. The lovely oak floor stained a chocolate brown.

"Yes."

"What about our guests?"

"This isn't available for guests," she said.

"It's not?" My eyebrows came together. Where were we? "Then what—"

"Just say yes." She clasped her hands in front of her chest. "Please?"

My gaze drifted to the couch. It was the same leather as the oversize chair. It could use a toss pillow or blanket, but otherwise, that was a couch for Friday-night movie marathons and Sunday-afternoon naps.

Everything was so nice and clean and fresh. Staying here would be a dream.

I couldn't afford dreams. Literally.

"How much is rent?"

Was I really considering this? Did it matter the price? It would be at least twice the amount I paid for in town. I couldn't afford this cabin. There was a reason I had a shitty rental. Shitty rentals came cheap. Sure, I was making a fantastic salary working for Indya, but I needed every penny at the moment.

"It's rent-free," she said.

I choked on my own breath, coughing for a moment. When I finally cleared my throat, I managed to eke out, "Rent-free? What?"

"I know things have been hard, and I want to make them easier. I can't do anything about the weather. But I can make your life a bit more comfortable."

Comfortable? Compared to my rental in town, this was as comfortable as a plush bathrobe and fuzzy slippers.

I worried my bottom lip between my teeth as I glanced into the kitchen. White cabinets with clean lines. Marble countertops. Stainless steel appliances that looked brand new.

Free. Rent-free.

"It's too much," I said. "This is too generous."

"Then you can pay the same rate you're paying for your place in town."

"Indya," I groaned. She wasn't making this easy for me. "I can't."

"Sure you can. Just say yes. It's easy."

Damn it. Was it easy? I didn't even know what easy was anymore. And this seemed too good to be true.

Indya must have read the indecision on my face. "How about you stay out here until after the party? Don't make any decisions yet. See if you like it first."

A one-week trial? That I could manage. I was about to agree when a knock came at the door.

Then Jax walked inside.

Wait. Why was he here? Where were we? Who lived in the big house next door? The questions started spinning.

"Hey." He jerked up his chin to Indya. "All good?"

"Yes?" Indya looked to me, nodding like she was expecting me to mimic the motion.

I glanced between the two of them. No. Not good. Not good at all.

Indya frowned, the hope on her face dying a quick death. "This is Jax's cabin. He lives in the house next door. I swear I was going to tell you. After you agreed to try it for a few days."

"Ah." Too good to be true. As expected.

It was smart of Indya not to tell me that at the start. I wouldn't have gotten into her car. "Look, I really appreciate the offer. But I think for right now, I'll stay where I'm at. I like being in town."

It wasn't entirely a lie. It was nice to be seconds from the grocery store, even if I did my best to go there as infrequently as possible.

"Are you sure?" she asked.

"I'm sure."

She sighed. "Okay. Well, if you change your mind, it's here."

"Thank you," I told her, then glanced at Jax, about to tell him the same. Except he was wearing the freaking smirk. God, I was tired of that smirk. It was condescending and arrogant and fucking hot. Damn him for being good looking.

"What?" I snapped.

"Nothing." He held up both hands, his smirk stretching. *Gah!* "Like Indya said, it's here if you change your mind."

"I won't." I walked over to my boots, pulling them on. Then I waited at the door for Indya to join me.

The ride back to the lodge was quiet. Awkward. Indya didn't ask why I had an issue with Jax. So far, I'd let her assume it was his chaotic, cavalier persona that rubbed me the wrong way.

Really, it was me.

It was always me. I was the problem.

And it all stemmed from that day at the grocery store. I couldn't look at him without thinking of that day. About how much I'd wanted a date. Or a kiss.

Why couldn't I forget it? Why couldn't he be just another coworker? Why couldn't we laugh about shopping carts?

Because I'd made it weird. Because I'd turned him down without reason. Because I'd tried to ignore him for months and keep everything strictly professional, but then I'd started thinking about him naked, and what the hell was professional about naked thoughts? Nothing.

Nothing. Nothing. Nothing. I wanted to see Jax Haven naked, and that was the crux of my problem.

Well, one of my problems. The list was long.

God, I was a mess.

We made it back to the lodge and retreated to our respective offices. I worked for the rest of the day, and after I'd spent an hour at the front desk, greeting guests on their way to the dining room for dinner, I headed to my car.

The drive home was slow and stressful—normal. And when I walked through my front door, the state of my living room was about as depressing as the balance in my bank account.

I didn't have a plush leather chair for reading. No couch for napping. No TV for watching. There wasn't a single piece of furniture in any room but my bedroom. Did an inflatable mattress count as furniture?

I had a lamp. That was something, right? And I had my laptop to watch Netflix. My subscription was the biggest splurge in my monthly budget.

The state of my cupboards was also depressing, but thankfully, I loved cold cereal. Fruity Hoops? Cinnamon Crunch? Honey Nut O's? My cupboard was stocked with store-brand knockoffs. I pulled down the box of Coco Roos, Eddie's favorite, and ate from one of three bowls I owned. Then I left it in the sink with an inch of chocolate milk in the bottom.

I'd clean it up tomorrow.

With nothing else to do, I retreated to my room and changed into a pair of sweats. Then I snuggled under my blankets and cuddled with a pillow, watching a movie until I fell asleep.

A pounding on the wall woke me with a jolt. I gasped, sitting up and shoving the hair out of my face.

"Fuck you!" a woman screamed outside.

I crawled out of bed, blinking away sleep as I rushed for the window to peel back the vinyl blinds.

A woman I'd seen a handful of times was standing in the middle of the street, both arms and middle fingers raised as she continued to scream obscenities into the night sky. "You motherfucker! I hope you rot in hell, bitch! Fuck you, asshole! Fuck you!"

"Shut up." I let the blinds snap into place as I banged my head against the wall. "Shut up. Shut up. Shut up."

For one night, for just one night, I just wanted to sleep without interruption. No power outages. No howling wind. No orgies next door.

No cursing women.

"I hate Montana," I muttered, trudging out of the room. Now that I was awake, there'd be no sleeping until the shouting stopped. Guess I'd wash my bowl from dinner.

Except I never made it to the kitchen.

Because as I was crossing through the living room, the front door burst open.

The locked front door.

A very drunk, very confused, very large man burst inside.

And vomited on the carpet.

～

Dear Eddie,

I miss you. I miss your cereal bowls in the kitchen sink. I miss you telling me you'll wash the dishes tomorrow. I miss your water bottles in every room. I miss tripping over your shoes when I come through the front door. I miss your laundry scattered everywhere. I miss your laugh. I miss your smile.

I miss you.

S

Chapter 5
JAX

The sound of clopping hooves mingled with voices outside my office. The guys were prepping for the day, getting horses saddled as they talked and joked around.

I enjoyed managing the guides and having that responsibility, but part of me missed the days when I was a trail guide. When it was just Wyatt and me running the excursions.

But Wyatt was gone now. He'd worked here for years until retiring this fall. He was a snowbird now, spending his winters in Arizona and summers in Montana.

Without him, I was the oldest person in the stables. At twenty-nine, I was in charge. How weird was that? There were days when I missed just being told what to do. When I didn't have to be the man with answers.

At least I had hiring authority. It was nice to choose my own staff.

When Indya had moved here, she'd brought on some high school kids to come and work during the summer. They'd been a huge help at a time when we'd needed it. Since then, I'd followed her lead, and we'd had a rotating crop of young men who worked different seasons.

It meant there was a steady stream of new faces. And while I hadn't minded the constant shuffling, it was strange this year without Wyatt. He'd provided a constant I hadn't noticed until it was missing.

There were only three guides working through the winter. On days when there wasn't much demand for excursions or private riding lessons, the guys would pitch in with snow removal or other jobs at the resort.

This summer, my staff would quadruple. There were four kids coming home from college who'd work for us during the busy season. The others I'd hire in early spring. There always seemed to be a ski bum or two who were bored in the summer, needed extra cash, and liked leading the guided hikes.

Meanwhile, I found myself at this desk more often than not. I'd cover if anyone called in sick. I'd lead rides for VIP guests if necessary, but otherwise, I made sure my team was trained and capable. And today was my weekly *organize shit* day. The papers on the desk rustled as I stacked them into a pile.

The conversation outside came to a grinding halt, the change enough to steal my attention toward the open door, papers frozen in my hands.

"Good morning. Is Jax here?"

Sasha.

I grinned. Finally, she'd ventured onto my turf.

"Morning, Ms. Vaughn," one of the guys said. "He's in his office."

"Thanks."

I tossed the papers aside and relaxed in my chair, folding my hands on my stomach as I waited.

Sasha approached the threshold slowly, each hesitant step accentuated with the click of her shoes on concrete. Then she peered around the corner and into the office like a rabid coyote was waiting inside to bite. She straightened, clearing her throat, when she found my waiting gaze. "Um, hi."

"Morning." I gestured to the chair on the other side of the desk. "Come on in. Coffee?"

"No, thanks." Her gaze flickered over the mess on my desk, her lip curling like it did when someone talked about the weather. As she sat in one of the leather guest chairs, her gaze surveyed the entire room.

"Want to take off your coat?" I asked.

"No, that's all right." Her black parka looked warm, but her nose and cheeks were rosy from the walk over. Though she did take off her gloves, tucking them into a pocket. "This is quite the office."

"I like it."

It was an office that Indya had originally designed for West, spacious with the same high-end finishes she'd incorporated across the resort. Except West preferred to work from his office at their house, away from the bustle of the guests. So with this space open, I'd traded up. The office next door that had originally been mine was now a break room for the guides.

"You've got a lot of, um . . . a lot." Her entire body shuddered as she grimaced at the mess.

I was so fucking glad I hadn't tidied up yet.

The couch against the wall was buried beneath coats and snow gear. My chaps were draped over the leather recliner I used for my afternoon power naps. There was an extra pair of boots tossed in the corner beside the tennis shoes I'd left behind this fall after a jog.

The bar where I kept my single-serve coffee maker and a few bottles of my favorite bourbons was in complete disarray. Dirty mugs. Used coffee pods. A wadded napkin.

My house was clean. I liked a clean house. But my truck and office never got the same treatment. My truck got cleaned only when the window was so filmy I couldn't see clearly. And this office, well . . . admittedly, it was overdue.

"Here to talk about excursions?" I asked.

Sasha tore her gaze from the disaster, meeting mine for a brief moment before she looked at the desk. "Maybe I should come back. Give you time to prepare."

"Nah. I'm ready." I shuffled a few papers around. "This won't take long. There is a method to this chaos."

"I don't think I want to learn this method," she muttered.

"Smart choice." I chuckled. "All you really need to know is that every week, I email Indya a list of the prior week's excursions. It summarizes each activity. The guide. The duration. The guests. I'll kick it your way too. If you need any other information, just let me know. Happy to add more detail."

"Do you just get that information from the reservation system database?"

"If by database you mean these, then yes." I picked up one of the papers on my desk and handed it over. It was an excursion report that the guides filled out after each activity.

"This is what you use." Sasha turned the paper over, probably searching for more. But it was just the one page.

"Yep. That's what we use. The guides fill out the details and turn them in at the end of every outing. I've found that it encourages the guys to learn and remember names. If there are any issues or incidents, they can add them to the comment section."

She scanned my desk, seeing the piles of summary sheets.

"I've already emailed Indya about these. Just haven't filed the originals away. I hate filing."

"Filing." Sasha blinked. "You mean actual, physical files."

I pointed to the cabinets beneath the bar. "Yep."

"So how do guests sign up?"

"There's a sign-up sheet for every excursion at the front desk. Guests just go down and register. Before each activity, guides go in and collect the final list, then round up the people going. This calendar right here"—I shuffled enough papers around that she could see the large desk calendar beneath the clutter—"is where I note which excursions are offered each day. Once a week, I take the sign-ups to the lobby."

"So paper. It's all tracked on paper." She pinched the bridge of her nose. "I feel like I've stepped back in time fifty years."

"Believe it or not, sometimes a pen and paper work just fine."

"It's just so . . ."

"Old fashioned."

"I was going to say inefficient."

"Let's use old fashioned. It's a nicer term." I grinned as her lip curled. Sasha didn't have a poker face. I liked that. A lot.

"I—" She stopped herself, holding out both hands. "Okay. Paper."

"You're not going to suggest I try out an app or software program?"

"Would you say yes if I did?"

"No."

"Thought so," she mumbled.

I laughed. "My grandparents used this system. It worked for them. Figured it was good enough for me too."

"So it's sentimental."

I shrugged. "You could call it that."

"All right." She dropped her gaze to the fingers fidgeting on her lap.

I waited, expecting her to scurry away to the lodge, to the world where Indya was in charge and had modernized the resort's systems. Every housekeeper carried an iPad. Reservations for the dining room were all made electronically. The same was true for the spa.

But instead of leaving, Sasha sank deeper into the chair, her shoulders finally resting against the back.

"This isn't related to your process. But if the offer is still available, would it be possible for me to stay in your cabin for a while?"

Huh. Well, that was unexpected. She'd left in such a rush yesterday that I'd assumed she'd either hated the cabin—not likely, because it was fucking awesome—or she'd loved it. And if Sasha loved something that was mine, she might have to admit it. Hence, the swift departure.

I smirked. "How hard was it to ask that question?"

The moment her nostrils flared, I regretted opening my damn mouth. Like a snake bit her in the ass, she shot out of the chair and stormed out of the door.

"Damn it." I got to my feet so fast that my chair's wheels skidded across the floor and it went crashing into the wall. "Sasha."

She kept walking through the stables.

"Would you just wait a minute?"

"Forget it," she barked over her shoulder. Her silky hair was down today, a rare change. It swished across her shoulders.

"Yes, you can stay at the cabin." I lengthened my stride, veering around her until I blocked her path to the door.

She drew up short so we didn't crash. Then she crossed her arms over her chest and leveled me with that glare I shouldn't have found so sexy. "If I move in, will you throw it in my face every five seconds?"

"No, I'm a cowboy. Once upon a time, I thought it would be fun to be a bull rider. We shoot for eight seconds, not five."

"Oh my God, this was a mistake." She shifted to move around me, but I blocked her path again.

"I'm kidding." I laughed. "I have no plans of throwing anything in your face, all right? The cabin is all yours, harassment-free."

She studied me for a long moment before finally dropping her arms. "Fine. Thank you. I'll come out after work."

"I'm almost finished remodeling the laundry room. I should have the washer and dryer in next week. You'll have to wait on laundry until then, or you can use my machines."

"No problem."

I glanced to the guides who—nosy shitheads—were all hovering by a nearby stall, trying to listen in. I jerked my chin and sent them a collective scowl to get back to work, then stepped closer to Sasha and lowered my voice. "For curiosity's sake, why'd you change your mind about the cabin?"

She tugged on her earlobe, something I hadn't seen her do before. It was cute. And, oddly, sexy too. What did it mean? Maybe if she was living next door, I'd have a chance to find out.

"My neighbors are idiots," she said. "They had a party or something last night, and one of their guests got mixed up on which front door to use. He came into mine and proceeded to vomit his dinner on my living room floor."

"What the fuck?" My voice was louder than I'd expected, and she jolted. "Sorry. You're serious?"

"Yep." She popped the *p*. "Not the best night I've ever had. My landlord is having the door's lock fixed and will get the carpets cleaned. If I could just stay at your cabin until then, that would be great."

Oh, she'd be staying longer than that. Not a chance in hell I was letting her go back to that shithole. But that would be a discussion we'd have later. "No problem."

"Thanks."

I stepped closer. "You okay?"

"I'm good." Sasha didn't look to the ceiling as she spoke, but I didn't need the tell to spot her lie.

I lifted my hand, my fingers itching to touch her face, but stopped myself. What was it about her that made me always want to touch? All the damn time. The pink cheeks. Her silky hair. Those freckles dusting her nose.

I shifted so close there was barely an inch between us, but she didn't shy away. This was the closest we'd been since the grocery store. That was something, right?

Sasha's eyes dropped to my mouth. Her gaze clung there, for just a moment, until it slammed to the floor.

So she liked my mouth. I knew it. I fucking knew it. This attraction wasn't one sided. Not even a bit.

When she looked up again, that cool stare was fixed in place.

It only made me smirk, which made her scowl deepen.

She could glare at me all she wanted. I didn't give a damn. I knew what it looked like when a woman wanted a kiss. And Sasha wanted to be kissed.

It took every ounce of willpower not to do a fist pump.

Was that why she'd been so prickly these past three months? Because she felt this attraction too?

"Want some help getting stuff from your place in town?" I asked.

She cleared her throat, shaking her head as she took a step back. "I can manage."

"You sure?" I stepped forward, keeping us so close that the toes of my boots nearly touched hers. "We could grab your stuff. Go do dinn—"

A horse whinnied.

The sound caught my attention just enough that I looked away. And that was all the window Sasha needed to escape. She sidestepped me faster than I'd expected and hurried to the door.

Only when she was gone did I let out a frustrated groan, tipping my head back to the rafters. "Couldn't keep the horses quiet for just a few fucking minutes, huh, guys?"

All three of the guides laughed. "Sorry, boss."

"No, you're not," I grumbled and retreated to my office.

It smelled like coffee and hay and horses, the usual scents. But beneath them was a hint of something sweet and fresh. Sasha's perfume.

I shut the door, hoping to trap it inside for a few moments. Then I got to work filing papers and cleaning up the office.

When the five guests for the midmorning excursion were gathered, I greeted them and shook hands before they left for their short trail ride through the snow. When they returned, I helped with the horses, then did it all over again for the afternoon ride.

Montana winter days were short, and by the time I left at five o'clock, it was dark. Sasha's car was still in the employee parking lot, so I headed toward home.

I parked in my garage, then walked over to the cabin, doing a quick sweep of the rooms to make sure there were no tools left behind that would get in her way. I ducked into the laundry room, took off the flannel I'd pulled on over a T-shirt this morning, popped in my earbuds, and got to work.

Sweat beaded at my temples after the hour it took me to apply the sealant to the stone tile. With it finished, I stood from my hands and knees, pulling out my headphones. Then I used the hem of my tee to wipe my face dry.

A tickle of cold air skated across my skin, drawing my attention down the hall.

Sasha stood in the open doorway with a suitcase in each hand. Her mouth was parted, her eyes locked on my flat stomach.

Another man might have dropped his shirt, but I had great fucking abs, so I kept it raised. "Hey."

She blinked, ripping her gaze away to glance around the room. Her face followed the movement of her eyes in a circle. "Hi. I, um, didn't realize you'd be here."

"Just finished for today." I dabbed my forehead again. It was dry, but I really liked the color that tinged her cheeks when she was flustered. And apparently, a six-pack was all it took to unravel Sasha Vaughn.

I reluctantly dropped my shirt and picked up the flannel off the floor as well as my sponge and the rest of the sealant bottle.

"Is there more in the car?" I nodded toward her luggage.

"Yes, but I can get it." She carried the suitcases out of the doorway, setting them aside before rushing outside again. By the time I was done washing off my sponge and hands, she'd hauled in three more bags, piling them beside the others.

"What about furniture?" I asked. "West and I can bring a horse trailer into town tomorrow to get your bigger stuff."

"Oh, that's okay." She waved it off as she closed the door, then bent to unzip her ankle boots, pulling them off to place neatly beside the door.

"You're just going to leave your stuff in the rental?"

"Yes, for now. I don't see any reason to bother with it if I'm only here for a short time."

There was nothing *short time* about this situation, but I'd let her fall in love with the cabin first. I'd let these walls do the convincing for me, then we'd move her furniture later.

"How was the rest of your day?" I asked.

"Fine. You?"

"Fine." I leaned against the counter, my hands gripping the edge as I crossed an ankle over the other.

Sasha's gaze traveled down my legs to my white socks—my boots were beside the door too. She stared at my feet like they were safer than my face.

I wiggled my toes.

She immediately sprang into action, moving for her belongings to put them away.

I waited until she was down the hall before I shoved off the counter and grabbed the rest of her bags, following her to the primary bedroom.

She had her face in her hands when I reached the door. Her suitcases on the carpet by her feet.

"What's wrong?"

She jumped, pressing a hand to her heart. "Shit. You startled me."

"Sorry."

"It's fine." She waved it off. "Thanks."

"Where do you want these?" I lifted up her bags.

"Anywhere is fine."

I stepped inside and set them on the bed.

Sasha gave me a wide berth, but it wasn't enough distance for me not to smell her perfume.

A perfume I wouldn't mind having on my sheets and pillows.

"Are you hungr—"

The flash of headlights flickered through the bedroom window.

Sasha shot out of the bedroom like it was on fire.

I threw a glare outside at whoever was here to ruin yet another attempt at asking Sasha to dinner. But my irritation was short lived as Emery's Jeep Wrangler parked outside my house. "Shit."

Sasha was standing in the center of the living room when I came down the hall. She'd put as many pieces of furniture between us as possible.

"I'll get out of your hair," I said. "Let me know if you need anything."

"Sure. Thanks again for letting me stay."

"No problem." I snagged my flannel from where I'd left it on the counter, quickly shrugging it on before I stowed the sponge and sealant beneath the kitchen sink and tugged on my boots. "Night."

"Good night." Sasha nodded as I lifted a hand and slipped outside.

Emery was at my front door when I walked over, my breath billowing as my boots crunched in the snow. There was an overnight bag by her feet.

"Hey."

"Hi." She smiled for three seconds before it crumpled.

Fuck. I hauled her into my arms as she started to cry. "You okay?"

"No."

"What happened?"

She didn't answer. Not that she needed to.

Calvin, her prick of a husband, was what had happened.

"What do you need?"

She pulled away and blew out a breath. "A stiff drink. And maybe a night on your couch."

"You got it." I bent to pick up her bag.

"Who's that?" she asked, her gaze trained past my shoulder at the cabin.

I turned just as Sasha moved away from the living room window. "Sasha. She's the new manager at the resort. She's got a place in town that's having some work done so she's crashing here for a little while."

"Ah."

A different night, I'd tell Emery all about Sasha. How we'd met. How she'd come to stay in the cabin. How I couldn't stop thinking about her.

But tonight was not the night.

Not when, even in the dark, I could spot the tear tracks down Emery's cheeks.

So I put my arm around her shoulders and steered her inside. "Let's see about that drink."

Chapter 6
SASHA

Four nights. That woman had been staying with Jax for four nights.

Who was she? How long had they been together? How did Mindi feel about another woman sharing Jax's bed?

"Why can't I stop staring out this stupid window?" I muttered to myself as I wiggled the back to my stud earring, trying to slide it on the post. "Just. Go. In."

This pair was always difficult. Or maybe it had nothing to do with the jewelry and everything to do with the irrational anger coursing through my body. An anger tied directly to that Jeep Wrangler next door.

I dropped my hands and closed my eyes. Then I willed this frustration to manifest somewhere other than my fingers.

It didn't matter who Jax was fucking. It did. Not. Matter. He wasn't mine. I had no claim over him and no reason to be jealous. So why couldn't I stop glancing out the living room window?

Was it because I'd caught a glimpse of his abs? It had to be. No real-life human being had abs like that. Jax had underwear-model abs. Chris Hemsworth Thor–style abs. Cover-his-skin-in-whipped-cream-and-lick-him-clean abs. And I didn't even like whipped cream—it gave me heartburn.

But just the glimpse I'd caught of his washboard stomach on Tuesday had haunted my thoughts. For days, my skin had felt too sensitive and my body too warm. If I even so much as thought of Jax's name, a dull throb would pulse in my core.

Was it really even Jax and his magnificent abs? Or was this sexual frustration due to the fact that I'd starved myself of physical touch these past few months?

I missed holding hands. I missed kissing. I missed hugs.

I missed strong arms and the way it felt to be held as I fell asleep. I missed Eddie. I missed my friends and my home and . . . my life.

But it was someone else's home now, wasn't it? It was someone else's job. Someone new was sleeping in my old bedroom. Someone new was working the Saturday shift with my friends.

Before I'd moved to Montana, I'd been the assistant manager at a wellness resort in Sacramento for five years.

After graduation, most of my friends had gone to college while I'd chosen to stay home and work, taking night classes until I'd finally earned my degree. Those had been a hard five years, but I'd worked my ass off, and my job at Serenity Rise Wellness Resort had been my reward.

The friends I'd made at work had been good friends. Maybe not lifelong friends, but good friends. We'd bonded over hectic schedules and long hours. Over snobby guests and ridiculous complaints. Over Friday-night martinis and *Vanderpump Rules*.

Our text thread had been quiet lately.

They probably had a new group chat going by now.

I'd hoped to make new friends in Montana, but it was different being the manager, not assistant manager. I couldn't gripe about the boss because I *was* the boss. The desk clerks wouldn't invite me to girls' night. The housekeepers didn't gossip with me in the halls.

It was hard not to think Montana was yet another bad decision in a line of horrible choices I'd made over the past ten years. But at least it was cheap. The cost of living was a fraction of what it had been in

California, and my paycheck was over double what I'd been making at Serenity.

Sure, moving here had come with a cost—my happiness. Though I hadn't exactly been a beaming ray of sunshine in California. But that light, however dim, was beginning to fade.

It was ironic, really. The first day I'd come here had started so badly with that incident at the grocery store. Then Jax had chased it all away. For three incredible blocks, back and forth, I'd thought it was all going to be okay. That I'd made a good choice. That Montana was right.

Except it wasn't right. This wasn't okay. *I* wasn't okay.

I hadn't been okay for a long, long time.

But I'd fake it. I'd keep faking it.

The sound of a door slamming put a halt to my pity party and tugged my gaze to the window. The woman who'd been sharing Jax's bed for four nights waved from behind the steering wheel. The lights from his porch were bright enough to illuminate her smile.

Jax, standing barefoot in his doorway, waved back. His jeans hung low on his hips. His white T-shirt strained across his chest. His hair was damp, like he'd just gotten out of the shower.

Probably from a lazy afternoon of sex and napping.

The grin he sent her made my insides twist.

"Ugh." This jealousy was eating me alive. Not that I'd ever admit it to him.

The woman was gorgeous. Of course she was gorgeous. Men who looked like Jax Haven were always attached to beautiful women.

Her brown hair was a few shades lighter than mine, the strands highlighted with blonde and caramel. She had a tall, willowy frame. Before her, I'd never seen a woman in Wranglers, but they made her legs look a mile long.

She was the cowgirl to Jax's cowboy. A perfect pair.

She belonged. And I did not.

Montana was not for me, but I had no choice but to tough it out through summer. Then, once the busy tourist season was over, I'd find a place to start fresh.

It wouldn't be California. After everything that had happened, I couldn't go back there now. Maybe Eddie would have a place in mind.

Before Jax caught me spying, I walked away from the window and focused on my earrings, finally getting them clasped. Then I retreated to the bathroom to blow-dry my own hair for tonight's party.

My black dress was already laid on the bed. The puffed sleeves cuffed at my wrists. The style was fitted around my torso and loose around the hips as the skirt draped to my knees. But the slit that ran up one side gave it a sexy edge, and the neckline was cut into a wide square that exposed my collarbones.

The material wasn't high quality. I'd bought it on sale. It was plain—boring. But this was a work function, and it was work appropriate. Besides that, it had been cheap. Someday, when I had time and money and lived somewhere with a mall, I'd go shopping again. For now, Amazon Prime was my best option.

With my hair dried and straight, I curled the ends to give it a bit of volume. Then I applied a heavier than normal layer of makeup, taking time to paint my lips a deep crimson red.

I was just fastening on my necklace—a gold chain with small diamond pendant that matched my earrings—when a knock came at the door. Considering that only a few people knew I was living in this cabin, it came as no surprise to find Jax standing on the stoop.

"Hi." His bright-blue eyes crinkled at the sides as the corner of his mouth turned up in that smirk.

My heart skipped.

Freaking smirk. It really, *really* shouldn't be hot. Or his cowboy hat.

It was black and clean, a different hat than the one he wore around the ranch for work. The brim shaded his face just enough to define the lines and angles of his features. His jaw, missing its normal stubble, might as well have been chiseled granite.

He wore a starched white shirt and dark jeans that draped to his polished square-toed boots. His belt buckle was the same that he wore every day, but it seemed shinier tonight, the gold and silver catching the light from inside.

Three months ago, I would have said a man in a fitted tux was the epitome of attractive. But apparently a spiffed-up cowboy was my new weakness. My knees wobbled.

Not once in my life had I experienced wobbling knees.

I wasn't a fan.

"You look beautiful." His voice was deep and smooth, missing that gravelly edge, like he'd stripped it away along with the dusty jeans and whiskered jaw.

"Thank you." What the hell was wrong with my voice? Why was it all breathy and pathetic?

Stupid freaking cowboy hat.

He stared at me, his gaze taking a lazy trail over my face, down my dress, and to the strappy heels on my feet.

The shoes were entirely impractical for the snow. I'd probably have frostbite before I even arrived at the party, but they'd been an impulse buy from years and years ago. From a time when life had been simpler. From a time when I'd been the type of girl who wore sexy heels and red lipstick.

I didn't let myself mourn that girl.

There were more important people to miss.

"Figured we could ride together," he said.

"Oh, um, I was going to drive." So I could leave early.

"Planning on sneaking out once the band starts?"

Damn it. "Yes," I admitted.

"Make you a deal. We'll ride together, and if you're having a miserable time, I'll bring you home."

"Or we can just drive separately. Then I can leave whenever I want."

"You can still leave whenever you want. But if I drive, you can relax. Have a few glasses of champagne."

Champagne? No, there would be no champagne. When it came to alcohol, I was a lightweight, and the last thing I needed was to get tipsy and lose my verbal filter at a party with every one of my employees in attendance. "This is a work event."

"A work event with champagne and whiskey." He winked. "My favorite type of work event."

"I still think I should drive. That way, you can stay."

He shook his head, that devilish grin stretching. "Do you have to make things so difficult?"

"If difficult means logical."

Jax laughed, shaking his head. "Fine."

"Good."

"We'll take your car."

"Whoa. Whoa. Whoa." *Shit.* "That's not what I meant."

He smirked. "I know."

I rolled my eyes. "How will you get home?"

Another woman? Mindi, maybe? Or would the woman with the Jeep come to his rescue? Maybe she'd just gone home to change for the party.

"Either I'll leave with you, or West can give me a lift."

"Oh." Did that mean the Jeep wouldn't be parked outside his house tonight?

"Are you ready, or do you need a bit longer?" he asked.

"You're not going to drive separately, are you? If I said I needed a few more minutes, you'd just wait for me."

His eyes sparkled. "She's catching on."

"Fine." I sighed and held up a finger. "One minute."

His chuckle echoed through the house as I rushed to get my purse from the bedroom, do a last-minute check of my hair, and spritz on perfume.

Really, I needed five more minutes, but I didn't want him to come inside. I was already struggling to forget just how comfortable and natural he looked in the kitchen the other day.

With my coat on and my keys in hand, I joined Jax outside. My heels clicked on the concrete landing. I hissed as I took that first step off the step and into the snow.

Jax's hand was instantly at my elbow, his grip light and ready to catch me if I slipped. "Careful."

"These shoes aren't snow appropriate."

"I won't let you fall."

My eyes flew to his as I froze.

No one had ever said that to me before.

It meant nothing. He was being literal. But something about his statement made my heart climb into my throat. Like maybe he knew I'd been walking on my own for too long.

"Good?" Jax asked.

"Yeah." I cleared my throat and took baby steps until I reached my car. Then I slid behind the wheel as Jax closed the door and rounded the hood for the passenger side.

The moment he was inside, I realized the magnitude of my mistake.

The Mazda was not a large car, but Jax was a large man.

His legs were so long that his knees pressed against the dash. His hat skimmed the ceiling. And his shoulders were so broad that his frame was just inches from my own.

The scent of his cologne filled my nose. Masculine and woodsy and clean with that hint of citrus. It wasn't a spicy scent. It wasn't overpowering or sharp. It was . . . Jax.

Delicious, tempting, playboy Jax who was not my boss but sort of was my boss. Off-limits, destined-to-break-my-fragile-heart Jax.

"Sure you don't want me to drive?" he asked.

I shook my head and started the car, then drove us to the lodge, ignoring the heat that radiated off his body. I ignored a lot on that drive, like the way his jeans molded to bulky thighs. Like his long fingers tapping on his knee and how never in my life had I found a hand so hypnotic. Like the way his shirt strained slightly at his biceps.

I blocked it all out and drove, following the trail of tire tracks that cut through the snow until we were parked outside the lodge. For once, I was grateful for winter. A clump of snow on my bare toes felt like a welcome relief to the heat coursing through my veins. The cold air cooled the flush in my cheeks before we entered the event space.

"Wow," I whispered as we walked inside the venue.

Lights had been strung across the rafters, casting the enormous room with a golden glow. Tall tables covered in white linens filled the open space. Employees and their dates milled around the room carrying cocktail glasses and flutes of champagne.

We'd had one wedding at the resort since I'd started working here, but it had been an intimate affair with an outdoor ceremony. They'd used the dining room rather than the former barn for the reception.

They'd missed out. If I ever got married, I wanted to celebrate in a place like this. A place kissed by soft, golden light and magic swirling in the air.

At the far end of the room was a dance floor positioned in front of a raised stage. The live band hadn't started playing yet, though their equipment was in place. Quiet background music drifted from the speakers, mingling with the hum of conversation.

In the corner, the bartender was grabbing beers from a stock tank filled with ice and mixing drinks while waiters carried trays of champagne and wine.

Our event coordinator, wearing a fitted green dress, waved when she spotted me at the doors. She was one of the few employees who'd be working tonight. Even Reid, our chef, was on orders to simply enjoy himself. We'd hired a local caterer to craft hors d'oeuvres and a buffet.

"Can I get you a drink?" Jax asked, helping me out of my coat.

I hadn't planned on drinking, but as a waitress passed with a tray of champagne, my mouth watered. "That would—"

"Uncle Jax!" Two twin boys crashed into his legs. Their tiny arms and legs wrapped around Jax's calves.

It was impossible not to smile at Kade and Kohen Haven. They were as adorable as they were rambunctious.

Jax's face softened as he bent to ruffle their blond, curly hair. "How are the monsters tonight?"

"Hungry." Kade pointed toward the table teeming with appetizers.

Kohen grinned up at his uncle. "Bet you can't walk all the way over there with us on your legs."

"Bet you can't hang on while I do." Jax picked up the leg with Kade, swinging it wide and shaking it furiously until both boys dissolved into a fit of giggles.

He laughed as he took two steps, then glanced over his shoulder.

I lifted a hand to wave.

He jerked up his chin.

With my coat on a hanger, I affixed my polite, professional smile and slipped into the fray.

For hours, I mingled with employees, meeting their spouses and significant others. I sipped from a single glass of champagne until the bubbles were gone and the half-full glass was warm. I listened from the opposite end of the room as the band played its first set.

But no matter what I was doing, where I looked, I could always find Jax.

There was an invisible tether between us. A tie that stretched tighter as the night progressed. He laughed with some of the guys as they clustered near the bar, shooting me that smirk when I glanced over. When his grandmother pulled him into a hug, his smile widened when he caught me watching. Every time I moved from one table to the next, he seemed to shift, too, keeping me in his line of sight.

It was unsettling how often I searched for him throughout the night.

It was unsettling how often his blue gaze was waiting.

The woman from the Jeep hadn't come to the party. Mindi had brought along a date.

Jax had come alone.

Actually, he'd come with me.

This wasn't a date. I refused to think of it as a date. But it was . . . something. The same something as the day at the grocery store.

A break in the music stole everyone's attention. Onstage, West held out a hand to help Indya up the rise. She looked stunning in a burgundy wrap dress that hugged her pregnant belly. The hem swished above a pair of intricately embroidered boots.

"Where's Jax?" she asked into the microphone, scanning faces. When she spotted him, she waved him up to the stage.

He took it with a quick step, lifting a hand to greet the crowd.

"Thank you all for coming," she said, smiling into the microphone as she kept her hand laced with West's.

Jax took up the space beside his brother, glancing out over the room. Searching. His gaze locked on me, and the corner of his mouth turned up.

My cheeks flamed as a few people close by glanced to me instead of the stage.

Why couldn't I look away? Why couldn't I break that stare?

Jax held me with those striking eyes as Indya continued. Through a crowded room, through noise and laughter and clapping, he held me captive.

"We're so grateful to celebrate you tonight," Indya said, her voice a dull murmur beyond my pounding heart. "This resort would not be the same without you. So on behalf of West, Jax, and myself, let's raise our glasses to another incredible year at the Haven River Ranch."

Glasses lifted as the crowd whistled and cheered. And even as Jax brought his own glass of ice and amber liquid to his lips, his focus stayed on me.

I felt the shift in the room. It wasn't just those nearby who glanced my way. Everyone in the party seemed to follow the path of Jax's gaze, including Indya and West.

What was I doing? This was not why I'd come to Montana. Not for a romance with my sort-of boss who'd had another woman in his bed for the past four nights.

It took everything I had, but my eyes dropped to the floor.

The wave of Jax's disappointment hit me from the stage.

There was a shuffling onstage as the band resumed their places. As they began a new song, I slipped toward a wooden pillar, doing my best to hide behind the beam.

Time to go home. Alone. Jax would have to get a ride from West.

The crowd shifted as people moved toward the dance floor. The music was louder, livelier, than it had been earlier. A crush of people was spinning and swaying. Smiling.

With the added noise, I made my break for the door. I hadn't even made it five steps before a large, warm hand circled my elbow. The same hand that had kept me from falling outside the cabin earlier.

Jax slid to my side, blocking my path like he'd done in the stables earlier this week. He stood just as close. Too close. "Hey, you."

My eyes dropped to his mouth automatically, lost in the way his lips formed words. I really needed to stop looking at his mouth. Our eyes collided.

It was worse. So much worse.

I saw the desire swirling in his blue eyes. It was the same desire I'd found in them all night. The rest of the party faded to a blur with one inhale of his cologne.

"Would you dance with me?"

It wasn't the first time in the past ten years that a man had asked me to dance. But it was the first time that I was tempted to say yes. So, so tempted.

Except there would be no dancing. Even if I got married in a room like this someday, I wouldn't dance.

"No, thank you."

Any other man would have let it slice his ego. Any other man would have let me leave. Not Jax. That sexy smirk stretched across his lips as he inched impossibly close. So close I could feel the heat from his chest. So close I had to lean back to keep his gaze.

"Not a dancing fan?" he asked.

"The last memory I have of my parents was them dancing together." The truth flew past my lips. I regretted it the moment the words escaped. Oh God. Why had I said that? "I don't know why I just said that."

His expression softened. "Sasha, I'm sorry."

"It's fine." It wasn't fine. "I just don't dance."

A waiter walked by with a tray of champagne.

Jax snagged a glass and handed it over. "All right. No dancing. How about a drink?"

I took the flute from his hand, raised it to my lips, and chugged until it was empty. "Good idea."

Chapter 7
JAX

Hiccup. Sasha giggled. "Sorry."

"Don't be sorry." That laugh. Every time she hiccuped, she laughed. I hoped those hiccups never went away.

"Champagne is my favorite, but it always gives me hiccups. What's your favorite drink?"

"Bourbon. Whiskey. A cold beer after a long day."

Sasha hummed, relaxing her head against the back of her seat. Another hiccup. Another giggle. "You know? I've never ridden in the passenger seat of my car before. I'm always the driver."

"And?"

She crossed and uncrossed her legs, her knees knocking against the glove box. "How did you even fit over here? You're huge."

"Sit at an angle." This wasn't the first small car I'd crammed myself into. The trick was sitting diagonally.

Sasha twisted, and this time, when she crossed her legs, she cleared the dash without issue. *Hiccup.* A giggle.

If I'd have known that all it would take were two glasses of champagne for her to finally relax around me, I would have been bringing bottles into the lodge every day for the past three months.

"Did you have fun tonight?" I asked her.

"Surprisingly, yes." Her smile was easy, unguarded. Her beautiful face was cast in shadows and the glow from the dashboard lights. "Did you?"

"Yeah. I had a great time." Especially the last two hours.

Sasha and I had stood at a table toward the back of the room, talking with each other and anyone who'd come over to visit.

She'd been quiet at first. Withdrawn. Probably because of that slip she'd made about her parents. There wasn't a doubt in my mind that she hadn't meant to share.

As much as I'd wanted to ask about it, there also hadn't been a doubt in my mind that she would have raced out of the building.

So I'd changed the subject. I'd gossiped with her about the guides. One of the guys had a crush on a masseuse, and I'd pointed them out in the crowd. Another one of the guys had just gotten dumped, and his ex had come on the arm of our weekend bartender—cheating rumors were running rampant.

Maybe it was the gossip, maybe it was the champagne, but Sasha had eventually relaxed. And then she'd charmed. Me. Employees. Everyone.

Her smile had been contagious. She was absolutely enchanting. With every visitor to our table, she'd been funny and smart. Her dry sense of humor made every person laugh, including herself. And God, when she laughed with those brown eyes dancing . . .

There was a very real chance I'd gone too far tonight. That I'd showed my hand to every employee on the ranch.

Except it had been impossible not to stare. Not to find her in the crowd.

The party had still been going strong when we'd left. The younger staff members would likely stay behind to drink and dance until the last shuttle left around two. But after West and Indya had taken the boys home, I'd ushered Sasha to the door.

There was a chance that us leaving together would start rumors of our own, but I didn't give a shit. Not when she'd gone willingly. Not when she'd let me help her into her coat. Not when she'd let me take her arm and escort her to the car to drive us both home.

Hiccup. She giggled. "Thanks for driving."

"Welcome." I'd stopped drinking after the toasts, not that I'd had much before that point anyway. My focus had been on Sasha all night, not the whiskey in my glass.

She leaned closer to her window, peering up to the heavens.

Winter nights were my favorite. When the moonlight glittered on the snow and the midnight sky sparkled.

"The stars are beautiful," she whispered, almost like she didn't want me to hear her admit it.

When my house and her cabin came into view, she sat up straight.

"Tired?" I asked.

"Not really."

"Want to come in for a drink?"

"As long as by *drink* you mean water. I've got a perfect buzz going but have no desire to be hungover tomorrow."

"You're in luck. I happen to have water."

"That is lucky." She laughed, no hiccup necessary this time.

I parked outside my house so she wouldn't have to walk far in the snow, then slipped out of the Mazda and rounded the trunk to open her door.

She stepped out, glancing to the sky one last time before following me to the house.

"Make yourself at home," I said, toeing off my boots and putting them in the rack beside the front door along with my hat.

Sasha bent to unstrap her heels before she took off her coat. Then she padded through the entryway, following me to the open-concept living room and kitchen. "This is lovely."

"Thanks." I filled a glass with ice water, handing it over before making myself a bourbon on the rocks.

"You did most of this yourself, right?" She ran a hand across the island's surface. "Indya mentioned these were built by your grandfather as employee housing but had sort of fallen to shambles."

"Yeah, I've been remodeling for a while now. Mostly here. I added on the garage and two bedrooms."

She wiggled her bare toes on the hardwood floor. "These are the same as in the cabin."

"They are." I took a sip, joining her at the island.

She leaned against one corner while I leaned against the other, three feet of smooth, polished granite between us.

"I like them," she said.

I liked her.

I liked that Sasha had taken off her shoes when we'd come inside because I'd taken off my boots. I liked that she hadn't batted those pretty eyelashes when I'd invited her inside. I liked that for the first time in months, she was the woman I'd met at the grocery store.

"Tell me a lie."

She arched her eyebrows, a smile toying on her mouth.

I liked that too.

"This again?"

I shrugged and took a sip of my drink. "Unless you'd prefer small talk about the weather."

"All right. I hate how you look in a cowboy hat." She lifted her water, hiding a smile behind the glass's rim. "Your turn."

"You look hideous tonight."

Pink tinged her cheeks as she dropped her gaze to a button on my shirt.

"Tell me a secret," I said, closing the gap between us to a foot.

Sasha didn't so much as blink. "I hate green beans."

"That's not a secret." My hand itched to twirl a lock of her silky, dark hair around a finger.

So I did.

This time, she blinked. It came with a hitch in her breath, and the entire world narrowed to her chocolate eyes.

"Tell me another secret," I said, my finger still twining that hair around a knuckle.

"You're handsome."

"Also not a secret."

She rolled her eyes as I chuckled. "I don't want to tell you another secret."

Another secret. She wasn't talking about the green beans. She meant her parents. That was the real secret she'd shared tonight. That was enough. "Want a secret of mine?"

"Yes."

"I want to kiss you."

She swallowed hard as her gaze dropped to my mouth. "Is that really a secret?"

"As secret as your hatred for green beans." I took the water glass from her hand and set it on the counter along with my tumbler.

Sasha shifted her weight from one foot to the next as I stepped close enough to dive into that hair, my fingers threading into the silky strands at her temples.

Her mouth parted, but before I could capture her lips, she whispered, "I want you to kiss me. That's a secret."

A grin tugged at the corner of my mouth. "Maybe for you. I thought it was fairly obvious with how you were staring at me all night."

She stiffened. "*You* were staring at *me*."

"Because I want to kiss you." I bent, brushing my lips across hers. It was a tease. A test.

Either she'd pull away and walk to the door. Or . . .

She leaned in. She lifted on those delicate toes.

Hell yes. This time when my mouth touched hers, there was no teasing. No gentle caress. I crushed my lips over hers, my tongue sweeping inside.

Sasha let out a soft hum that shot straight to my cock. She melted against me, her hands sliding up the starched cotton of my shirt.

I slanted my mouth over hers, banding my arms around her back to haul her close. Then I savored the way her tongue tangled with mine, delving into every corner of her mouth until I'd licked them all.

The way she fit against me was perfect, like puzzle pieces snapping together.

Her hands snaked around my waist, her hands sliding up my spine until she couldn't reach any higher. Then she fisted the fabric of my shirt, clinging to me for dear life.

Not that I had any intention of letting her go.

I kissed her until she whimpered, until my pulse pounded through my veins. Until my entire body thrummed with heat and my arousal strained against my jeans.

"Damn, baby." I tore my lips away and kissed a line across her jaw before dropping to lick her throat.

"Jax." Her hands threaded through my hair, tugging at the roots. "More."

I bent lower, sucking and tasting every inch of her neck. My hands roamed up to her shoulders, then down her ribs, drifting lower until I cupped her ass in my palms and squeezed. Hard.

She moaned. "Yes."

"I want you, Sasha. So fucking much."

"Then take me."

I pulled away, meeting her gaze.

Those beautiful eyes were clear. Confident. When she gave me a slight nod, that was all the invitation I needed to pick her up and carry her down the hall.

My bedroom was cast in silvery shadows, the dim light from a clear winter night slipping through the windows. It was just enough light to see Sasha's eyes widen as I laid her on the mattress.

Her hair fanned out on the charcoal bedding as I came down on top of her, capturing her lips in another kiss.

My hands continued to wander, memorizing every inch, every curve, until I reached the bare skin of her thigh and skated beneath the hem of her skirt.

She broke the kiss, panting as she arched into my chest. "Jax."

Every night. I wanted my name on her lips every night. My clothes felt too tight, too hot. I needed skin. Hers. Mine. I wanted this dress off her body and to cover her with mine. But I forced my hand to slide up her leg one inch at a time, savoring the trembling in her limbs as I moved higher.

Sasha reached between us, frantically working the buttons on my shirt loose until it was open to my navel. She pushed at the cotton, trying to get it off my shoulders. "Take this off."

"Patience."

She squirmed beneath me, her legs widening. "Touch me. Please."

What was better? My name? Or hearing her beg?

I peppered her collarbones with kisses, my hand beneath her skirt stalling. The moment my fingers stopped inching toward her apex, she let out a frustrated groan.

"Just wait."

"I don't want to wait." She grabbed my chin, forcing my face up as she slammed her mouth onto mine. Her tongue pushed between my teeth, flickering before it twined with my own.

I let her have control for a minute, let her take what she needed. Then I broke away and stood to yank my shirt from my jeans and finish with the buttons. The clang of my belt filled the room as I unbuckled the latch.

Sasha pushed up on her elbow, reaching for the waistband of my jeans, but with a hand over her heart, I eased her back onto the mattress.

She frowned.

I liked that frown.

When I slipped my hands beneath her back, reaching for the zipper on her dress, she shifted up to help, but I stopped her with a shake of my head. "I'll do it."

She pulled her bottom lip between her teeth as I stripped the fabric from her body. First her left arm, then the right. I eased it off her naked breasts, dragging it over her ribs and down her stomach.

It was like unwrapping a present, and tonight, I wasn't going to rush.

"I've been wanting to take this off you all night."

Her mouth parted as the cool air kissed her skin. Those nipples, pebbled and pink, made my mouth water. I bent, taking one between my teeth to pull into my mouth.

"Oh God." Her hands dived into my hair as she moaned.

I sucked harder, earning a hiss, before moving to the other nipple to give it the same treatment. My hands kept moving, tugging until the dress was over her hips and she wiggled, kicking it to the floor to join my shirt.

The moment my bare chest pressed into her skin, I groaned, a nipple still in my mouth. The heat between us was scorching. A zing shot down my spine, my erection becoming painful behind my zipper.

Sasha arched into my mouth, her eyes fluttering closed as I kept her pinned to the bed, tormenting her breasts. While my mouth worked one nipple, my fingers rolled the other, pinching and plucking until a string of mewls escaped her lips. That grip she had on my hair tightened.

"Could I make you come just from this?"

She nodded, her mouth parted.

I let my hand trail along her belly, tickling her ribs before slipping beneath her black lace panties. "Are you wet for me?"

She gulped.

That was a yes. I stroked a finger through her slit. "Drenched."

Sasha brought a hand to her face, covering her eyes as she tried to bring her knees together. "Oh my God."

"Don't hide, baby." I wrapped my hand around her wrist, pulling it away. "It's so sexy that you're wet for me."

She nibbled on her lower lip again as I pulled her panties to the side, dragging a finger over her clit. She bucked into the touch. A cross between a moan and a cry echoed off the walls.

I kissed her inner thigh, about to yank those panties off, when she shifted, her knees closing.

"I don't like it." She pulled on my forearm, a feeble attempt to drag me into the bed.

"You don't like it?" Seriously?

"No. Not really. I don't . . . I just . . ." She squeezed her eyes shut. "Just fuck me, okay?"

There was more to this, but for tonight, for this first time, I'd let her make that call. But sooner rather than later, I wanted her sweetness on my tongue. I wanted to taste every inch of her body and feel her come apart beneath my mouth.

I stood and gripped the sides of her panties, yanking them off her legs. Then I unzipped my jeans, shoving them and my boxer briefs to the floor.

Sasha's eyes widened as she stared at my cock. "You're . . ."

Huge. Like she'd said in the car. A grin stretched across my face as I fisted my shaft, giving my dick a few hard strokes. She watched, eyes fixed on my every move. Her tongue darted out to lick her bottom lip.

Someday, I'd taste her. Someday, I'd have that mouth around me. Someday, we'd play.

Because I'd be damned if this was the only time she was in my bed.

I reached for the nightstand and fished out a condom from the drawer. And when I was sheathed, I settled into the cradle of her hips, framing her face with my elbows.

Her eyes darted around the room, looking anywhere but at my face.

"Sasha," I murmured.

She closed her eyes.

"Don't shut me out." I pushed a lock of hair off her temple, waiting until she met my gaze. "We can stop this right now."

"No, that's not . . ." She sighed. "I'm nervous. I don't . . . I'm not good at this."

"This?"

"Sex," she whispered.

"Who said?"

She shrugged. "I said. I have a hard time, um . . ."

Orgasming. Either because she'd had morons for past lovers, not something I wanted to think about at this very moment, or because she was stuck in her own head.

Both problems I'd be happy to solve.

I kissed the corner of her mouth as I reached between us, dragging the tip of my cock through her center and up to her clit. When she gasped, I kissed her again, rocking against her.

"We're going to fuck. And tomorrow, when you wake up, we're going to fuck again. Then you can decide if you're not good at this. But not yet."

Sasha's mouth parted. "I—"

Whatever she was going to say, I captured with my lips, kissing her until she clung to my shoulders, her nails digging into my skin. When she started to rock against me this time, seeking that friction, I lined up at her entrance and thrust home.

"Fuck," I hissed. Tight. She was so tight. "God, you feel good."

"Jax." Those nails dug deeper as she stretched around me. "Move."

I gave myself a moment so I wouldn't come like a teenager, then I eased out and drove forward again.

Her inner walls were already fluttering.

Not good at this? Her entire body sparked mine. That bite of her nails. Those nipples dragging along my chest. Her long, toned legs wrapping around my hips.

"So damn good." I gritted my teeth. This was going to last five minutes if I didn't rein myself in.

Sasha let out a shaky breath, but instead of sinking deeper into this, of letting go and enjoying the ride, a tension crept into her body.

"Eyes on me, baby."

She opened them, reluctantly, and this time when I kissed her, it was sweet. Gentle.

I rocked us together slowly, flicking the tip of my tongue against hers as I matched the rhythm. And the whole time, I held that dark gaze.

It took five strokes before she finally melted beneath me. Until that fluttering in her pussy returned, stronger and faster.

Every time she tried to look away, I'd take her mouth, forcing her to stay with me.

"Look how you take me." I glanced between us to where we were connected, slowing so she could watch my cock sink inside. "It's fucking magic, Sasha."

Her entire body trembled. "Oh God, Jax."

I pistoned faster, loosening the hold on my control, just a little.

Her eyes drifted closed as her breaths turned ragged. Her face twisted, like she was trying so hard to get there except that beautiful mind of hers was still in the way.

I bent and sucked a nipple into my mouth. Then I reached between us and found her clit.

"Yes," she moaned. "Don't stop."

I circled the bundle of nerves with my finger, faster and faster. Until finally, her neck arched, her back coming off the bed. And she shattered.

Pulse after pulse she quaked. Her face was unguarded as pure ecstasy washed over her features. Her lips parted in a silent cry as the orgasm rocked through her, shaking every muscle, head to toe.

She'd never looked more beautiful.

I closed my eyes, savoring the sound of her incoherent moans. Then I let go, joining her as we both toppled over the edge.

"Fuck, Sasha." I poured inside her, my mind gone to anything but her.

Every bone trembled through the release, every nerve ending buzzing. It was like being shaken upside down and whirled right side up. Like I was spinning faster than the earth itself and gravity lost its hold.

There was thunder in my chest, lightning zapping through my limbs. Reality returned slowly, like a morning fog clearing off a spring meadow as the sun burned it away.

I collapsed on top of Sasha, burying my face in her hair as I inhaled.

Damn. That was the best sex I'd had in, well, ever. That changed . . . a lot.

She clung to me, her legs wrapped around my hips and her arms locked over my shoulders. Our bodies, still connected, were slick with sweat. Our heartbeats raged, and our chests heaved. But neither of us made a move to untangle, not until the stars fully cleared from my eyes. Then I rolled to the side, hauling her onto my chest.

I needed to deal with the condom, but I kept her tucked close, not ready to lose her quite yet. "Still think you're not good at this?"

She pushed up onto an arm, staring down at me with that adorable crease between her eyebrows.

"It was an easy question, Sasha. With an easy answer." I pushed a lock of hair off her forehead, threading my fingers through the tresses until I reached her nape. Then I urged her close until our mouths fused.

We burned through three more condoms before we collapsed into a pile of twisted limbs. Her back was tucked into my chest, and as I closed my eyes, exhausted, I breathed in her hair.

"Good night, Sasha."

She burrowed into my hold. "Good night, Jax."

∾

It shouldn't have surprised me to wake up alone the next morning. Not after she'd been keeping me at arm's length for three months.

But damn if it didn't burn.

It really fucking burned.

Chapter 8
SASHA

The lodge was quiet for a Sunday morning. When I'd walked in at seven, the lobby had been nearly silent. The front desk clerk was miserably hungover from last night's party and keeping the trash close by. But with the guest count low, hopefully today would be easy for everyone.

Me included.

But considering where I'd woken up this morning, I wasn't holding my breath.

There were emails in my inbox, each of them bold and screaming, "Read me first!" But rather than move my mouse or touch my keyboard, I sat with my hands on my lap, watching the doorway from the corner of my eye.

Was Jax awake yet? It was nine. He was probably awake. Was he mad that I'd snuck out of his bed before dawn? Or was he relieved that he could skip the awkward morning after a one-night stand?

Not that Jax would have made it awkward. I couldn't imagine him saying, "Well, that was fun. Thanks for the sex. See you at work." He'd been nothing but a dream.

But rather than face him, rather than take a chance at an honest conversation where I let my guard down, I'd left.

God, I was such a coward.

Last night had been . . .

Mind blowing. Earth shattering. Life changing. I'd never felt like that before. I hadn't even known I *could* feel like that.

It terrified me how much I wanted him again. Over and over. Mine and only mine.

But that was impossible. There were too many obstacles between us, and at the end of it all, I was leaving Montana. Not today, but someday. Sooner rather than later.

Getting attached to Jax was guaranteed to break my heart. And I'd survived enough of that in my twenty-eight years to last a lifetime.

So I'd snuck out of his bed, then run to the cabin barefoot in the snow just to put some distance between us.

Losing control wasn't an option. Neither was losing this job.

I needed this job.

And I really, really shouldn't have slept with my sort-of boss and landlord.

Why was I such a mess? I dropped my face into my palms, letting out a frustrated groan.

At the sound of footsteps in the hall, I lowered my hands and held my breath, eyes glued to the open doorway as I waited. But when the bathroom door opened and closed, I exhaled and sagged in my chair.

If Jax decided to track me down today, it wouldn't take much effort. I didn't have a great place to hide. No friends who'd invite me over to spend the day on their couch or family members who'd let me crash a Sunday dinner.

This office was my safe place at the moment. Work was my retreat. How pathetic was that?

Maybe I could have driven into town and spent the day at a coffee shop, but I'd been too scared to get in my car parked at his place, so I'd walked to the lodge. I'd trudged through the snow, bundled in my warmest coat, boots, and gloves, all so I wouldn't have to face the man who'd given me four orgasms.

Four. How was that possible? It was usually a miracle if I could fake one.

There'd been nothing fake about my body's reaction. Somehow Jax had known exactly what to do, exactly how to move, and I'd come alive under his touch.

It was hard for me to shut off my brain during sex. I couldn't relax. So I'd learned how to fake it. The few men I'd slept with hadn't seemed to notice.

If I had faked it with Jax, would he have noticed? Probably.

"Oh God." I buried my face in my hands again. What the hell had I been thinking?

First at the party, blurting out the truth about my parents. Then the champagne. I hadn't been drunk, but it had definitely lowered my inhibitions. Enough to let Jax carry me to his bedroom and fuck me senseless.

It was the hat. It had been that cowboy hat. He'd looked so sexy wearing it all night, and then I'd gotten this ridiculous thrill that I was the woman who'd been with him when he'd taken it off. "Stupid. Freaking. Cowboy hat."

"Don't blame the hat."

My hands flew wide, my heart leaping into my throat as my gaze streaked to the door.

Jax stood with his arms crossed, leaning against the frame with an ankle crossed over the other. He was the epitome of casual. Relaxed. Friendly.

Except there was tension in his jaw and fire in those blue eyes.

Was he going to come into the office? Or linger in the doorway?

Linger. *Please linger.* I didn't trust myself to keep my composure if he came too close.

He held up a hand and jingled my car keys. With a quick flick of his wrist, they sailed across the room for me to catch.

"Thanks." I gulped. *Shit.*

He'd brought me my car. Did that mean he was good with me sneaking out? Or pissed?

His lips pursed.

Pissed. Definitely pissed.

"Sasha—"

"Wait." I held up a hand and cut him off before he could say anything that might change my mind.

I had to say this. I had to end this.

Before I screwed everything up, if I hadn't already.

"I need you to forget last night happened." The words tasted sour but necessary, like a bitter pill we both had to swallow. "Please. I can't be one of the many who flit in and out of your bed."

His jaw flexed, the corners so sharp they could have cut glass. But he didn't speak. He didn't move other than to blink and breathe.

"We work together," I said. "You're my boss."

He arched his eyebrows.

"Boss-ish," I muttered. Ugh. Why was it so hot in here? Was it the thermostat? Or the heat from his blazing glare? "I need this job, Jax. I *need* it."

At the moment, it was the only thing keeping me afloat.

"Please." My voice cracked. "Can we forget it?"

He stayed silent, staring as my heart galloped faster and faster until I feared it would race out of my chest. I fought the urge to squirm and take it all back. To tell him that last night was the best night I'd had in years.

That he made me laugh, and it had been a long time since I'd laughed.

Three months, actually. I hadn't truly laughed since the grocery store.

I wanted to tell him that he was the best kiss I'd ever had. That even though I'd woken up early, the hours I'd slept in his arms were the most peaceful I'd had in months. I wanted to tell him that I *liked* him. I liked him so much.

Except nothing had changed. Me liking Jax would probably end in disaster, and at the moment, that wasn't a risk I could afford.

So I kept my mouth shut and let him glare until he stood tall and walked away.

My heart cracked a little when the sound of his boots faded.

I closed my eyes, breathing through the pain in my chest. When the quiet returned, when I knew he'd leave me alone for the rest of the day, I sagged in my chair, pulling up my knees and hugging them to my chest.

This was the only way. This was the best choice.

Jax wasn't the relationship type. I had no desire to become fodder for gossip at the resort over a casual affair that would likely end in my broken heart.

It was better to stop this now. Then when I left this job, I could walk away without any ties.

Better. This was better. So why didn't I feel better?

I was good at faking it. Sometimes, I could even fool myself.

Not this time.

My stomach knotted, and my temples began to throb. I bit the inside of my cheek to stop my chin from quivering, then shook my mouse, waking up my computer to check my personal email.

The top of the inbox was a bill.

That's all I seemed to get these days. Just bills and spam.

Nothing from Eddie.

I opened the invoice, then clicked through the payment system until it was processed. Then I pulled up my bank account, cringing at the tiny balance.

When was I going to get ahead? How long would it take to feel like I was moving forward, not just running in place?

I really, *really* shouldn't have had sex with Jax. How uncomfortable was this going to get? It would all be made worse by the facts that he was my neighbor for the time being and we worked together.

For three months, I'd tried to avoid and escape him. It was next to impossible.

Where had my head been last night? Sex was not the reason I'd come to Montana. A fling with a hot cowboy was not why I'd uprooted my life to endure a miserable winter.

The knot in my stomach doubled in size as I reached for a piece of paper and a pen.

My handwriting was sloppy, more scribble than script. It didn't matter. This was just another letter that would go unanswered.

A letter I crumpled into a ball when it was finished.

A letter I would never send.

~

Eddie,
I'm sorry.
I'm so sorry.
I messed up.
S

Chapter 9
SASHA

Six weeks later . . .

I'd messed up. *Oh God.* I'd messed up. This wasn't happening. This couldn't be happening.

My hands were shaking, my palms clammy. I walked out of the bathroom and collapsed on the bed, hugging a pillow to my chest.

Did I cry? Or scream?

I hugged the pillow tighter, letting numbness spread through my veins like a fog. The faint echo of a car door slamming drifted through the windows.

It certainly wasn't a visitor here to see me. I didn't get visitors. No, it was probably Jax's girlfriend.

She'd been around fairly often over the past two weeks. Did she know that Jax had slept with me after the party in January? Maybe she didn't care. Maybe they hadn't been officially together yet. Well, if she didn't know, she would soon enough.

I squeezed my eyes shut as my stomach roiled.

"Oh God." I buried my face in the pillow as a sob escaped.

What was I going to do? What would Jax say?

We hadn't spoken in six weeks. Not a single word. He'd email me his weekly excursion summaries. He'd nod if we crossed paths in the lodge—which rarely happened now that Indya was on maternity leave and he didn't stop by her office to visit.

If we both happened to be outside of our houses at the same time, he'd look at me, but that was it. Either he'd get in his truck to drive away, or he'd retreat inside his house.

He'd finished the laundry room the week after the party. He'd come in while I was at work and installed the new washer and dryer. But he hadn't left a note. Hadn't texted to tell me it was done. Nothing.

It wasn't like I'd tried to talk to him either. It had become so awkward that if I saw him, I turned and went the other direction. My rent checks were slipped under his front door whenever I was sure he wasn't home.

How was I supposed to face him? How was I supposed to tell him I was—

Another sob escaped. My insides churned, and the dinner I'd nibbled threatened to make a reappearance, but I wasn't about to puke on my bed, so I swallowed it down, breathing through my nose.

How did I tell Jax when I couldn't even think the word, let alone speak it?

A car door slammed again, forcing me off the bed. I trudged to the bedroom window and tugged back the corner of the curtain to look outside.

Jax stood in the front door's frame, his posture relaxed and easy. He lifted a hand to the Jeep Wrangler woman as she reversed away.

Not a sleepover then?

Damn. I was kind of hoping she'd be there all night. It would be easier to convince myself to put this off, to delay until tomorrow or the next day or the next, if he had a guest.

I let the curtain fall and dropped my forehead to the wall. *Shit.*

Delaying this would only make it harder. So before I lost the nerve, I forced myself out of the bedroom and to the cabin's door. I bundled up in my warmest coat and boots, then slipped outside and into the cold.

Winter was endless. For nearly a week, Mother Nature had gotten my hopes up that we'd seen the last blizzard. The weather had been warm enough to melt the roads, and while there were still patches and drifts of white, the meadows around the ranch were mostly mud and damp tufts of golden-brown grass.

I'd started repacking my belongings, preparing to return to the rental in town now that the drive wouldn't be so treacherous. My landlord had promised that the carpet was not just cleaned but new, and that the door's latch and lock had both been replaced.

The last time I'd talked to him, about two weeks ago, he'd seemed desperate to have me move back. Probably because I'd refused to pay while I wasn't living there. But also because my lease was month to month, and I had a feeling he didn't get a lot of takers on vacancies.

Nope, just me. The idiot who was new to Montana and didn't realize the people next door were prone to late-night parties and raucous sex.

As shitty as the rental was, it was better than being next door to Jax. So I'd planned to leave the cabin tonight while Jax was at the Saturday barbeque at the lodge.

But a massive storm had blown in three days ago, killing my hopes of spring and thwarting my plans to move.

I wasn't willing to risk the roads. And it wasn't like I particularly wanted to move.

This cabin was a dream. It was cozy and warm. It was clean, and I'd gotten used to having furniture. To sleeping on a real bed.

But as much as I wanted to stay, paying rent on two properties was ridiculous, especially on my budget. My landlord would expect a rent check if I didn't cancel my lease. And he, unlike Jax, would cash the checks I left.

Things hadn't been great over the past six weeks, but they'd been fine. Now? This wasn't fine. I wasn't fine.

Where did I go from here? What did I do?

Forward. One step at a time, like I'd done for the past ten years, no matter how hard it was to pick up my feet. So I forged a path through the snow to Jax's house. I took a fortifying breath when I reached his porch, steeling my spine and raising a finger to press the doorbell.

My heart hammered as it chimed. When the knob turned, I was sure I'd vomit. Again.

But then he was there, his blue eyes narrowing and his jaw flexing.

Even angry, he was gorgeous.

Jax crossed his arms over his chest. *State your purpose* might as well have been written on his forehead.

I didn't bother with a hello or small talk. I didn't bother with a smile.

Tonight, I wasn't here to tell him lies. But I did have a secret.

"I'm pregnant."

Chapter 10
JAX

I'm pregnant.

Two words in six weeks. Two fucking words.

I'm pregnant.

Those two words had been ringing in my head since Sasha had stormed back to her house an hour ago.

She'd gotten mad when I'd stood there, eyes wide and mouth agape.

Say something.

What had she expected me to say?

"We used condoms" clearly wasn't the right choice because she'd leveled me with a glare before walking away.

Pregnant. She was pregnant?

"Fuck." I reached for my tumbler, the ice rattling as I brought it to my lips. When I tipped it back, the bourbon inside was gone. "Shit."

Time for another refill.

Rather than stand from the kitchen floor where I was sitting, I stretched for the bottle on the counter above my head. The lid was . . . somewhere. Whatever.

I didn't need the lid. Not when I planned on finishing every last drop in the bottle.

With it pressed to my lips, I didn't swig—I chugged. Bubbles rolled through the amber liquid. The alcohol burned a flaming trail through my chest, settling hot in my gut.

The liquor was supposed to be helping. Why wasn't it helping?

I'm pregnant. Sasha's voice was ringing in my head, really fucking loud. Sitting on my kitchen floor, working on a hell of a hangover, wasn't helping either.

What was I supposed to do? Maybe West would know. My brother was good at this kind of emergency stuff.

My phone was on the other side of the living room, so leaving the bottle behind, I shoved to my feet, swaying slightly as I walked. Either the booze had kicked in fast, or I was still reeling from Sasha's visit.

Probably both.

For six weeks I'd been waiting for her to knock on my door. To acknowledge my existence. But she'd avoided me entirely. She hadn't breathed a word in my direction since the morning after the party when she'd asked me to forget.

Forget one of the best nights of my life? Nope. Forget my name on her lips? Not a chance. Forget how she felt in my arms? Absolutely not.

I didn't want to forget, so damn it, I wasn't going to forget. She couldn't make me, so there. Instead, I'd given her time and space to miss me.

She'd missed me, right?

I'd missed her. Sasha and I were practically strangers, but I missed her. That was weird, right? What did that even mean? I'd never missed a woman I'd slept with before.

I missed the look on her face when she'd spotted me from a distance, and for a split second, before she could hide it, her eyes would go all soft and sparkly. I missed the way she laughed. I missed the way she scowled.

Why couldn't she just admit that she liked me? She liked me. She had to like me, right?

How could she forget our night together? I'd been playing it on repeat for six freaking weeks. Over and over and over. I couldn't stop. I couldn't get that woman off my mind, no matter how hard I'd tried.

There was something between us that felt . . . different. Important. There was a spark. A connection. A potential.

And . . . a baby.

What. The. Fuck?

We were seriously having a kid?

I was halfway to the living room when I veered off course, changing paths for the door. The bourbon seeping into my blood made hopping into my boots a challenge, but after I crashed into the wall twice, they were on my feet, my jeans bunched around my calves. I yanked open the door, slamming it behind me as I followed Sasha's path through the snow.

The cold wasn't as sobering as it should have been. Halfway to the cabin, I lost my balance and slipped, crashing to my hands and knees. But I managed to stand, and when I finally made it to the cabin, I braced an elbow on the door's frame to hold me up as I knocked.

No answer.

Goddamn this woman. I knocked again. "Sasha."

Her feet pounded on the floor before she ripped the door open.

There was a toothbrush in her mouth. Her hair was tied up in a messy knot, and she was dressed in a pair of faded black sweatpants and a green tank top that molded to her breasts.

There was a gray pallor to her face. Her cheeks looked sunken. Her eyes were red rimmed and tired.

"You look like hell."

Sasha yanked the toothbrush from her mouth, her lip curling. "That's what you come over here to tell me? That I look like hell?"

"You do look like hell. And you're still the most beautiful woman I've ever seen."

The fury on her face vanished, pink rising in her cheeks.

"Getting ready for bed? Or are you sick?"

"Sick." She popped the toothbrush back in her mouth as she shifted to the side so I could come in.

As I shut the door and wrangled my boots off my feet, she disappeared down the hallway, probably to the bathroom.

I wandered into the living room and took a seat on the couch. The house smelled like her. Sweet and fresh and unique. A scent that was only Sasha. I'd missed that smell.

With my elbows on my knees, I dropped my face into my hands and scrubbed. The liquor was soaking in, making the world fuzzy at the edges.

Sasha came back, without the toothbrush, and sat in the oversize chair on the other side of the room.

"I'm drunk," I announced.

"Fantastic," she deadpanned, tugging idly on an earlobe.

"Why do you do that?"

"Do what?" she muttered.

"Pull on your ear."

She stopped instantly, her hand falling to her lap like she didn't even realize she did it. Maybe it was a nervous habit. Something she did when she was anxious or uncomfortable. "What do you want, Jax?"

I stared at her, wishing I knew what the hell I should say. "We used a condom."

"Back to that again, huh?" She hugged her knees to her chest. "I'm aware we used a condom. Multiple condoms. One of them didn't work."

She rested a cheek on her knee. She looked small. Exhausted. Withdrawn. The more she curled into herself, the more I regretted that bourbon. With every passing second, she was shutting me out, and my head was too muddled to stop it.

"Sasha."

Her eyes flickered to mine.

"I'm sorry."

"Me too," she whispered.

I gave her a sad smile, then lay back, resting with an arm behind my head. The couch was too small, and my feet extended off the opposite end, but the world had tipped upside down tonight. It was spinning too fast, and if I didn't slow down, Sasha wouldn't be the only one puking tonight.

"I fixed this place up," I said.

"I know."

I lifted an arm, pointing to the ceiling. "There's a swirl in the texture that looks like an elephant up there."

Sasha was quiet for a moment, then she barked a hollow laugh. "This is what we're talking about."

"Stick with me, sweetheart. I ramble when I'm drunk." I let my arm fall to my side. "I fixed this place up."

"You said that already."

"Don't move out." I turned my head to look at her. "I don't want you to move out."

She swallowed hard. "I have my place in town."

"Let it go."

Her gaze dropped to an invisible spot on the rug beneath the coffee table.

"Everyone thought I should just tear this place down. But I thought it would be a good spot if I ever had company or if a friend like Emery needed to crash here for a while."

"Who's Emery?"

"My best friend. She's been staying at my place on and off. Her husband is a dickhead. I wanted this place to be ready when—if—she ever decides to leave him. Chances are she never will. But just in case, I wanted a safe place for her to stay."

"Oh." Sasha blinked, giving her head a slight shake. "I thought—"

"That she was my girlfriend? Nope. Eww." I grimaced. "I kissed her when we were thirteen. It was gross."

A ghost of a smile tugged at her lips.

"I don't have a girlfriend. I haven't been with anyone since you."

Something like relief crossed her expression. "Um, me neither."

"Yeah, I know."

Sasha was at home every night. She didn't seem to have friends. She'd never invited another person to the cabin. If she wasn't at the office, she was at home.

I'd been paying close attention.

Because had another man showed up at her door, I would have dragged him the hell off my property.

"Your friend's husband. Does he hit her?" she asked.

"Verbal punches. They count too."

She nodded. "I'm sorry for your friend."

"Me too." I shifted to stare up at the ceiling again, at the elephant I'd always see from this point on. "I don't know what to say."

"Neither do I." Her voice trembled. "I never expected this."

I blew out a long breath. Well, at least I wasn't alone in the shock. "How long have you known?"

"What time is it?"

I shifted to dig my phone from my jeans pocket. "Eight thirty-nine."

"Then I've known for one hour and thirty-nine minutes. I haven't been feeling great lately. Things have been, um, tender. And I'm late. I went to the store after work and bought a test. I took it not long before I came to your house."

Not long before Emery had left.

Part of me wished she would have stuck around tonight instead of heading home to work on shit with Calvin. If she had been there, she would have known what to say. That, or she would have smacked me upside the head the moment I reached for the bottle of bourbon and told me to get my ass to Sasha's place.

"Tell me what to say," I said.

"I don't know," she murmured. "I can't believe this is happening."

"Same."

There wasn't a single time I'd had sex without a condom. Not once. I'd had such confidence that they just . . . worked. Every time. Except one hadn't worked. And now I was going to be a father.

Holy fuck.

I was going to be a dad.

Definitely, definitely not ready. Not even a bit. I didn't even have a dog. Or a cat. My horses were the closest things I had to pets, and they didn't take much. What the hell did I know about being a father?

Yep, I was going to puke.

"Tell me a lie," I blurted.

"I'm excited for this baby." Sasha sniffled, and when I glanced over, she was wiping beneath her eyes.

My heart squeezed. Maybe from the tears she was fighting. Or the reality that this might all go away. This didn't have to be a monumental life change, not if she was against it.

My stomach pitched and tipped, like I was about to get bucked off my damn horse.

"Tell me a story."

She dabbed at her eyes again. "What kind of story?"

"Anything." At this point, I'd take scraps. Anything to know her better.

Anything to delay the question I'd have to ask eventually.

Her gaze roved down my legs, stopping at my feet. "My parents were sticklers for taking shoes off in the house, especially my dad. He wore plain white socks, like you. The day I moved in here, when you were working on the laundry room and had your boots off, it reminded me of him and his white socks."

I wasn't sure what to say to that, so I wiggled my toes.

"I'm scared, Jax."

The dread of what she might say next manifested as a lump in my throat. "What do you want to do?"

Sasha shrugged a shoulder but otherwise stayed quiet.

"My mother abandoned me."

"W-what? I thought Lily was—"

"Not my mother. West's mom. Not mine. It's fine." I waved it off like it wasn't a big deal.

It wasn't a big deal. Not really. Or maybe I'd been waving it off for so long that I'd convinced myself it wasn't an issue. Tonight was not the night to figure that shit out.

"I never knew her. I was a baby when she left," I told Sasha. "She had a one-night stand with Dad in Vegas. Brought me to Montana after I was born. Dropped me off. Never came back."

"Jax, I . . . if you're worried about that, I would never abandon my child." There was an edge to her voice.

"That wasn't meant as an accusation. I told you, I ramble when I'm drunk. My point was that she had me. Even if she left me, at least she had me. Then she gave me to Dad."

"Oh."

I shook my head, wishing I knew how to do this the right way. Was there a right way? How did other men react when a woman dropped the pregnancy bombshell?

What I needed to say wasn't something to say lying down, so I swung up to a seat, ignoring the spinning in my head as I held Sasha's gaze. "I'll understand if you don't want to go through with this. Promise. But I think . . . I think I do?"

It sounded like a question. Was it a question? No. Even with only an hour for it to sink in, that was all the time it had taken for my heart to decide. My brain had some catching up to do, but in my heart, I knew what I wanted.

Somehow, even drunk and shocked, I knew what I wanted.

"I want to go through with this," I said. "If that's okay with you."

Was I ready to be a dad? Not really. But I could get ready. I had time to get ready, right?

"I think . . ." Sasha swallowed hard. "I think I do too. Want to go through with this, I mean."

"Really?"

She lifted a shoulder. "Yes. I'm not sure I can even articulate why I feel like this. But I think . . . I want this baby."

"Thank fuck." The air rushed from my lungs as I hung my head. Then I shifted to lie down again because the drunkenness wasn't as bad if I just kept staring at the elephant. "We should probably get to know each other."

"Probably."

"What's your favorite flavor of pickle? Dill? Or bread and butter?"

"Dill."

"I like both. I like bubble gum ice cream. The kind that turns your tongue blue and has actual gum in it. You can't really get it in a lot of places, but every summer during the county fair, there's a waffle-cone booth that has it. Do you like the county fair?"

"I've never been to one."

"I'll take you. We'll get bubble gum ice cream and ride the Sizzler. Not the Zipper. Those cages are death traps. I won't do it. Deal?"

"Deal." Sasha shifted in the chair, curling sideways so she could rest her cheek against the back. "What's your favorite movie?"

"*The Notebook*."

She lifted her head. "Seriously?"

"No."

The corner of her mouth turned up, and that barely there smile was enough to loosen some of the pressure in my chest.

"I love old Westerns. Anything John Wayne or Clint Eastwood. If I had to pick a favorite, probably *Lonesome Dove*."

"I've never seen it."

"We'll fix that soon enough," I promised, closing my eyes. "Are you scared of any animals or insects?"

"I'm terrified of snakes. I don't love spiders."

"You told me the day we met. About the spiders. I don't mind snakes or spiders. But I think hyenas are creepy."

"Hyenas?"

"Yeah. Why are their necks so long?"

A faint giggle drifted across the room. That laugh was my win for the night. "No hyenas. Got it. Cats or dogs?"

"Both," I said. "But I don't have pets. I don't love the idea of animals inside. My grandparents are like that too. How old were you when you got your first kiss?"

"Sixteen. You?"

"Thirteen. Emery and I thought we should be boyfriend-girlfriend in eighth grade. So I kissed her at a high school football game underneath the bleachers." It had been sloppy and wet. We'd both cringed afterward, and from that moment on, she'd been nothing but my best friend.

There weren't many things I didn't tell Emery. But for some reason, I'd kept Sasha a secret.

Emery knew *about* Sasha. That she worked as manager at the lodge. That she was staying in the cabin for the time being.

But I hadn't wanted anyone to know about our night together. Not Emery. Not Indya. Not even West.

Sasha was mine and mine alone.

How were we going to tell people she was pregnant? How were we going to handle this? Maybe she should move into my house. It would be easier if we were under the same roof. Or did she want to keep some separation?

"Would you go to dinner with me tomorrow night?" I asked, holding my breath for her answer.

Except the room was quiet.

I cracked my eyes open, glancing at the chair.

Sasha's body sagged against the cushions, her eyes shut and her mouth parted as she slept.

I pointed to the elephant on the ceiling. "I see you now, buddy."

Then I closed my eyes and fell asleep.

Chapter 11
SASHA

A throat cleared at my office door, pulling my focus away from my monitor.

Jax leaned against the threshold, arms crossed over his chest.

Hello, déjà vu. It was like a blast to six weeks ago, the morning after the party. This was another Sunday morning when I'd snuck out of a house to hide in my office. And Jax had found me.

Jax had been asleep on the couch when I'd slipped out of the cabin at dawn. As quietly as possible, I'd climbed into my car and made my way to the lodge. And for the past thirty-ish minutes, I'd been staring, unblinking, at my screen, wondering how long it would take for him to show up.

Thirty-ish minutes.

"Hi."

"Hey." He was wearing a baseball hat, the brim casting a shadow over his eyes. The ends of his dark-blond hair were damp from a shower. He was wearing a pair of faded jeans and his brown cowboy boots. But rather than his typical button-down shirt, he was in a hoodie. Montana State was embroidered in white letters on the navy cotton.

"Is that where you went to college?"

He nodded. "Yes. You?"

"A community college in California." Not the kind of school where you bought official apparel or proudly sported its colors.

Jax looked tired this morning. Probably because he'd spent the night on a couch too small for his large frame.

When I'd woken up in the chair, drool dripping down my chin, he'd been snoring softly. I didn't remember him snoring the night I'd spent in his bed. Maybe he rambled *and* snored when he was drunk.

"Hungover?" I asked.

He lifted a shoulder. "I've felt better, and I've felt worse."

I nodded, not sure where to look, so I stared at a spot on my desk. It had been easier last night when he'd carried the conversation. When he'd filled the quiet moments, babbling about elephants on my ceiling.

"I'm going to make a doctor's appointment," I said. This morning, I'd woken with a thousand questions exploding in my brain.

If we were doing this—*were we really doing this?*—I wanted to prepare.

When was my due date? What were the off-limits foods? Could I drink my morning coffee? I'd skipped it today, and the headache blooming between my eyes was the result.

"Can I come along?" Jax asked. "I'd like to go."

"Sure." My chest felt too tight, like I couldn't fill my lungs, and I was either about to cry or laugh or scream. Maybe all of the above.

I wrapped my arms around my waist, holding tight.

"Sick?" Jax shoved off the door, standing tall and ready, like he'd rush to grab a trash can if I was about to puke.

"No." I shook my head. "Sort of. It's just . . . overwhelming."

"Yeah." His arm crashed against the door's frame again, the weight of this settling heavy on his shoulders. "Are you going to hide out here all day?"

"If I said yes, would you let me?"

The corner of his mouth turned up. "No."

"Figured," I muttered. "I can't concentrate anyway."

"Hmm." He rubbed a hand over his jaw, his palm scraping against the stubble. "So you hate Montana."

"I don't hate Montana."

Jax smirked. "Liar."

There was no use denying it. "It's not my first choice of home locations," I admitted, reaching for my water bottle to take a sip.

"I'm going to make you fall in love."

The water spewed from my mouth, a few drops even coming out of my nostrils as I coughed and choked. "W-what?"

"With Montana. I'll make you love it."

"Oh." I coughed again, clearing the last of the water. *Phew.* Not Jax. He didn't want me to fall in love with him. Just Montana.

That was a relief, right? Why didn't I feel relieved? The last thing we needed was romance. This was complicated enough with the pregnancy. And after the baby was born . . .

How would this work when I left Montana? Where was I going? What about Eddie?

Eddie. My stomach pitched, and it was my turn to search for a trash can.

He hadn't crossed my mind today. Last night either. Why hadn't I thought about Eddie? I'd been reeling from the moment I'd peed on that pregnancy test, and he'd been forgotten. God, I was the worst.

Well, now that Jax knew the truth, I could think beyond the next five minutes.

Sooner or later, I'd have to tell Eddie. I'd have to admit to a one-night stand with Jax. To being careless and reckless.

Would he hate me? Would this break his heart? Or had we already hurt each other so much that this would just be another wedge driving us apart?

"Sasha." Jax took a step into the office, his eyes narrowing in concern. "What?"

"It just . . . everything changed. The world keeps flipping upside down."

He gave me a sad smile as he walked to the desk, holding out his hand. "Come on. Let's get out of here."

"And go where?"

Jax smiled. It was soft and gentle and sweet. It was a smile I had only seen once. The night of the party. And just like then, my heart tumbled.

He kept hold of my hand as we walked out of my office and down the hallway.

I wiggled my fingers as we made it to the lobby, trying to shake loose, but he just clamped down tighter.

"Jax," I hissed.

He shot that infuriating, adorable smirk over his shoulder.

My nostrils flared.

Mindi was working at the desk this morning. Either he didn't give a damn what she thought, or he was holding my hand to make a point.

I kept wiggling.

He kept holding.

People were going to talk. The resort would be abuzz with rumors.

Except they were always going to talk, weren't they? There was only so long I could hide a pregnancy. Maybe it was better for people to think we were together. That this baby wasn't a huge mistake that would derail all of my plans.

"Jax." I pulled on his arm the moment we were outside, bringing us both to a stop on the lodge's sweeping porch. "I don't ever want this baby to think he or she is a mistake. I don't ever want to say this was an accident."

He studied me for a long moment, then nodded. "Okay."

The air rushed from my lungs, forming a white cloud in the cold. Eventually, we'd have to figure out a story to tell, but for now, as long as we had that understanding, it was enough.

"Do you think it's a boy or girl?" he asked.

"Girl." It was wishful thinking. Most expectant mothers would probably answer that they didn't care as long as the baby was healthy.

But I wanted a girl. "If it's a girl, I want to name her Josephine, after my mother."

"Josephine." Jax spoke the name like he was sampling a fine red wine, letting it swirl on his tongue to see how it tasted. "It's beautiful."

"Thank you."

He squeezed my hand, keeping that constant grip, then continued on down the stairs and to his gray Silverado waiting in the parking lot. He opened my door, helping me in before going to the driver's side. Then as the engine revved and the heat blasted through the vents, he pulled away from the ranch.

"Where are we going?"

"You'll see." Jax drove with one hand on the wheel, the other leaning on the center console. It was relaxed yet confident and wholly attractive, sort of like his swagger. And that freaking baseball hat. When had I become such a sucker for hats?

My pulse beat faster and my breath caught as I tried not to stare. Was it the pregnancy hormones already? When did they kick in?

"What?" he asked.

"Nothing." I tore my gaze away, keeping it on the gravel road ahead. "Where are we going?"

"You asked me that already."

"Thought maybe you'd tell me this time."

His chuckle was deep and smooth, filling the truck's cab. "I need to get Grandpa his lottery tickets."

"Oh," I groaned. "We're going to the grocery store, aren't we?"

"Returning to the scene of the crime."

There was one and only one grocery store in town. There'd been no avoiding it in the months that I'd lived in Montana, but I always tried to go at night, when the owner was gone and the clerks were teenagers working after school.

Last night, when I'd gone to buy the pregnancy test, there'd been a boy with severe acne at the register. He hadn't so much as blinked as he'd scanned the test because he'd been too busy trying not to gawk at the teenage girl in line behind me.

"We could stop by your place too," Jax said. "In case you want to pick up anything."

"That's okay."

"So you're just going to leave your stuff in town, keep paying for a shitty rental, but live on the ranch."

"Yes." Maybe. It made zero financial sense to keep the rental. But it was the safety net. "Are you going to cash my rent check for the cabin?"

"No."

"Didn't think so," I muttered. "That was the agreement I made with Indya."

"Indya doesn't own the cabin."

I sighed. "I don't like freeloading."

"You're carrying my Josephine. That's not exactly freeloading."

My Josephine.

The emotions swelled so fast I couldn't breathe. I opened my mouth, but nothing came out. My eyes flooded, the world a watery blur.

My Josephine.

Two words and he made it real. He made it special. He made it so I wasn't doing this alone.

Jax's hand stretched across the cab as the tears slipped down my cheeks. His fingers slid beneath my hair to my nape. His palm was warm as he cupped my skin. His thumb traced a line down the column of my neck, up and down, as I wiped my face dry, fighting to fill my lungs.

"I don't have stuff," I blurted when I could speak again. "Everything I own fits in my car. So the rental is empty. There's nothing for me there to pick up."

His thumb stilled. "What about furniture?"

"Nothing."

"Your bed?"

"Just an air mattress."

The pressure of his grip tensed as his jaw clenched. "Then you don't need it. Call the landlord. Put in your notice. Today."

"But—"

"Today, Sasha. Or I'll call for you."

I blew out a shaky exhale. It was the right decision. Deep down, I knew it was the smart decision too. In no way, shape, or form did I want to live there again.

Goodbye, safety net.

"Fine." Maybe I should have put up a fight, except I didn't want to trade the plush bed in the cabin for a leaky air mattress. I didn't want loud neighbors or a questionable hot-water supply.

And Jax had called her *my Josephine.*

So I pulled out my phone and called the landlord, promising to drop the keys in the mail while he would do the same with my deposit. "Done."

"I'll cash your rent check if that would make you feel better."

"Yes, please."

He nodded, slowing on the highway as we reached town. Then, before I was ready, we were parked outside the grocery store.

We passed an older woman exiting as we walked inside.

"Jax!" She let go of her cart, loaded with paper bags, to open her arms as wide as her smile. "Oh, it's so good to see you."

"Hi, Mrs. Miller. How are you?"

"Dandy." Mrs. Miller's eyes flicked my direction, but Jax didn't introduce us. "And you?"

"Doing great. Running a few quick errands this morning before we've got to get back to the ranch."

"Well, then I won't keep you. Potatoes and bacon are on sale."

Jax dipped his chin, giving her one last sideways hug before he led the way inside. "Mrs. Miller was my third-grade teacher. She's retired now. Sorry I didn't introduce you. But she would have kept us out there chatting for an hour."

"Ah." Who was my third-grade teacher? I couldn't remember her name.

Instead of heading for the cashier's lane, he snagged a basket from the rack beside the door and wandered to the produce section, getting a bag of potatoes and an onion. Then he made his way to the back of the store, grabbing a carton of eggs.

"Normally, I get eggs from my grandma's chickens. But there was an incident with a chicken hawk a couple weeks ago. It was a bloodbath."

"A chicken hawk." What the hell was a chicken hawk?

Before I could ask, a man in tan overalls stopped at Jax's side. "Mornin', Jax."

"Morning, Hank." They shook hands, then the man got his own carton of eggs as Jax walked to the dairy cooler.

When we reached the meat section, Jax grabbed three packs of bacon as another man, dressed in jeans and a canvas coat, smacked him on the shoulder.

"Jax. What's happening?"

"Hey, Mike. How are you?"

"Can't complain."

"Mike, this is Sasha. She's the manager at the resort." Jax shifted out of the way so I could shake Mike's hand. "Mike is a local contractor. He's the one who remodeled most of Haven River."

"Oh, you've done incredible work. It's lovely to meet you."

"You too." Mike smiled, giving Jax another clap on the shoulder, then left us to resume our shopping.

"Do you know everyone in town?" I asked as we meandered down the cereal aisle.

"Not everyone but close. That's just how it is when you grow up in a small town." He shifted the basket to his other forearm so he could take my hand.

This morning, while the world kept flipping, I let him hold it.

"You'll get used to it," he said.

Would I? A jolt of panic quickened my heart rate. Montana had never been permanent. This was my chance to make some money while everything with Eddie was up in the air. Then we'd find a place together. We'd start over.

But there was no starting over, was there? Not anymore.

The blood drained from my face. My head started spinning as my feet stopped moving. Surrounded by colorful boxes of cereal, standing beside a man who might as well be a stranger, I felt my entire future go up in flames.

"What's wrong, babe?"

I gulped, closing my eyes to try and find my balance. "Everything keeps flipping."

"Just hold tight. It'll stop."

After a few deep breaths, I started down the aisle again. "How are you so steady?"

"I'm not." He shifted closer, dropping his lips to my hair. It wasn't a kiss, not really. It was more like he was resting against me, breathing me in.

Leaning on me.

So I leaned on him.

We stood together, in a private bubble, until a woman approached, pushing a shopping cart. The rattle of the wheels broke us apart.

"Excuse me," she said, steering past us.

Jax pulled me into his side, his arm around my shoulder, and walked us to the checkout.

Carla, the owner, was the cashier today. She took one look at me, and her smile morphed to a sneer.

"Good morning," I said, helping Jax take things out of his basket.

She turned her glare to Jax, and though she stayed quiet, her expression screamed *Traitor.*

He just chuckled. "Hello, Carla."

The barcode on the eggs dinged as she swept it past the reader, her scowl never faltering.

"And my weekly lottery tickets," he told her, digging out his wallet from his back pocket.

She scanned and glared.

I squirmed, eyeing the door.

The moment the last pack of bacon was in a paper bag, I swept it into my arms and made a quick getaway.

"She hates me," I told Jax as we walked to the truck.

"Yep."

"How long is that going to last?"

"Until Josephine is ten or eleven."

Josephine. He kept saying her name. He kept making it real.

"What if it's a boy?" I whispered when the groceries were loaded and we were sitting in the truck.

"It's a girl."

Neither of us had a damn clue. But I needed to believe this was a Josephine, at least today. And somehow, he knew I needed to hear it too.

Jax waved to every person we passed on the drive back to the ranch. It wasn't a normal wave. He rolled two fingers over the steering wheel and toward the windshield, almost like a salute.

A white Tahoe rolled past, and he did it again.

"Who was that?"

He shrugged. "No idea."

"But you waved."

"Yeah."

"Why? You don't know them."

"Why not?" He shot me a smirk. "It's nice."

I couldn't think of a time I'd ever been waved at while driving. At least not in a friendly way.

"Try it," he said as another vehicle approached from the opposite direction.

"No, it's weird from the passenger seat." Besides, that was something for Montanans to do. Something for people who belonged here.

"It's just a wave, honey." He glanced over, a challenge sparkling in his blue eyes.

They were truly beautiful eyes. I hoped this baby, girl or boy, would get them.

As the gap closed with the other car, he rolled his wrist, getting the same wave in return.

I tucked my hands between my knees.

The sparkle dimmed in Jax's gaze, the only sign of his disappointment. "What kind of music do you like?"

"Pop. Some rock. You?"

"Country." He turned on the radio, letting the music keep us company on the rest of the drive.

When we pulled up to the lodge, West's truck caught his attention, and instead of taking me to my car, he headed for the stables, parking beside his brother.

The sound of two wild boys and the scent of horses greeted us as we walked through the door.

"Hey." Indya's face lit up when she spotted me with Jax. In her arms was baby Grace, bundled in a tiny pink snowsuit and wrapped in a fuzzy blanket.

"Oh, um, hi." *Shit.* I should have thought of what to say before we'd stopped. Maybe asked Jax not to stop at all.

We'd have to tell them. Did we do it today? We should wait, right? Until later? But what if Jax wanted to tell them? What was he going to say? How were they going to react? Was Indya going to be mad? What did this mean for my job?

With every question, the world flipped. *Flip. Flip. Flip.*

My gaze roamed the room, finding a clump of straw in the corner. That was my spot. That was where I'd puke.

Except before I could dart away, West carried over two ropes. "Hi. What are you guys up to today?"

"Groceries," Jax said, putting more space between us than he had all morning. "We carpooled into town."

The air rushed from my lungs. *Thank God.*

"Uncle Jax!" Kade was standing on a bale of hay, peering over a stall's gate. "Wanna come riding with us?"

"Sure." Jax took a rope from West and headed for his nephew.

"Mommy." Kohen raced over, his index finger raised in the air. "I got a sliver. It hurts really bad."

"Oh no."

"There are tweezers and a first aid kit in the bathroom," Jax said as he opened the gate, walking into the stall to join a pretty brown horse.

"Okay. Would you mind holding her?" Indya glanced to Grace, shifting the baby into my arms instead of waiting for an answer.

Not that I would have said no. I hadn't gotten to hold Grace yet. The day Indya had brought her into the lodge last week for the first time, there'd been so many people clamoring to hold her that I'd let others go ahead. By the time it was my turn, Grace had been fussy and ready to go home.

As Indya followed Kohen to the far end of the building toward Jax's office, I studied the baby's face.

Grace was two weeks old and light as a feather. Her soft eyelashes formed crescents above her smooth cheeks. Her pink mouth was pursed in a tiny bow.

She was perfect. She was precious and terrifying.

In nine months, I'd have one of these. A perfect, precious, and terrifying baby of my own.

My Josephine.

Flip. But this time, I didn't let the flipping sway me on my feet. Not while I had Grace in my arms.

When I glanced to the stalls again, Jax's blue eyes were waiting.

He gave me a soft smile, like he knew holding a baby today was freaking me the fuck out, but I was holding a baby anyway. He winked at me before moving back to the brown horse.

He was the handsomest man I'd ever seen in my life. Rugged and masculine and hypnotic. He was so beautiful it almost made me want a boy who'd look just like his father.

Almost, but not quite.

Grace whimpered, kicking her legs.

"Shh." I rocked her side to side. It had been a long time since I'd held a baby, but some things were hard to forget.

I hoped the other pieces would come back to me too.

"Do you think I can do this?" I whispered.

Grace opened her tiny mouth.

And wailed.

～

Eddie,
You were never a mistake. Not to me.
   S

Chapter 12
JAX

We'd been parked in front of the hospital for five minutes, and Sasha still hadn't moved to open her door. If we waited much longer, we'd be late to the appointment. But if she needed to sit here and stare at the Pioneer Medical Center, then I'd sit here too.

I'd needed the extra five myself.

She'd scheduled this initial visit with the doctor two weeks ago. Since, she'd reminded me about it seven times. I'd figured that the moment I parked, she'd be out of the truck and speed walking inside.

But Sasha surprised me more often than not. She'd pause when I expected her to rush. She'd stay quiet when I expected a snarky reply. She'd build her walls up higher just when I thought I was beginning to break them down.

I understood her hesitation. The moment we walked through the hospital's doors, this was real. This was happening.

We were having a baby.

"Sorry," she murmured as she finally reached for the door. "I just needed a second."

"Take your time."

She gave me a small smile, then hopped out.

Here we go. Ready or not. I climbed out, too, and followed her across the lot, tucking my hands in my jeans pockets to hide their slight tremble.

Sasha wasn't the only one freaking out. But she needed me to be steady right now. So I was saving my panicked moments for when I was alone. My anxiety had its time to shine in the middle of the night when I couldn't sleep.

Could we do this? Could I be a father?

God, I wanted to talk to West. Or even Dad. They always knew what to say, but until this appointment was over, until we learned more from the doctor, I'd keep my mouth shut.

It had been the longest two weeks of my goddamn life.

I wasn't good with secrets.

Sasha led the way through the hospital's entrance. To the left was the emergency room. Straight ahead, the doors to the nursing home. To the right, the small local clinic where the family medicine doctors practiced.

We checked in at the reception desk, then Sasha spent ten minutes filling out forms on a clipboard while I sat in the chair beside hers, fighting the urge to bounce my knees.

"I don't, um . . . I don't know your birthday." Sasha handed the paperwork over. "Can you fill out your information?"

"Sure." I took the pen and clipboard, balancing it on a thigh as I quickly checked boxes and scribbled down my address. "November third. I'm twenty-nine."

"I'm twenty-eight. My birthday is January first."

"New Year's." Wait. She'd been working at the lodge on her birthday. "We didn't have a party on your birthday."

"Indya offered." She waved it off. "I didn't want one."

I frowned and handed back the paperwork so she could finish.

Birthdays had become a big deal at the resort. Indya always made sure we celebrated an employee's special day, either with cake or cookies or a dessert of choice. She'd get balloons and a card to pass around. I didn't remember signing one for Sasha.

And birthdays had become a big deal in our family, too, ever since West and Indya had gotten married.

West always planned a party for Indya's. She did the same for him. One or both planned something for mine. And the celebration for the twins was a massive affair, usually involving inflatable bouncy houses or a petting zoo.

Had anyone celebrated with her? Did she have any friends in town? Or had she just worked the whole day, then gone home to an empty house and an air mattress?

A fucking air mattress.

Why didn't she have furniture? She'd been here for months before moving into the cabin. That was plenty of time to get something ordered and delivered.

It was on the tip of my tongue to ask, just like it had been for the past two weeks. But I swallowed down the questions, saving them for after this appointment. Saving them for a time when Sasha might actually answer.

She'd gone back to avoiding me over the past two weeks. I'd let her. Other than a daily stop at her office to make sure she was feeling all right, I gave her space.

I'd needed some space myself. Time to get my head wrapped around everything. I wasn't there yet, not even close, but I was trying.

A door across from the small waiting area opened, and a nurse dressed in pink scrubs called, "Sasha Vaughn."

She shot to her feet, the clipboard clutched to her chest.

I put my hand on the small of her back as we walked across the space to the nurse.

Sasha glanced over her shoulder to where my thumb was drawing circles on her black sweater.

If she wanted me to stop touching her, well . . . tough. There was something anchoring about having a hand on her. It was a reminder that we were figuring this out together. A reminder that if I lost my shit, she'd fall apart. And I wasn't going to let that happen.

The nurse was older than me, probably in her forties. She gave us a kind smile as we walked through the doorway, and I sent up a silent thanks that I didn't recognize her or the receptionist. Not that they could tell anyone, but I wanted my family to know before people around town.

When should we tell West and Indya? Wasn't there a wait time or something? Three months or whatever?

"We're in here." The nurse waved us into the closest exam room, then closed the door behind us.

I sat in another stiff, uncomfortable chair while Sasha was on the table having her blood pressure and temperature taken.

When the nurse handed her a paper gown and told her to strip down to nothing, she swallowed hard.

"Want me to go?" I asked when the nurse left us alone so Sasha could change.

"It's not like you haven't seen me naked," she murmured, the tissue paper on the table crinkling as she jumped down.

Yeah, I'd seen her naked. Every glorious inch. But that was not something I needed to be thinking about right now. Not something that would make her more comfortable. So I slipped off my baseball hat and covered my face to give her a moment of privacy. "It stinks in here."

"In this room?" The sound of rustling clothes filled the room as she started to undress. "I don't smell anything."

"No, in my hat. Is this what my hair smells like?"

"Jax." Sasha let out a tiny laugh. It was my win for the day. "You don't need to do that."

Yes. Yes, I did.

Where Sasha was concerned, my dick seemed to have a mind of its own, so I really did need to keep my eyes covered. The last thing I needed was an erection in this sterile, cold room. And if I watched her get naked, my body would have a reaction.

"Okay, I'm done. You can stop breathing in your stinky hat." The tissue paper crinkled again, and the exam table creaked as she resumed her spot.

I uncovered my face and found her chocolate gaze waiting.

She clutched the gown over her heart. Her knees were pressed together, and her shoulders curled in. She looked stiff and uncomfortable.

"Maybe I shouldn't have come," I told her.

"I think if you weren't here, I'd still be in the parking lot."

"Sasha—"

Before I could finish my sentence, not that I was really even sure what I was about to say, a knock came at the door, and the doctor stepped inside.

Hers was a face I did recognize. *Oh shit.* My stomach splattered to my boots. *Robin.*

"Hi, Sasha. I'm Dr. Anderson." She extended a hand for a shake, then turned to me, her eyes widening. "Jax?"

I gulped. "Hey, Robin."

She looked between Sasha and me, putting the pieces together. "So you're . . ."

"Having a baby," I finished, doing my best to keep my expression neutral despite my racing heart. "Didn't realize you were back in town."

"Yes. I moved home last month when I finished my residency. Dr. Smith is retiring, and I'm taking his place."

Did Emery know about this? If so, I was going to chew her ass for not giving me a warning.

Sasha's forehead furrowed. Of all the things I didn't want to explain today, the reason why I knew Sasha's doctor was at the top of the list.

"Robin and I grew up together," I said. It was only part of the story, but the rest would have to wait.

"We go way back." There was an edge to Robin's voice, but she swallowed it down and put on a polite smile before giving her undivided attention to Sasha. "Congratulations. How are you feeling?"

"Um, fine."

"She's been sick a little," I said.

Robin tensed at my voice, and I had a feeling if Sasha weren't here, she would have told me to shut the fuck up.

Sasha noticed it too. Her eyes flickered between us, trying to read that tension. She was a smart woman. She'd jump to a conclusion.

The right one.

"Nausea is normal at this stage," Robin said. "Are you still able to eat? Keep a meal or two down every day?"

"Yes, it hasn't been that bad." As Sasha spoke, she kept her attention on Robin. And Robin spoke only to Sasha.

There might as well have been a curtain in the room to shut me out. Between their collective cold shoulders, I was glad I'd kept my coat on. And when Sasha had a full breast and pelvis exam, I pulled my hat over my face again.

"Everything looks great," Robin told her when they were finished. "It might still be early, but let's see if we can hear the heartbeat."

Sasha's eyes finally flicked to mine from where she was lying on the table.

I gave her a smile as my heart galloped so fast it nearly raced out of my chest.

"You can get one of these for home." Robin squirted some gel onto Sasha's belly, then held up a box that looked like a walkie-talkie attached to a wand. "But we'll check the heartbeat at every appointment. Some patients find it causes more stress to try and locate it at home than just waiting for their next visit."

"Okay." Sasha nodded as Robin moved the wand through the gel.

There was a woosh and a bit of static, but then a heartbeat filled the room.

Luh-dub, luh-dub, luh-dub. It was fast. Steady. So incredible I couldn't breathe past the lump in my throat.

Sasha stared at the ceiling. She swallowed hard, then looked at me again.

A thousand different emotions swirled in her pretty eyes.

Fear. Hope. Excitement. Dread. Love.

I mirrored each and every one.

"Very healthy heartbeat," Robin said before she removed the wand.

The sound was gone too soon, and with it, Sasha blinked and tore her eyes away, once more focusing on the ceiling.

"Given the date of your last menstrual period, we'll put your due date on October nineteenth."

"Oh." Sasha paled as a flash of panic crossed her face. "October nineteenth."

Was there something wrong with October? Or was it just another detail that made the pregnancy all the more daunting?

October nineteenth. That was months away. We could do this, right? We could figure out how to become parents before this fall?

Why hadn't I paid more attention when the twins were babies? Maybe I should start babysitting Grace. I didn't know how to change a diaper or make a bottle.

Indya and West had spent that first week walking around like zombies because Grace didn't sleep for more than two hours at a time. I didn't function without sleep. They'd come home from the hospital in Bozeman and been—

Wait. "Is this a good enough hospital?"

Both Sasha and Robin looked in my direction.

"Should we be planning to have the baby in Bozeman or Billings?"

Sasha's eyes bulged, not having considered that yet.

Robin's narrowed into slits. "This facility is fine."

"But most people have their babies in a bigger hospital, right?"

"Yes," she admitted. "Some choose to go to Bozeman or Billings. If that's your decision, I'll be happy to coordinate with the physicians there. But we're perfectly capable of delivering babies at Pioneer."

Capable. But this was a small-town hospital with small-town limitations. If there was an emergency, I wanted Sasha in a larger facility. We'd plan that as we got closer to October.

"Good to know," I said.

Robin went back to ignoring me as she reviewed a list of recommendations with Sasha. They talked everything from vitamins to diet changes to appointment scheduling. She gave Sasha instructions for urine and blood tests, then handed over a litany of pamphlets for expectant mothers. Then she held out two for me to take, dropping them into my lap before I had a chance to grab them.

"Thanks," I muttered.

This was going to be a problem, wasn't it? Sasha and I didn't need more problems when we had plenty of our own. I wasn't going to skip these appointments just because Robin was pissed at me for something that had happened a decade ago.

"Lovely to meet you, Sasha," Robin said, then without so much as a glance in my direction, she left the room.

Fuck. It was easier to breathe with her gone.

Sasha moved quickly to get dressed and stuffed the paper gown in the trash. "What was that?"

"Not even going to wait until we're in the truck?"

Her glare was lethal.

"Robin and I dated our senior year in high school."

"Was it serious?"

"Sort of?" I shrugged, keeping my seat as she stood above me, fists braced on her hips. "I don't know. We broke up freshman year at MSU. It, uh, wasn't mutual. I hooked up with her roommate three hours after I dumped her, and she's pretty much hated me ever since."

"Seriously?" Sasha scrunched up her nose.

"Not my finest moment." I raked a hand through my hair.

For the first time in my life, I regretted the casual hookups from the past. The one-night stands and the women I'd taken home from the bar. Sasha would meet others. In this town, there was no avoiding it.

"I had no idea she was back and working here," I said.

"It's fine." She waved it off, going to the hooks on the wall to get her coat. "Just . . . awkward."

"We can get another doctor."

Sasha stayed quiet, ducking into the bathroom next door while I waited in the hallway. Then after she'd stopped at the lab to have her blood drawn, we headed for the exit.

We were three feet from making our escape when the double doors slid open.

Lily walked inside, dressed in navy scrubs, with her purse and a lunch box tucked under an arm.

Fuck my life. Wasn't she working the night shift?

"Jax?" She did a double take when she saw me, then scanned me head to toe. "Are you okay?"

"All good."

It was foolish to hope that she wouldn't recognize Sasha. The moment her gaze landed on the pamphlets in Sasha's hand, her jaw dropped. "Oh. I, um, I didn't know."

"No one does," I said, my voice sharp. "And we'd like to keep it that way."

Lily gulped. "Of course."

My hand found the small of Sasha's back, pressing her forward.

She arched her eyebrows as I kept pushing but, thankfully, kept walking.

"Wait. Jax?" Lily called before we reached the doors.

"What?" I glanced over my shoulder, not bothering to fully turn.

"Congratulations."

No. This was wrong. It was all wrong. I didn't want Lily to be the first person who knew about the baby. I didn't want her to have anything special when it came to Sasha or my kid. I didn't want her saying congratulations. Not before West or Indya or Dad.

Sasha slowed, giving me a sideways glance, like she expected me to say thanks.

I wasn't saying anything. So without a word, I left them both behind and walked outside.

How well did Sasha know Lily? Did they spend time together? Were they friends the way Lily had become friends with Indya?

My lip curled as I stalked to the truck. I was sitting behind the wheel, fuming, when Sasha caught up.

"Why didn't you have furniture?" I asked the moment she had her seat belt fastened.

"What?"

"Furniture. At the rental. Why didn't you want furniture?"

She shrugged. "It wasn't that I didn't want furniture. But I wasn't in a hurry to spend a bunch of money when I was rarely at the house."

"Not even a bed?"

"Beds are expensive, Jax."

There. That was the reason. Money.

She was earning a great salary, right? Indya wasn't the type to skimp on paying employees. Was Sasha in debt? Was she trying to pay off college loans or something?

But I'd asked my question, and I wasn't getting another.

"What was that with Lily?"

"It's complicated. Lily and I haven't spoken much lately." If *lately* meant most of the previous decade.

"Why?"

"Long story." I started the truck and pulled out of the lot. "What's wrong with October nineteenth?"

Sasha threw my own words in my face. "Long story."

That's how it was going to be, huh? Vague answers. Fine. If neither of us was in a mood to share, we'd listen to music. I turned up the volume on the radio, letting the latest country hits fill the silence as I drove us to the ranch.

When we reached the lodge, Sasha got out of the truck without a word. Then she disappeared inside to the safety of her office while I retreated to my own, working in the stables until dark.

The lights in the cabin cast a golden glow into the night when I finally made it home. My truck seemed to steer itself to the empty space beside Sasha's car.

She answered the door before I had the chance to knock. She'd changed out of the jeans and sweater she'd worn earlier and into a pair of orange sweatpants and a black tank that showed the straps of her pink bra. The toothbrush was in her mouth again.

"I'm grumpy," I warned.

She popped the toothbrush out of her mouth. "Me too."

"Want to be grumpy together?"

Sasha shrugged.

"Come on." I reached inside and plucked her coat from the rack. "We're having breakfast for dinner."

"I'm not hungry."

"You don't have to eat."

She took the toothbrush to the kitchen, leaving it on the counter, then rejoined me at the door, stepping into a pair of tennis shoes before tugging on her coat. Then she followed me outside and into the truck.

I parked in the garage and escorted her inside, taking off my boots as she did the same with her shoes before we entered the living area. "Want a tour?"

"That's okay." She curled into one side of my leather couch as I built a fire in the fireplace.

And when I moved to the kitchen to start on dinner, she sat on a stool at the island, watching me cook.

It should have been strange to have her here again. Maybe a bit awkward, considering she'd spent a whole five minutes here last time before I'd taken her to the bedroom. But it felt easy. Natural.

I took a chance that she was hungry. When I took the seat beside hers, I slid over a plate of pancakes with roasted strawberries before diving into my own.

Sasha picked up her fork and dived in.

"Your first breakfast for dinner?" I asked.

"Yes. This is really good," she said as a shiver rolled over her shoulders.

I set my fork down and went to my bedroom, then returned with a hoodie.

"Thanks." She smiled before pulling it over her head. "I get really hot when I don't feel good. Then it passes, and I'm freezing all the time."

The sweatshirt was three sizes too big and pooled at her wrists, but damn if I didn't love seeing her in my clothes.

"Tell me a lie," I said as we kept eating.

She poked at a strawberry, pushing it around her plate. "It doesn't bother me at all that my doctor is your ex-girlfriend."

There was jealousy there. Any other situation, and I probably would have gotten a little thrill from that envy. Except this wasn't her being jealous about a former girlfriend and claiming me as hers. Sasha was uncomfortable. And that was not okay.

"We'll get another doctor. I can, uh, ask Lily for recommendations." The last phone call I wanted to make, but I'd make it.

"Are you sure? I can ask around too."

"We don't have a great relationship, but she's worked at the hospital for ages. She'll recommend the best doctor."

"Thank you."

"Sure." I ate another bite, taking a moment to sort out exactly how to explain this. "About Lily."

"Jax, we don't have to talk about this."

"No, you should know." I wiped my mouth and swiveled sideways to face her. "Lily's the closest thing I've got to a mom. When I was little, she did everything a mother would do. Taught me how to tell my left boot from my right. Made me breakfast, lunch, and dinner. Read me books, and tucked me in at night. But if I called her Mommy, she'd correct me. She'd tell me to call her Lily."

Sasha's forehead furrowed. "Really? How old were you?"

"Two. Three. Four. I can't remember a time when I didn't call her Lily. It was just her name. West called her Mom. I called her Lily."

And maybe if she hadn't done everything else, if she hadn't treated us the same in every other way, it wouldn't have bothered me.

"She hugged me. Teased me. Scolded me. After she and Dad got divorced, she'd come visit and check up on me. West stayed at her place in town more often, but I was mostly here on the ranch. Not always, but usually. If I had a late-night practice after school and the roads were bad, I'd stay at her place with West. She'd cheer me on at my football games and help with the fundraisers at school. Most people assumed she was my mom. That was the role she played. It was what we both let people believe. Until I realized it wasn't enough."

I didn't want to pretend that Lily was my mother. I didn't like having to explain to my friends why I called her Lily—or dodge the question entirely. I was tired of wondering why she couldn't just love me.

"Before I left for college, we got into a fight. I told her she could either be in or out. Told her I was either enough of a son that she could fucking act like it and let me call her Mom. Or I was done."

Looking back, the whole fight had been impulsive. She'd asked me out for dinner to spend an evening together before I left for Bozeman. But we'd bumped into one of my friends and his parents as we were leaving the restaurant.

My buddy's mom had made a comment about requiring Sunday phone calls to give proof of life to our mothers.

Lily hadn't asked me to call her. She hadn't asked me to check in regularly or keep her posted about my classes or grades. Maybe she'd just been relieved that I was finally leaving. That the child of the woman who'd ruined her marriage was in another county.

All I'd wanted, as a teenage kid about to leave home, was to call a mother on Sundays if I was homesick.

Not once in my four years of college had I called Lily on a Sunday. Or any other day.

"She made her choice," I told Sasha. "And I haven't spoken to her much since."

"She told you to keep calling her Lily?" Sasha asked.

"Yeah."

Her jaw clenched, then she was off her stool, swiping my plate and hers to take to the sink. They clanked and clattered as she rinsed them off, then practically threw them into the dishwasher. Then she slammed the door and turned, her arms crossed over her chest.

"That's not right, Jax."

My chest felt too tight. Her rage on my behalf made it hard to breathe. "No, it's not."

"I was nice to her at the hospital. After you stormed outside, I was nice because I felt bad for her because you were being a jerk. Now I wish I hadn't been nice."

I'd seen Sasha angry, always at me. It was adorable the way her cheeks flushed. Beautiful, really, especially when that anger wasn't aimed in my direction. "You can be nice to Lily."

She scoffed. "Not a chance."

God, she was something. Flushed and frazzled and absolutely drowning in my hoodie. "Tell me a lie."

She was still fuming as she leaned against the counter. "Breakfast for dinner is gross. Your turn."

"You look horrible in that sweatshirt."

The compliment softened her frown but didn't make it vanish. Not entirely. It took every ounce of willpower not to leave my seat.

Not to kiss that frown off her face.

Except that wasn't the point of dinner tonight. That wasn't the point of any of this. So instead of kissing her, I grabbed one of the pamphlets I'd brought in from the truck and opened it to the first page.

Chapter 13
SASHA

With a fortifying breath, I raised my hand and knocked on Jax's door. My pulse had been racing since, well . . . all day. Since he'd come into my office this morning and invited me over for another dinner.

I'd had an excuse at the ready. A headache. But before I could tell him the lie, he'd said please.

Please? Have dinner with me.

He didn't have to say please to have dinner with a woman, did he? Most probably jumped at the chance to share a meal with Jax Haven. Besides that, he hadn't asked me for much in the past month. He hadn't pushed me for anything, even my time.

So here I was, standing on his porch, my heart beating so fast I worried it would fly out of my chest.

The knob turned, and there he was, a dish towel in hand and a smile on his face. A smile that stole the sliver of air left in my lungs.

"Hey, you."

My stomach dipped. "Hi."

God, this was a stupid idea. He looked gorgeous. His hair was disheveled, sticking up at odd angles. He hadn't shaved this morning, and the stubble on his jaw was sexier than was safe for my well-being.

"Hungry?" he asked, shifting out of the way for me to come inside.

"Yeah." Starving. The nausea I'd battled in the evenings during my first trimester had vanished. An insatiable appetite seemed to have taken its place, and I was famished. The scents of bacon and maple and vanilla made my stomach growl.

Jax steadied my elbow as I toed off my shoes on the mat in the entryway.

So far, spring had been wet and muddy. But I'd never minded the rain. Every morning for the past week, I'd woken to the musical prattle of drops on the cabin's tin roof.

"Come on in." He jerked his chin for me to follow him into the open room, where he had a fire burning in the hearth.

Jax headed for the kitchen stove, where a frying pan sizzled with hash browns. His jeans draped down long legs to bare toes.

He was relaxed and casual. It was magnetic. I couldn't tear my eyes from his plain black T-shirt that stretched across his broad shoulders and strong chest, straining at the biceps.

"Pancakes okay?" he asked.

"Sure." I slid onto a stool at the island and watched as he moved around the space, mesmerized by how such a large body could be so graceful.

"Haven't seen you much lately," he said. It was just a statement without a hint of accusation in his tone.

I hadn't been purposefully avoiding him, but I hadn't exactly sought him out either. Mostly because I was three and a half months pregnant.

And three months was when couples generally started making announcements.

I wasn't ready to make announcements, not yet.

"It's been busy at work." Not entirely a lie.

With Indya still out on maternity leave, there was plenty to be done. Reservations were beginning to ramp up with the spring weather, and the resort was busier now than it had been since the holidays.

Just like it had been when I'd first moved to Montana, work had been my salvation over the past month. It gave me an excuse to ignore the disaster that was my personal life.

I went into the office around six each morning, and if I came home by seven, it was an early night. Either it was the pregnancy or the long hours, but I was usually so exhausted by the time I walked through the cabin's door that I didn't have time to panic about the baby. Or Jax. Or Eddie.

Ignoring problems was my newest party trick. And if it ever failed me, there was always my trusty standby. *Fake it until it breaks you.*

People at work thought I actually had my shit together. The joke was on them.

"Feeling okay?" Jax asked over his shoulder.

I nodded. "I'm good."

"Doctor's appointment tomorrow."

"Yep. One o'clock. If you don't want to come—"

"I'll be there."

The relief was staggering.

Maybe I wasn't sure how to cope with all of this yet. I'd probably be a lousy mother. Except it was happening. Whether I was ready or not, this was happening.

I'd only had the one doctor's appointment so far. This early on, I'd go in once a month. Tomorrow, I couldn't ignore reality. And if he came with me to the appointment, then at least I wouldn't be alone.

In case something bad happened, for once, I didn't want to handle it alone.

"Thanks," I said. "And thanks for talking to Lily about a new doctor."

"Welcome." He opened the oven door and took out a baking sheet lined with aluminum foil and crackling bacon.

We wouldn't be meeting with ex-girlfriend Robin tomorrow. The trade-off was that my physician was now a man. I'd never had a male doctor before, but he came highly recommended, and he'd been Indya's doctor, too, during her pregnancy. Not that I'd asked Indya about her experience. This was all information from Lily.

I think I hated her for what she did to Jax. Maybe. Probably. It would be easier to hate her if she wasn't so . . . nice.

Why did she have to be nice? Every time I'd spoken to Lily, she'd been sweet and kind. She'd come out to the resort to visit Indya or West, and she'd always made it a point to pop into my office and say hello.

Before Jax had told me about their history, I'd liked Lily. A lot. Now? *Hate* was a strong word. And I'd probably gone overboard with my reaction the night Jax had told me the whole story.

But being a mother wasn't always about blood.

Lily had made the wrong choice. She should have chosen Jax.

If I were him, I wouldn't have talked to her either. With any luck, we wouldn't bump into her at the hospital again.

"Can I help with anything?" I asked.

"Nah. I've got it."

While he cooked, it gave me a chance to study more of his house. From the warm, forest green cabinets to the granite counters flecked with gold. The island was massive and separated the kitchen from the open living room.

The rawhide leather furniture was clearly expensive, but it was also cozy and welcoming. The random scratches across the couch gave it character and charm. It had a similar style to the cabin, rugged yet modern. Except something about his couch was more inviting than mine. I wanted to curl under his tan-and-black-striped throw blanket, soak in the heat from the fireplace, and sleep for ten hours straight.

I yawned, unable to hold it back.

"Tired?" Jax asked as he pulled two plates out of a cupboard.

"Yeah. I'm tired a lot at the moment."

He hummed, finishing our dinner. When he set a heaping plate in front of me, my eyes bulged.

"This is more than I'll be able to eat."

"It's all right." He lifted a hand and pushed a lock of hair off my temple.

Tingles raced across my skin as his fingers lingered at the shell of my ear. Then his hand was gone, and I couldn't seem to remember how to breathe.

He poured syrup over his pancakes as I forced an inhale.

What were we doing? What did he want from me? What did I want from him?

No idea. But I liked that he touched me. I liked that he was affectionate. Even if it was confusing and reckless and would only complicate things more than they were already.

I liked being here, at this island, having breakfast for dinner again. Maybe I shouldn't have ignored so much for the past month. It was easy to slip back onto this stool. I liked that it was easy to be here, around him.

But that was everyone in his life, wasn't it? People liked Jax; they fell into his orbit. I was just another one of those people. The one who happened to be having his baby.

"Tell me a story," he said.

"What kind of story?"

"Anything." He nudged my elbow with his, giving me a playful smile. "We haven't done a great job in the past month getting to know each other, have we?"

"No, I guess not." Still no accusation in his tone.

Maybe because he could have tracked me down too. Maybe I wasn't the only one not sure how to navigate this. Maybe I wasn't the only one happy to ignore it for a bit.

"I was prom queen my senior year in high school," I said.

"Ah." He smirked. "You were the popular girl."

"Pretty much. I was a cheerleader."

"Dating the star quarterback of the football team?" he teased.

"Yes." My smile dimmed.

When was the last time I'd thought about high school? About the girl I used to be?

That had been a different life. The girl who'd worn ball gowns and tiaras hadn't survived the death of her parents.

Where would I be if Mom and Dad were still alive? What would have happened with me and Eddie? Maybe it would have turned out exactly the same. Maybe not.

But I doubted I'd be in Montana. I wouldn't have met Jax. I wouldn't be having a baby.

Flip. There went the world again, flipping upside down.

"Tell me a secret," he said.

For once, I didn't have to think long. "I caught Tara making out with Reid in the hallway yesterday."

"What?" Jax's jaw dropped, his fork frozen in midair. "Reid? The chef Reid? And Tara?"

"Yep."

Tara had worked at the lodge for years as a housekeeper, then as an assistant manager. She was fiery but honest. When I'd first started at the resort, she'd gladly answered my questions and welcomed me to the staff.

Reid had been rather cantankerous at first, not wanting to take orders from me when he'd reported to Indya for so long. But eventually, we'd found a groove. I let him do his job, and he realized that when I made suggestions, I was simply trying to do mine.

"I don't know how I feel about this." Jax set down his fork and raked a hand through his hair. "Tara's like my aunt. She's worked at the lodge my whole life. She's Lily's best friend. I love Tara. And Reid is, well . . . Reid. He's a grumpy bastard most days. They always bicker. I figured they didn't like each other."

I shrugged. "Maybe that bickering was foreplay."

"Eww. Now I can't get the image of them together out of my head." He grimaced. "It's like thinking about your parents having sex."

"Sorry." I laughed.

"Save those kinds of secrets for when we're not eating." He chuckled, diving back into his meal.

"Your turn."

"Secret or a story?"

I shrugged. "Your choice."

Jax hummed as he chewed. Then he set his fork down again, turning sideways to look at me. "When I was a kid, I used to imagine my mother showing up. She'd tell me she was sorry for leaving me here, but she was helping other kids around the world who didn't have a safe place to live like I did on the ranch."

"Jax." I wasn't sure what to say. That wasn't a secret I'd been expecting either.

"I've been thinking a lot about her lately. Since we talked about her. I don't ever talk about her. Not to anyone."

Except me. He'd confided in me. "Do you have any idea where she is?"

"Yeah." He picked up his fork to poke at his scrambled eggs. "Not saving children around the world. I was curious a few years ago. Mostly I wanted to know if she was still alive. So I hired an investigator to track her down. She's currently serving a seven-year sentence in Nevada for drug trafficking."

"W-what? Oh my God."

"No one knows that," he said. "Appreciate it if you'd keep it between us."

"Of course." He didn't even need to ask. That wasn't something I'd ever share without his permission.

"I hate drugs."

"Me too." On that, we'd always agree.

"Sorry. That was, uh, not exactly the lighthearted dinner conversation I'd planned. But . . . figured you should know."

We could share random facts and easy secrets. But we were tied together, forever. We should share the hard and heavy too. I couldn't keep everything to myself, not with Jax.

"Thanks for telling me."

"Of course." He put his hand on my shoulder, massaging lightly. I leaned into his touch as he continued to knead with his fingers. The tension seeped out of my muscles. My eyes drifted closed, and I swallowed a moan.

God, he had great hands. How had I forgotten that from our night together? Jax delivered the perfect amount of pressure and strength and tenderness.

Was this what I'd been missing all month? Breakfast for dinner and a shoulder massage to melt away the stress?

"You know, if you stopped avoiding me, this could become a regular thing," he said like he could read my mind.

"I haven't been avoiding you. You know exactly where I am."

"So this is my fault?"

"Basically."

His quiet chuckle called me on the lie. "How about we go out for dinner in town tom—"

A knock at the door stopped him from finishing the invitation.

His hand dropped as he stood and walked to the entryway.

We should have heard a vehicle approach. There should have been a flash of light outside. But I guess neither of us had been paying much attention to anything beyond each other.

"Hey," Jax answered. "Come on in."

"Sorry." A woman's voice carried from the hall. "I tried calling but you didn't answer."

"It's all right."

"It smells good in—" The beautiful woman who drove the Jeep emerged carrying a backpack, coming to a halt when she spotted me at the island. "Oh. I'm so sorry. I'm interrupting."

Jax stood behind her and gave me a sad smile.

"You should have told me you had a date." She stretched behind her and smacked Jax in the gut.

"It's not a date," I said at the same time he said, "I have a date."

She rolled her eyes at him, then walked over, hand extended. "Hi. I'm Emery."

"I'm Sasha."

Emery was stunning. Even with red-rimmed eyes and splotchy cheeks still damp with tears, she was gorgeous. Her hair fell in thick, wavy sheets around her shoulders. She had a slender, willowy frame despite her boxy sweatshirt.

The same sweatshirt I'd worn a month ago at this island.

Jax's sweatshirt.

Why was she wearing Jax's sweatshirt?

"It's nice to finally meet you," she said. "Jax has told me so much about you."

"It's nice to meet you too," I lied. Maybe it would have been nice. If she wasn't wearing his clothes.

Wait. How much had he told her? Did she know I was pregnant? My eyes flicked to him, and he gave a slight head shake.

Phew. We really needed to talk about how and when we were going to tell people. But not with Emery here. And not until we figured out what to say.

Everyone would know that I was Jax's drunken one-night stand. Everyone would realize I was a hot mess.

"I'm sorry to interrupt," Emery said. "I'll get out of here. Let you get back to your dinner."

I opened my mouth, about to tell her that it was fine and she should stay. Especially since she'd been crying—hard from the looks of it. But before I could say anything, Jax put his hands on her shoulders, massaging her muscles like he had with me earlier, and steered her for a stool.

His stool.

He sat her right beside me, rounded the corner of the island, and turned on the stove. "How many pancakes?"

"Two," she said, abandoning her seat. "But I can make them myself. Finish eating."

"I'll do it."

"Get out." She shooed him out of the kitchen, then went to work, mixing up pancake batter in a bowl.

Emery moved around the kitchen with the same ease as Jax. She knew where everything was located, from the pancake mix to a whisk to a plate to a bowl.

When the pancakes were cooking, she set a plate in the space beside Jax, leaning against the counter. "How do you like the cabin?" she asked me. "Isn't it cute?"

"Very cute."

"You should have seen it before Jax worked his magic. This place too. Talk about a couple of dumps."

"Hey." Jax flicked the tip of her nose. "It wasn't a dump."

Emery swatted his hand away. "It was a total dump. I can prove it too."

Jax groaned as she dug out her phone. "Here we go with the pictures."

"He thinks I take too many pictures." She swiped through her phone, shifting out of reach when he tried to snatch it away. When she found the one she'd been looking for, she held out the screen. "See? Total dump."

It was old but not awful. It wasn't all that worse than my rental in town.

"Flip your pancakes, Hill."

"Don't boss me around, Haven." Emery stuck out her tongue, then went to the stove to flip her pancakes.

It wasn't exactly flirting. There didn't seem to be a lick of chemistry between them. The playful touches and teasing were just . . . friendship.

Except he'd done the same with me. The smirks. The shoulder massage. The hoodie.

Was that how he saw us? Friends? Was I reading more into this than necessary?

A relationship between us was impossible. With the baby. With Eddie. With my job. It would never work. We needed to be friends. Stay friends.

I couldn't—*shouldn't*—want more.

"How was work?" Jax asked Emery.

"Fine." She shrugged. "You know that filing-system overhaul I've been working on? I think I finally finished. We're officially digital. Maybe someday you'll move out of the dark ages, too, and join the rest of us in the cloud."

He chuckled. "Only if Sasha makes me."

She knew about his paper filing system? Of course she knew. She'd probably spent plenty of time in his office. More than me.

"What did you do today?" she asked him.

"Worked. Managed to get in a ride this afternoon. Went up to the north ridge."

The north ridge. I had no idea where that was. But the way Emery nodded, she did. She'd probably been there too.

I realized as they kept talking that I was the third wheel. I was the outsider. I was the silent observer of a conversation between friends.

A headache bloomed behind my temples. Time to go home.

"I think I'm going to head out," I told him as Emery poured syrup on her pancakes. "Thanks for dinner."

"What? No. Don't go." His blue eyes were pleading. "Not yet."

"You should talk," I said quietly, my gaze darting to Emery. If I was gone, he could ask her why she'd been crying.

He sighed. "Okay."

"Good night."

"You're leaving?" Her eyes widened, dread filling her expression. Either because she felt bad for interrupting, or because if I was gone, then Jax would make her talk about whatever it was that had sent her to his house. "You should stay."

"It's been a long day." I quickly took my plate to the sink, then I waved goodbye and headed for the entryway.

Jax joined me as I pulled on my shoes. "See you tomorrow?"

"Yeah. See you tomorrow." I opened the door, stepping out into the night.

He lingered outside until I was at the cabin, lifting a hand before I disappeared inside.

This was fine. Better, actually. It was better this way.

As I got ready for bed, I pretended like this disappointment in my heart wasn't disappointment at all.

Jax and I should just be friends.

Friends who were having a baby together. Nothing more.

At the end of the day, I was doing this alone. I needed to stand on my own two feet. If I relied too much on Jax, well . . . I couldn't take that risk. I couldn't depend on him, not when so much was at stake.

So we'd be friends. Friends who should stop having breakfasts for dinner. Friends who didn't need to share secrets and lies.

Friends. That was better.

When would it feel better?

～

Dear Eddie,

You know what we never made for dinner? Breakfast. I've had breakfast for dinner a couple times lately. Pancakes. Bacon. Eggs. Hash browns. All the things I never took the time to make us in the mornings.

Remember when we used to eat ice cream for dinner? Only ice cream. We'd stay up late and watch some stupid show on TV and pig out on ice cream. Just the idea of Cherry Garcia makes me sick to my stomach. We took it too far, didn't we? Not just with the ice cream. Sometimes I think we just didn't know how to stop and reset. We liked something so much that we went wild. I'm rambling now. Anyway. When I see you again, let's have breakfast for dinner.

S

Chapter 14
JAX

Meet you at the hospital.

Sasha's text had been grating on my nerves since she'd sent it before lunch. It could be nothing. Maybe she just wanted to ride separately for some reason today. But considering we'd planned to ride together, that for her last appointment she'd hardly gotten out of my truck, it made no sense.

We'd agreed last night to go together. Why the change?

One step forward, three steps back.

Every time I thought Sasha was relaxing around me, something would spook her. She was more skittish than a wild horse.

You'd think after I'd bared my damn soul last night, told her all that shit about my birth mother, she would have opened up, just a little. *Nope.*

No matter how much I laid out there, she was as guarded as ever.

Though maybe our night would have ended differently if Emery hadn't shown up.

I loved Emery. She was the closest thing to a sister I'd ever had. But for fuck's sake, her timing was shit.

I should have made her leave, but with how rocky things had been with Calvin, I couldn't do it.

Until she left him, my house had become her safe space.

That hadn't bothered me in the slightest until last night. It made me a selfish bastard, but whatever. I'd wanted that time alone with Sasha.

We didn't have a relationship. I didn't really do relationships. But we should have something, right? Something beyond the occasional dinner and a child that had half her DNA and half mine?

Maybe if Emery hadn't interrupted dinner, then I wouldn't be in a bad mood, parking next to Sasha's car in the hospital's lot.

I headed inside, scanning the lobby as I made my way toward the doctors' offices. No familiar faces. Thank fuck.

The fact that we'd been able to keep this pregnancy under wraps for three months was a damn miracle in and of itself. It was time to tell people, at least family and friends. It felt like a lie, keeping news this massive to myself.

Was Sasha ready to tell people? Or was she wanting to keep up the secrecy? Was that why she'd wanted to drive separately?

It was time to start telling people. Maybe today, after we got through this appointment.

My boots were a muffled thud on the hallway's thin carpet. I combed my hair with my fingers a few times before I reached the office's door.

The waiting area was busy. A mother in the corner watched as her son played in the small toy area. Another couple occupied a pair of chairs. An older woman sat alone reading a magazine. And Sasha was in the back row, sitting with her hands tucked beneath her legs and as far away from anyone else as possible.

"Hey, you." I took the seat beside hers, leaning in to kiss her cheek.

"H-hi." She stiffened as my lips brushed her skin.

What the hell? I frowned as I pulled away. "What's wrong?"

"Nothing." Her gaze flicked to the ceiling.

"Thought we were going to ride together."

"I needed to run a few errands. Post office. Gas station." Her eyes flicked to the ceiling as she lied.

"I could have ridden with you. Or gone along on errands."

She stayed quiet, her eyes dropping to her lap.

Shutting me out. Again. "If this is about last night—"

"It's not." She was arguably the worst liar I'd ever met.

There was no use calling her on it, not here. So I crossed my arms over my chest and waited in silence until a nurse called Sasha's name.

We stood in unison, and my hand went to the small of her back. It was automatic. She was close, so I touched.

She stiffened again, quickening her strides.

What the actual fuck?

My teeth ground together so hard my molars cracked. Then I shoved my hands into my jeans pockets, not so I wouldn't be tempted to touch Sasha, but so she wouldn't see them in fists. I trailed behind her and the nurse, the silent observer as she stepped on a scale.

"Okay, Dad." The nurse, a different woman than Robin's from last month, motioned me into the guest chair once we hit the exam room. "You get that seat."

Dad. She was the first person to call me Dad.

It was wrong to have that first come from a stranger. It should have come from West or Indya. Anyone other than a nurse who used the term because she hadn't bothered to learn my name.

I sat down, elbows to knees, and kept my eyes on the floor while the nurse measured Sasha's blood pressure and pulse. When she left us to get the doctor, I sat straight and looked at Sasha.

"What's wrong?"

"Nothing," she lied again. "What's wrong with you?"

"I'm in a shit mood."

She blinked, startled that I hadn't lied too. But I wasn't going to hide the truth from her. I didn't want bullshit between us. She'd get honesty, always, even if it sucked.

Sasha sat on her hands again, staring blankly at the floor. So I did the same until Dr. Green knocked on the door.

He didn't bother with pleasantries. He shook Sasha's hand, then mine, making introductions before launching into his short exam. She didn't have to change out of her clothes today, only pull up her sweater so he could listen to the baby's heartbeat. Then we were dismissed.

He wasn't cold. It was better than the awkward visit with Robin. But Green was succinct. Clinical. There'd be no warm, fuzzy feelings during these visits, would there?

When he left the room, Sasha hopped off the table as I stood. "He's . . . different," I said.

"Better than *Robin*," she muttered as she pulled on her coat.

My nostrils flared, but I kept my mouth shut. Yeah, Green was better than Robin. Had I said I wanted Robin? No. Was everything I said today going to piss Sasha off?

"I have to use the bathroom." She swiped the urine cup that Green had left behind off the counter. "You don't need to wait."

I'd been dismissed. "Fine."

She walked out of the room first, taking a right for the restroom while I headed left for the exit.

One step forward. Three steps back.

The moment I climbed into my truck, I pounded a fist against the wheel. "Damn it."

I should go back inside. I shouldn't let her shove me away. But it would probably just make her mad. So I turned the key and started for home.

Later. We'd talk later.

There was a line of trucks parked outside the stables when I made it to the ranch, most belonging to the guides. Now that spring was here and most of the snow had melted, we'd been busy.

It was still slow compared to the summer season, but I'd hired on three more guides, pairing them with my experienced staffers so they could learn the ropes over the next few weeks.

Harry, one of the guides who worked year round and my best hand with the horses, jerked up his chin when I walked inside. "Hey, Jax."

"Harry. How's it going?"

"Good." He pointed to a sorrel mare in a stall. "Was just going to take this one out for a ride. One of the new guys rode her yesterday and said she was acting like a shit. Figured I'd squeeze in a quick ride to find out if it's the horse or the rider."

Sometimes, horses knew their rider was green. They'd act one way with one person and entirely different if an experienced rider was in the saddle. But I didn't like snotty horses. If she was prone to misbehaving, well . . . this wasn't the ranch for her.

"I'll take her out," I said. This wasn't a horse I'd ridden before. West had given her a test run before we'd bought her last fall. I doubted she had an attitude. West wouldn't have bought her otherwise.

Each of the guys I'd hired had riding experience on their résumés. But it wouldn't be the first time an employee had exaggerated their skill set. At this point, I was more loyal to the horse, but a ride would give me a better idea of the situation.

"You sure?" Harry asked.

"Yeah." A long, hard ride sounded a hell of a lot better than being stuck at my desk. "Let me grab my hat and gloves."

I ducked into my office and changed my coat for a thicker one. Then I put on my favorite Stetson. I swiped a pair of leather gloves from the mess on the couch and was about to head out when a knock came at the door and Dad stepped inside.

"Hey," he said. "Harry said you were heading out on a ride."

"Yeah. What are you up to?"

He shrugged. "Was hoping I could join you."

Well, shit.

If Dad came along, he'd want to talk, and I wasn't in the mood for company. What I needed were a few hours to clear my head. Think about Sasha. Figure out what the fuck I was going to do. "Dad—"

"Please? It's been ages since you rode with your old man."

Damn it. "Uh, yeah. Sure."

"Good." His exhale was loud, like he'd been holding his breath. "I'll get a horse saddled."

I waited until he was gone to groan. Then I shoved past my frustration and walked out to get my horse.

It didn't take us long to ride away from the ranch, and once we made it to a clearing, I nudged the mare with my heels and let her run.

Dad kept pace for a while but slowed. But I kept going, continuing past a grove of trees and around a bend that took us to the river. Once I reached the water's edge, I turned around and made my way back to Dad.

"Well, this horse seems fine to me," I told him. "If there was a problem, maybe it was a fluke."

"She's a pretty thing," Dad said. "She's got a nice stride."

"Yeah, she does." I settled into an easy walk next to Dad, drawing in a deep breath. The air was infused with grass and earth and pine. It smelled like home.

It smelled like Montana.

I'd promised Sasha I'd get her to fall in love with it here. So far, I'd done a lousy job. Other than a trip to the grocery store, we'd spent next to no time together.

We were already three months into this thing. If she hated it here, would she want to move? How would that work?

She couldn't leave. No way. Maybe I couldn't convince her to stay at the cabin forever, but Sasha couldn't leave the state. Not with my kid.

"Fuck," I muttered, dragging a glove over my face.

"What's wrong?" Dad asked.

I almost lied. I almost brushed him off. Instead, I blurted, "Sasha's pregnant."

Dad swayed, and for a split second, I thought he might fall out of his saddle.

"Whoa." I reached out a hand, but he'd already steadied himself.

"I'm okay." He shook his head. "Just surprised me."

"Yeah, shocked the hell out of me too."

"How far along?"

"Three months."

He blinked in surprise. "Oh. I, uh, didn't realize you two were dating."

"We aren't." I sighed. Not for my lack of trying. I'd lost count of the times I'd invited her to dinner—or been interrupted before I could ask. "We hooked up after the party."

"Ah." Dad nodded. "Well. A baby. That's something good."

"Yeah." It was something good, wasn't it? Scary, sure. But it was good news. News I wanted to share—had shared.

A weight lifted. I'd always figured West would be the first to know. But this worked too. Dad and I might not be all that close. We'd grown apart some after he'd sold the ranch to Indya. But he was still my dad.

A sniffle drew my attention, and I glanced over in time to see Dad dab his eye with the fingertip of his buckskin glove.

"Are you crying?" My heart warmed. Yeah, he was crying. Because this was good news. "Pull yourself together, old man," I teased.

"Oh, shut it." He scowled. "I'm allowed to get a little emotional at my age. Especially knowing I'm having another grandbaby."

"Did you cry when West told you about their kids?"

"Might have shed a tear or two. But I'll never admit it if you tell him."

I dragged a finger across my mouth. "My lips are sealed."

"You doing okay?" Dad asked.

"Anxious. Excited. Scared."

"That sounds about right."

"I've read three pregnancy books this month. Mostly when I can't sleep. I can't decide if it makes it better or worse." With every page, it made me realize how little I knew about babies. "Were you nervous? Before West was born?"

Considering he hadn't even known my mother was pregnant, all I could ask about was my brother.

"Yeah, I was nervous. Mostly that I'd screw everything up. And looking back, I fucked up plenty. But you and West are both better men than me. So maybe I did a few things right."

We'd been hard on Dad over the past seven years, hadn't we? Too hard.

When he'd sold the ranch to Indya in secret, West and I had both taken it as a betrayal. Maybe it was time to let the hard feelings go. For good.

So that when my baby was born, he or she didn't have my baggage weighing down a relationship with *Papa*.

"Does anyone else know?" Dad asked.

"No. Well, Lily does."

He blinked. "Lily?"

"She was at the hospital when Sasha and I went in for an appointment last month. But otherwise, we haven't told anyone."

"All right. Consider it a secret. Until you tell me otherwise."

"Thanks, Dad."

"You're welcome, Son." As he smiled, his eyes turned watery again.

"More tears," I teased. "Really?"

"Fuck off." He laughed, dabbing at his eyes again. "You know, one thing I regret is not being more open with you and your brother. Not just about the ranch sale. I know I screwed that up by not talking to you both first. But everything else too. I guess I always thought you'd think I was weak if I asked for help. If I admitted I couldn't do it all on my own. I'm working on that. Working on being around more in case you need me."

There was a vulnerability in his voice I'd never heard from my father before. "Appreciate that."

He swallowed hard, clearing his throat. Then he adjusted his grip on his reins. "Wanna race?"

Before I could answer, he shot ahead, his laugh carrying on the breeze.

I grinned, counting to ten to give him a head start. Then I clicked my tongue and nudged my horse to follow.

She was fast. Faster than Dad's gelding. But I held her back enough that Dad could win.

Once we were in the stables, the horses turned out to graze and our saddles hung on their racks, Dad waved goodbye before heading home. I spent the rest of my afternoon catching up on work, visiting with the guides, and reviewing summaries of today's activities.

The sun was inching its way to the jagged mountain horizon when I left for home. The soft evening light made the colors of the land brighter. The greens and blues and golds were a vivid kaleidoscope, and spring was just beginning.

Maybe I wouldn't have to sell Sasha on Montana. Maybe Montana would do that all on its own. Convince her to stay.

Her car was parked outside the cabin when I made it to the house. She was safely locked behind her doors, where she'd hide the rest of the night.

Something Dad said on our ride echoed in my mind.

I always thought you'd think I was weak if I asked for help. If I admitted I couldn't do it all on my own.

Was that why Sasha was so withdrawn? Was she scared I'd see her as weak if she leaned on me? Or was she scared people would let her down? That I'd disappear?

She wasn't alone in this. She knew that, right? I was here.

Maybe all we really needed was time. Time for her to see I wasn't going anywhere.

I parked in my garage but didn't go inside. I walked the distance between our houses and knocked on her door.

She answered wearing the same sweater and jeans she'd been in earlier, her hair still in that slick bun. "Hi."

"Hi. Sorry about earlier."

"I'm sorry too. I was in a bad mood."

"Truce?"

She nodded. "Truce."

"Sorry about Emery interrupting us last night. I should have told her to leave."

"No." Sasha sighed. "She was upset. It's good she has a place to go. Is she okay?"

"Hope so. He called her last night and apologized. She went back home around midnight. For now, they're getting along. I doubt it lasts, it never does, but we'll see."

"Does she, um, know about the baby?"

"No, I haven't told her. But I did tell Dad today."

Her eyes widened. "You did?"

"This isn't exactly something we can keep a secret, honey."

"I know." She worried her bottom lip between her teeth. "I think we should wait a while longer."

"How long is a while?" A few hours? Sure. Maybe a couple more days. But eventually, there would be no more hiding this.

"Until the ultrasound."

"Over a month?" My voice bounced off the walls. What the fuck? It had been hard enough as it was to keep it from my family for this long. But another month? "Sasha—"

"Please, Jax. Just until the ultrasound. I know we can't keep it a secret forever. But I need . . ."

I waited for her to finish. When she didn't, when she dropped her eyes to the floor, I shifted closer, hooking my finger beneath her chin and tilting her face to mine. "You need what?"

"Time to figure out what to say." Her shoulders sagged. "People are going to ask questions. I'm not exactly looking forward to telling my employees or my boss, who happens to be your sister-in-law, that that we had a one-night stand and a condom broke. It sounds reckless."

"It was reckless." I chuckled, letting my thumb trace along her cheek. "But that doesn't mean it's less important."

"Everything will change when we tell people," she whispered.

"Everything has changed already."

"I know that." The pleading in those pretty eyes was my undoing. "Please? Just until the ultrasound."

The ultrasound was the halfway mark. "That's six weeks. Not a month," I grumbled.

Sasha might not have a poker face. But damn if she wasn't good at negotiating. She was worse than West's twins, who always begged for five more minutes to play. Three more minutes in the bathtub. One more hug before bedtime.

I had a feeling that if I didn't agree to six weeks, her next offer would be eight.

"Fine," I muttered. "Until the ultrasound."

By that point, at least we'd know if we were having a boy or a Josephine.

"Thank you, Jax." A tiny, smug smile tugged at her pretty mouth.

It took everything I had not to kiss it off her face.

Chapter 15
JAX

The ultrasound room was dark and cramped. My chair was squeezed into a corner, and any time I shifted, my knees knocked against the table where Sasha was lying.

"What if it's not a girl?" she whispered.

Why was she so set on having a girl? "Then we'll have a boy."

"Obviously." She shot me a frown. "I don't know what to do with boys."

Ah. That was the reason. "Well, I do."

I was more confident in my parenting skills with boys than girls. But either way, we'd figure it out.

My confidence didn't earn me Sasha's smile. She was still worried about doing everything on her own, wasn't she?

"It's a Josephine," I said.

"You don't know that."

"We will soon enough." I shifted, trying to get comfortable, but all of the chairs in this hospital were so damn little. "Think they could have us in a smaller room?"

It was no bigger than a storage closet, and with the ultrasound equipment and exam table, hardly any space remained.

"Maybe we should have gone to Bozeman for this." At least we'd get to be in a larger hospital for the delivery.

Sasha blew out a long breath, her fingers tapping over her belly.

In the past six weeks, her body had begun to change. Her breasts were fuller. There was a roundness to her stomach when she'd pulled up her shirt earlier for her exam with Dr. Green.

I doubted anyone else had recognized the differences, but soon, there'd be no hiding this pregnancy. Maybe once it was out in the open, Sasha would finally stop hiding from me too.

I'd invited her over for dinner five times in the past month and a half. And with each invitation, she'd had an excuse.

I've had a headache all day.

I'm planning to work late tonight.

I was going to make an appearance in the dining room tonight and mingle with guests.

I'm swamped.

I'm exhausted.

Granted, the resort was absolutely hectic now that we were at the end of May. Indya had returned from maternity leave, but she was only working part time until Grace was older, which put a lot on Sasha's plate.

But it was more than a busy schedule that kept her from saying yes.

Did she get a thrill from shredding my ego on a regular basis? Any other woman, I would have walked away. Moved on. But Sasha had been stuck in my head for months.

And it had nothing to do with our baby.

I liked her.

I didn't even know what to do with that. I hadn't liked a girl enough to ask her out on a real date in, well . . . years. Probably not since Robin was my girlfriend in high school, and that had ended in a dumpster fire.

Commitment wasn't exactly my forte. Not that I was asking for a commitment. I just wanted . . . something. What did I want?

For starters, I wanted her to stop denying the chemistry between us. When Sasha was in the room, she was like a magnet. It took a conscious effort *not* to touch her. This wasn't a one-way street. She felt that pull too. So maybe we could find a middle ground. We could get to know each other, see what was happening here, and . . . something.

I couldn't articulate that something, not yet. Wasn't that the point? To figure it out?

"After this, let's go to—"

The door opened before I could finish my sentence, and the ultrasound tech came inside carrying a chart. "Sasha Vaughn?"

"Yes." She nodded.

The tech did a double take when she spotted me in the guest chair. "Hey, Jax."

"Hey." I lifted a hand to wave. What was her name? I recognized her from around town but wasn't sure we'd actually met.

She took a seat on a rolling stool, explained the process, and readied her equipment. Then she had Sasha lift up her shirt and shift down the waistband of her slacks. "Do you want to know the baby's sex?"

"Yes, please." Sasha sucked in a shaky breath as the tech squirted cold gel onto her belly.

My eyes locked on the monitor, watching as the waves of black and white and gray swirled until finally—

"Holy fuck," I whispered. That was a head. A baby's head. *My* baby's head.

My hand found Sasha's.

"There's your baby," the tech said, moving the wand. "There's an arm and a leg. And it looks like you're having a girl."

The air rushed from my lungs at the same time Sasha squeezed my hand so hard my knuckles cracked.

I bent, dropping my head to hers. "Josephine."

That was our girl. On a screen, in fuzzy black and white. My daughter.

"Let me get you some photos." The tech finished with the wand and wiped off Sasha's stomach. Then the printer in the corner buzzed as it rolled out a series of pictures. She handed them over, then spent a moment on the computer before taking Sasha's chart and heading for the door. "Congratulations."

The moment the tech was gone, Sasha's face crumpled. She covered her face with her hands to hide the tears, but she couldn't mask the shaking of her shoulders.

"Hey." I stood and sat on the edge of her table, hauling her into my arms. Then I wrapped her up tight as she buried her face in my shoulder and cried.

The tears didn't last long. She sniffled and leaned away, wiping beneath her eyes. "Sorry."

"Don't be." I brushed a lock of dark hair away from her face.

She'd been wearing her hair down more often lately. Was that because she didn't want her hair messed up when she lay down on the exam tables? Or was it because she was relaxing and finally adjusting to the casual vibe at the lodge? I hoped it was the latter.

Sasha righted her shirt, then adjusted the elastic waistband of the slacks she'd worn today, before climbing off the table.

I folded the ultrasound photos carefully, then inched my way around the room to meet Sasha by the door.

She'd let me drive her to town. That was my win for the day. I didn't take it personally when she stayed quiet as we returned to the ranch. She stared out her window at the fields of lush spring green and the indigo mountains kissing a clear blue sky.

"Let's have dinner tonight," I said before pulling up to the lodge. "We'll get Reid to pack us up a couple of cheeseburgers or something."

"Maybe." Her maybes were code for no. "Um, can we see how the rest of the day goes?"

"Sasha—"

But she was already gone, out of the truck the moment I was stopped and disappearing into the lodge without a backward glance.

"Fuck." I rubbed a hand over my jaw, then put the truck in drive.

Before I'd headed into town for the ultrasound, I'd made sure everything with the guides was covered for the day. So rather than go to my office in the stables, I drove across the ranch, following dirt roads until I found my brother.

"Hey." He jerked up his chin as I climbed out of my truck parked beside his.

"Hey. What are you up to?"

The gasoline, metallic scent of a two-stroke chain saw engine filled the air, mingling with the smell of fresh-cut pine.

"A couple trees were getting too close to the fence, so I'm just clearing them away." He took off his gloves, tucked them in a pocket, then shifted the safety glasses off his face to the brim of his baseball hat. "What's up?"

I swallowed hard, then handed over the neatly folded ultrasound photos. "I'm, uh, having a baby. With Sasha."

West blinked.

Then his jaw hit the dirt.

∽

Before I'd even climbed the porch stairs to Grandma and Grandpa's place, the door opened.

"You're just in time." Grandma hauled me into a hug the moment I was close enough. "Dinner's about ready."

It was barely after five. Normally, I'd eat at six thirty or seven. But after my conversation with West, I was emotionally drained, and Grandma's comfort food sounded like a damn good idea.

"Working today?" she asked as we made our way through the halls of the farmhouse where she and Grandpa had lived for decades.

"Yeah. Was just out with West for a bit."

After he'd recovered from the shock of my news, he'd hauled me into a hug.

I hadn't even realized that I'd needed a hug.

Then we'd spent a few hours cutting up the trees he'd felled and clearing logs from the fence line, all while I told him what had happened at the party in January. And everything since.

Telling Dad had lifted some of the burden. But talking to West was what I'd needed.

He hadn't overloaded me with advice. He hadn't asked a lot of questions. He'd just listened and let me talk. He'd let me voice my fears and tell my story, and when we were done, he'd shaken my hand and told me I'd be a good dad.

I really loved my brother.

"I made a casserole," Grandma said as we reached the kitchen. It smelled like onions and hamburger and garlic. "It's a new recipe."

"Is that my warning?"

"She's been experimenting a lot." Grandpa emerged from the living room, holding out his hand to shake mine. "I had diarrhea for two days after the last casserole."

"Alan," Grandma scolded as she pulled on two oven mitts. "They call that an overshare."

"I don't care what they call it, Sarah. It's the truth. I'm never eating tuna again."

Grandma held a hand in the air, probably flipping Grandpa off, even though neither of us could see her fingers. "Jax, grab a place setting. Then both of you sit down."

"Yes, ma'am." I chuckled and followed orders, keeping out of her way as I went to the cupboard for a plate and the drawer for silverware.

Grandma liked cloth napkins. Tonight, she had out the linen set I'd bought her for Christmas, so I found a matching third and took a seat beside Grandpa at the table.

The dining room was wallpapered in roses. The oak table was scratched and dinged from fifty years of use. My chair creaked slightly under my weight, but the moment I was seated and Grandma carried out the casserole, it felt like home.

This house was as familiar as my own. It was as much a part of my childhood as Dad's place.

After Lily and Dad got divorced, Grandma had filled the role of mother. On nights when Dad was busy at the resort, I'd spend my evenings here. She'd read me books. Grandpa taught me to play cards. And until I was a teenager, their guest bedroom had belonged to me.

Next time, maybe I'd bring Sasha. I'd never brought a woman to my grandparents' place before, but they'd make a show of it.

Grandma would use the china from her hutch. She'd pair the dishes with her fanciest set of embroidered napkins. And she'd make my favorite pot roast with homemade biscuits.

Grandpa would take out the old photo albums, teeming with black-and-white and sepia pictures of the lodge in its infancy. He'd tell her stories from the old days, and since there'd be four of us, he'd offer to teach her pinochle.

"I've got some news," I told them once we'd said grace and our plates were dished. "You know Sasha? She works at the lodge."

"The savior." Grandma laughed. "That's what Indya calls her. Sounds like she sure does a great job running the resort."

"Yes, she does."

"What about her?" Grandpa asked.

"She's pregnant. We're having a baby."

Grandma blinked. "O-oh. I didn't realize you were an item."

"Well, we're not exactly."

The room went quiet.

Grandma and Grandpa shared a sour look.

Wait. Were they actually upset by this? I wasn't sure what I'd expected in telling them tonight, but it certainly wasn't a disappointment so ripe it could wilt the wallpaper roses.

"Well, that is news." Grandpa cleared his throat. "Are you getting married?"

"No."

He arched a bushy gray eyebrow as Grandma's frown cut deep lines into her weathered face. She went back to eating first. Grandpa followed suit.

All while I sat there watching them chew and avoid looking at me entirely.

What the actual fuck? How was this their reaction?

Was this why Sasha had been so adamant about not telling people? Thank God she wasn't here tonight.

Manners kept me in my seat. Manners made me eat the meal. Manners sent me to the sink to rinse my plate and put it in the dishwasher.

It took effort not to scowl as I thanked them for dinner and stalked out of the house, not sticking around for the apple pie dessert.

Damn it. They hadn't shown even a shred of excitement. Not enough curiosity to inquire about Sasha's due date. Not enough fucks to give to ask if it was a boy or a girl.

My grandparents were old fashioned. I respected their take on life. But for the first time in mine, I was disappointed in them.

My frustration only seemed to get worse as I drove home. By the time I reached my house, I had half a mind to turn around and call them on their bullshit. But I parked in my garage and walked to Sasha's place instead.

If my grandparents were going to be disappointed in me tonight, I might as well tack Sasha onto that list too. Our secret was out, whether she liked it or not.

My knock was more of a fist pound than a knuckle tap.

When she opened the door, she was still dressed in her work clothes. Her shoes were still on, so she must have just gotten home. "Hi."

"I told West. And my grandparents at dinner."

"Oh, okay." Her shoulders sagged, relief softening her eyes. "Thanks."

"I figured you'd be mad."

"No. You were right. We shouldn't have kept it a secret for so long."

165

I gave her a sideways glance, then put the back of my hand against her forehead. "Are you feeling okay? Because it sounded like you said, 'You were right.'"

A smile tugged at her mouth. "I take it back."

"Too late." I tapped the tip of her nose, the anger from earlier fading into the night. "West says congratulations. I'm sure he'll tell Indya, so I'd expect her in your office tomorrow morning."

"All right. Thanks for the heads-up."

"Welcome." I turned to leave, to give her the space she so clearly desired, but I stopped myself before I could walk home, turning to face her.

We'd been tiptoeing around each other for months, and I was so goddamn sick of it I could scream.

Maybe it was because of Grandma and Grandpa's reaction. They'd shocked me enough that I'd lost my cool. Or maybe it was because, for a split second, when Grandpa had asked if Sasha and I were getting married, I'd wanted to say yes.

Me, the guy who'd shied away from commitment, had actually entertained the idea of marriage. What was happening?

Maybe instead of fighting it, I should just go for broke. Lay it all out there and see where we landed.

"Robin told me once that I came on strong. I always thought that was a funny statement, considering she was my girlfriend at the time. But I do come on strong when I see something I want. And if the situation was different, if you weren't pregnant, I'd be in your face so much that you'd never be able to get rid of me."

Sasha gulped. "Jax."

I stalked to the door, leaning in close. Our gazes clashed, blue searching brown. "I'm scared to push with you. I'm afraid I'll push you away. But damn it, Sasha, I want to push."

She stared up at me for a long moment, her eyes wide and unguarded. "Maybe I need to be pushed."

The corner of my mouth turned up. "Careful. If you give me permission, you'll be stuck with me."

She gave me a sad smile. "That's what I'm hoping."

So my guess had been right. She was scared of going it alone.

"It's a promise, sweetheart." I clamped my hand over her wrist and pulled her outside.

"Where are we going?"

"My place. I'll make you dinner."

"You said you already ate dinner with your grandparents."

I shifted my hand to hers, lacing our fingers together. "Does that mean I can't make *you* dinner?"

That earned me a blush. "I guess not."

Chapter 16
SASHA

Jax was in his kitchen making me a grilled cheese sandwich.

I didn't like grilled cheese, something I'd told him the day we'd met at the grocery store. Something he remembered. But he'd promised me this grilled cheese would be different, so I was humoring him. Just this once. He'd told me I didn't have to finish it if I wasn't a fan, and it wouldn't hurt his feelings in the slightest.

So I was letting him make me grilled cheese—*blech*.

While he cooked, I wandered into his living room. To the book on the coffee table. It was a guide for expectant dads.

"What's this?" I held it up for him to see.

He shrugged as he stood at the stove, a spatula in his hand. "Oh, just something I've been reading on the nights when I can't sleep."

I had the same book, though for expectant mothers, on my nightstand.

"I might be freaked out about this," he said. "But no one can say I haven't done my best to prepare."

My heart thumped too hard. He always seemed so sure. So steady. Eager instead of anxious. Calm instead of crazed. In the beginning, he'd had a few freak-out moments, but those had long since passed. "You're still freaked out?"

"Well, yeah." He turned off the burner, moving my sandwich out of the frying pan to a plate. Then he sliced it in half diagonally before getting out a jar of strawberry jelly from the fridge. "Water? Milk? Orange juice?"

"Water. This time of night, I'll have miserable heartburn if I drink anything else."

"You get heartburn at night?"

"Sometimes." I took a seat at the island as he set down the plate. "You didn't need to make me dinner."

"I wanted to, babe." He shifted a stool around the corner so we could face each other.

"Thank you. What's the jelly for?"

"Your sandwich. Put it on top. Give it a try."

"Really?" I twisted the lid off the jar and spread a small amount on a corner. A moan escaped at the first bite. "It shouldn't be good. I don't like grilled cheese."

He grinned. "That's the limit of my culinary skills. Breakfast. Or grilled cheese."

"Noted. My turn next time."

"I'll hold you to that." His eyes crinkled at the sides. "Tell me a secret."

"I think Tara and Reid are engaged."

"What?" He sat up straight. "Seriously?"

"Last week. I saw them coming into the lodge one morning together. He kissed her before heading to the kitchen, and she pulled off a ring before going to the front desk."

Jax blinked. "Why would they keep it a secret?"

"I don't know." I shrugged. "Maybe they just wanted to keep it to themselves for a while. Like us."

"Yeah." His shock vanished into a soft smile. "Like us."

I ate a few more bites as Jax leaned his forearms on the island. "How did your grandparents take the news?"

"They're, uh, old fashioned."

169

"Ah." So, not great. Maybe they thought I'd gotten pregnant intentionally in some plot to weasel myself into the Haven family wealth.

I might be broke, but I didn't want Jax's money.

"They'll come around," he said. It sounded like reassurance more for himself than for me. "Tell me another secret."

I picked up the knife, about to tell him some trivial lodge gossip, but I stopped myself.

Jax had confided in me about his mother. About Lily. It couldn't have been easy for him to share those secrets. Yet the most personal thing he knew about me was that I'd spent a few months crashing on an air mattress.

So I set the knife down.

"My parents died on their way home from a wedding." Not exactly a secret, but it was something no one in Montana knew. "The wedding was for an older couple. My dad was an instructor at a golf course, and the groom was his boss. I was working at the pro shop that summer, and they'd hired a few of us to help with the setup for the reception. I hung around for a while, after my parents arrived. They were dancing when I left to go home."

Smiling. Laughing. Twirling. Oblivious to anyone else in the world when they had each other.

"They were really in love," I said past the lump growing in my throat. "I think it would have destroyed Dad to bury Mom. She wouldn't have recovered if she'd had to say goodbye to him. So in a way, I'm glad they went together."

Even if that meant leaving me behind.

"I'm sorry, honey."

"Me too," I whispered. "They were driving home and got into a head-on collision with a truck driver who fell asleep at the wheel and crossed the center line."

"Fuck." Jax hissed.

"He shouldn't have been driving. He was over the limit on hours and going too fast. Mom and Dad died on impact. The truck driver died in the ambulance on the way to the hospital." I reached for my water, my hand trembling as I lifted the glass to my lips.

"How old were you?" he asked.

"Eighteen."

Legally, an adult. Legally, the person who had to settle their affairs. Realistically, a kid who'd lost her parents. But I'd never once complained. I'd carried every burden without question, even when they'd nearly crushed me to dust.

"It's been a strange ten years," I told Jax. "Every time I think I'm getting settled, something changes. Something knocks me off balance."

Maybe that was why I always seemed to prepare for the worst. Because for ten years, I'd never managed to find my footing. I was constantly being shoved sideways, and by the time I was standing tall again, something else came along to trip me up.

I picked up the knife again, adding more jelly to my sandwich. Then I ate it too fast so I could stop talking about my parents.

The knife stayed in my hand the entire time.

"Why did you come to Montana?" Jax asked, stealing the utensil from my grip.

"This job." Mostly, this job.

It was a half truth. But I wasn't ready to tell anyone about Eddie. Not yet. And especially Jax.

"I was working at a resort in California when I stumbled on the job posting that Indya had put online. When I submitted my résumé, I was sure that I'd get a canned rejection email. But she called me, and I had to pinch myself to believe it was real."

"You didn't think you were qualified?"

"Not really. Not compared to other people who applied."

"You're selling yourself short. You were Indya's first choice."

"Seriously?"

He nodded. "She interviewed three other people, I think? She said you were the only one who made her laugh."

Probably with an awkward, sarcastic joke.

"Whatever the reason, I'm glad you're here." Jax stood and grabbed my now-empty plate, then took it to the sink.

I followed with my water glass. "Me too."

"Even if this baby threw you for another loop?"

"Yeah." Was I scared? Absolutely. Nervous? Definitely. "This was unexpected. But not a mistake. Never a mistake, okay?"

"I was a mistake. You don't need to convince me never to use that term about our kid."

No, I guess I didn't. "Sorry, that dinner conversation got heavy."

"Broad shoulders, darlin'. Lay it on me."

He made it seem so easy. He made it seem like it would all be okay.

"Be honest. Thoughts on the grilled cheese?"

"I liked it."

He narrowed his gaze. "Really?"

"Yeah." I tugged on my earlobe as his eyes stayed locked on my face. It was a nervous habit I'd developed years ago. I caught myself and dropped my hand, but not before Jax noticed.

"Why do you do that?" Where my fingers had been, his took their place, tugging lightly.

A jolt raced down my spine, and my breath hitched. "It's, um, a nervous habit."

"Why are you nervous?"

You. Because he was standing so close. Because he was still touching my ear. Because his gaze dropped to my mouth, and my entire body seemed to liquify.

"Tell me a lie," he whispered.

"I don't want you to kiss me." It came out so fast I couldn't stop it. What was I doing? What was I saying?

His tongue darted out to lick his bottom lip. "Tell me a secret."

Only one secret came to mind. A secret I really, really shouldn't say. But I did anyway. "I always want you to kiss me."

He moved so fast I gasped as he sealed his lips over mine. He took advantage of my open mouth, his tongue sweeping inside.

A moan rebounded between us. Was it mine? His? Both? Did it matter? Jax was kissing me, and for the first time in months, I didn't let myself overthink.

The kiss wasn't sweet or gentle. It was hard, nearly demanding, like I was being punished for not kissing him all this time.

God, he was good at this. Why hadn't we been kissing all this time? There were reasons. He was my boss—sort of. I was leaving Montana—probably. Jax was a cowboy playboy, and a romantic entanglement would only break my heart—definitely.

Except all of those reasons flittered into the ether as he wrapped me in his strong arms. He picked me up off my feet like I weighed no more than a feather and set me on the counter. Then he shifted his hands into my hair, threading his fingers through the strands as he slanted my head to plunder.

A groan rumbled in his chest, the vibration racing straight to my core.

I looped my arms around his shoulders, my fingers pressing into the firm muscles along his back. It was like caressing warm marble.

That masculine, fresh scent wrapped around me as I savored his taste. It was better than I remembered. So, so much better.

We should have been kissing all along. All this time.

I whimpered as he sucked on my bottom lip, pulling it into his mouth. I wiggled on the counter, shifting closer, widening my thighs so he could stand between them. Desire coiled in my belly, a pounding throb blooming as heat pooled.

Maybe it was the pregnancy hormones. Or maybe it was just Jax. Not a man alive had ever turned me on so quickly.

Before I was ready for the kiss to end, he growled and tore his mouth away.

We panted, breaths mingling and chests heaving, as we stared at each other.

His hands were still in my hair. Mine were still locked behind his neck.

"I'm going to carry you to my bedroom." There was an edge to his voice. A threat. A promise. "I'm going to make you come so hard you scream. I'm going to make our night in January look like foreplay. Unless you tell me to stop. Right now."

"Don't stop."

Tomorrow, I'd suffer the consequences. Tomorrow, I'd berate myself for being so weak. Tomorrow, I'd find a decent excuse for why this shouldn't—couldn't—happen again.

But tonight, I just wanted Jax.

"Last chance, Sasha."

I didn't wait for him to kiss me. I pulled him to me until his mouth was on mine.

He did exactly as he'd warned, sweeping me off the counter and carrying me down the hall to his bedroom, not once breaking the kiss.

The lights were off, like last time. Maybe someday I'd see Jax's bedroom in color, but tonight, it was only blacks and grays and a faint glint of silver streaming through the window.

He laid me on the bed, his elbows bracketing my face as he nipped at the corner of my lips. He was careful with his weight, hovering above me. But his hips fell into the cradle of mine, and the moment he ground his arousal against my center, I nearly bucked off the bed.

"Yes." Every nerve vibrated with anticipation. My body pulsed, head to toe, its rhythm saying *again, again, again.*

My fingers shifted between us, tugging at his shirt until it was free from the waistband of his jeans. Then I started on the buttons, fumbling thanks to the frantic energy in my fingertips. But I managed to undo them all, bottom to top, and shoved at the cotton until it was over his shoulders.

My victory was short lived. He had a cotton T-shirt on underneath. It was in the way. When I needed the heat from his skin, this damn T-shirt was in the way.

Jax broke us apart, reaching behind his nape to rip the shirt away as I shoved up to a seat, grappling with the hem of my sweater. He was faster, his shirt flying over his shoulder to the floor. My sweater was yanked over my head with a whoosh and landed with a plop.

Then the music to my ears: the clank of his belt buckle. The sound that made my entire body shiver. A sound I hadn't forgotten since January.

"Jax." My hands went to his chest, pressing against smooth skin and hard muscle as they traveled up his washboard abs to his chest. His nipples were small and pebbled.

I flicked them both with my thumbs, earning a hiss through his gritted teeth.

"We'll play later, baby." His voice was low and gravelly as he moved to my slacks, tugging them and my panties over my hips, dragging them off my legs, inch by torturous inch.

He'd seen me naked. He'd seen my belly. But a sudden rush of self-consciousness caused me to wrap my arms over my stomach.

"Sasha." He shot me a frown, then took my wrists in his grip and lifted my hands to cup my breasts. "Work on that bra, baby."

He dropped a kiss to my navel, a gesture that was as sweet as it was sexy. But before I could undo the clasp on my bra, his mouth trailed lower, causing a wave of tingles to skate over my skin. "Bra, Sasha."

Right. I had a job to do. I propped up, unclasping the back, then slid it off my arms. My nipples were hard, desperate for his mouth.

He leaned back, a smirk stretching his soft lips. "You look so fucking pretty, naked on my bed."

Heat bloomed in my cheeks, that throbbing in my core becoming an ache.

"Lie down."

I obeyed, my heart hammering as his knee hit the edge of the mattress.

He didn't reach for his nightstand.

"Jax. What about—" I swallowed hard. "Do we need, um . . ."

"A condom?"

I nodded.

"Have you been with anyone?"

"No."

"Good." He ran his tongue over the curve of my breast. "Neither have I."

"Oh, thank God." I sighed and dived into his hair, holding him to me as he sucked on a nipple, my mind blanking as his teeth scraped over my skin.

He cupped me in his hands, squeezing and sucking to the point where pain met pleasure.

I writhed beneath him, arching my hips toward his cock. It was pressed hard and thick against my leg, not at all where I wanted it to stay. "I need to feel you inside."

"Not yet." He kissed my sternum, then skimmed his lips over the curve of my belly. For a moment, I thought he'd stop there, but as he pushed my knees apart, a flash of panic popped my eyes open as I pushed up on an arm.

"Jax, I—"

"Do you trust me?" he asked, his eyes hooded.

I gulped but nodded.

That earned me another smirk. It shouldn't be sexy. It really shouldn't. My pussy clenched.

Then my thoughts dissolved as he dragged his tongue through my slit, and I collapsed on my back, my hands coming to my face.

Why was this embarrassing? He was down there, and it felt good—*so good*—but he was down there, and I was dripping wet. Was it normal to be this wet?

I closed my eyes, trying to relax, but I stiffened as he kissed and lapped at me with his tongue. *Relax. Just relax.* Why couldn't I relax? My friends all loved this. They always boasted whenever they found a guy who'd go down on them. It had been rare. For all of us.

A chore, not foreplay. It was what a man did to guarantee he was getting fucked.

I'd never come like this before. But I'd faked it.

Except Jax hummed against me, the sound sheer pleasure. "You taste so fucking good, baby."

Really? He licked me again before pushing a finger inside.

I gasped, my eyes flying open.

"Good?"

"Good," I panted.

Jax fluttered his tongue over my clit, and a cry escaped my lips.

Not good. Fantastic. My heart raced as scorching heat spread beneath my skin. My legs fell open, my hips lifting to his mouth as he continued to lick and suck. My limbs trembled as sweat beaded at my temples.

"Jax?" It came out as a question right before he latched on to my clit.

And every star in the galaxy exploded behind my eyes.

Incoherent screams tore through my throat. They echoed in a plea for Jax not to stop. Never stop. And I shattered into a million pieces, every cell in my being rattling as my orgasm racked my body in crushing waves.

It lasted an eternity, and it was too short. When I finally breathed, my body collapsing, utterly spent, on the mattress, Jax rose to his knees, that smirk even wider.

His cock jutted between us, the size making my breath catch. He fisted the shaft, pumping slowly. Watching him as his head lolled to the side, pleasure on his face, was the most erotic moment of my life. I'd just had the best orgasm, but I needed more. I needed him.

"I want you on my tongue every night, Sasha." He looked at me and brought a finger to his lips, the finger that had been inside me, and sucked it into his mouth. His eyes closed as he hummed, like he was tasting honey.

Okay, *that* was the most erotic moment of my life.

"Jax." My voice sounded pathetic. Pleading and desperate. I didn't have it in me to care.

He came down on top of me, his eyes locking with mine as he hovered. His body covering mine. His hand shifted to my hair, brushing it off of my temple. It was the first tender, sweet gesture he'd made since the kiss in the kitchen.

Another erotic moment. Entirely different than the others. Equally powerful.

He positioned himself at my entrance, waiting for me to give him a slight nod. Then he drove home, clenching his jaw as I clung to his shoulders, my body stretching around his length. "Fuck."

"Jax." My whole body shuddered. My inner walls squeezed as the coil of another orgasm began to twist.

"You feel so good." Jax eased out to slam inside again, driving impossibly deep.

I closed my eyes, savoring every moment as he set into a steady rhythm. It was better than the first time. How was that even possible?

A string of moans and whimpers poured from my throat without permission. I was too lost in Jax to do anything but feel.

One of his hands began to wander, massaging my curves and skin. His touch was electric, and with every piston of his hips, bringing us together, I wound tighter and tighter and tighter.

"Yes." My nails dug into his skin as I writhed beneath him.

His lips were a whisper against the shell of my ear. "Come, Sasha."

It shouldn't have worked. He shouldn't be able to command an orgasm with a single order. But I came apart, shattering around him as he fucked harder, faster.

His name filled the room as I screamed it loud. My bones felt like they were shaking loose as I pulsed around him, losing all touch with reality. I was not a person who liked to be out of control. But this? I would let go of every shred of control to feel this again.

"Sasha," Jax groaned, his body tensing. Then he came on a roar, pouring inside me until he collapsed. With a quick roll, he spun us both, breaking our connection as he positioned me on his chest.

My ear was pressed to his thundering heart, its beat matching my own. Our skin was sticky, and the room smelled like sex. His come and my wetness were leaking down my inner thighs.

But I breathed. For the first time in what felt like months, what *had been* months, I breathed.

Jax shifted to drag the covers over us both. Then he kissed my hair, murmuring, "Night, Sasha."

"Night, Jax." I yawned, burrowing into his neck.

Maybe I should have gone home. Maybe I should have put some sort of flimsy boundary between us. But as Jax wrapped me in his arms, as he cocooned me in his warmth, I closed my eyes.

And for the first time in a long, long time, I fell asleep with a smile on my lips.

Chapter 17
JAX

The sound of a car door slamming dragged me from sleep. I came instantly awake at the noise, my eyes popping open.

My body was curled around Sasha's, her back pressed against my chest. Her face was buried in a pillow, her mouth slightly open.

I peeled myself away, trying not to shift the bed as I slid out from beneath the covers.

But when the mattress dipped, she stirred. "Jax?"

"Someone's here."

She pushed up onto an elbow, shoving her hair away from her face. "Who?"

"I don't know. Go back to sleep."

It didn't surprise me in the slightest that she whipped the sheets from her legs and climbed out of bed, scanning the floor for her clothes.

"Here, babe." I swiped up my T-shirt and tossed it over, before pulling on my jeans.

She tugged the cotton over her head, the hem hitting her below the ass. Then she shimmied into her panties. Her lip curled when she picked up her slacks.

If she wasn't at work, she liked her sweats.

I ducked into the walk-in closet, grabbed a flannel off a hanger and a pair of folded sweatpants, handed them over. "You can wear these."

"Thanks."

The clock on my nightstand glowed 1:14 a.m. If someone was here this late, something was wrong.

"Maybe I should just go home," she said as she pulled on the pants, rolling the waistband three times so they'd stay on her hips.

"Don't go." Not a chance I was letting her walk home alone in the dark, even if it was only fifty yards.

"Okay." She pulled on the flannel first, the sleeves draping well past her fingertips, while I grabbed a hoodie and yanked it over my head.

Then, when we were both dressed, I clasped Sasha's hand and walked out of the bedroom.

A faint knock sounded at the front door. Through the living room windows, I spotted Emery's Jeep parked out front. "Fuck. It's Emery. This can't be good."

Emery was the type who was in bed by nine. If she and Calvin were fighting, it was usually right after they both got home from work. He'd come home in a shit mood and take it out on her, which was the equivalent of chasing her out of the house because rather than argue, she'd just leave. These days, she seemed to always have an overnight bag at the ready.

Either they'd been fighting late tonight, or the fight they'd started early had lasted hours.

"Come on in," I hollered, since I hadn't bothered flipping the lock earlier. The lights were still on in the kitchen and living room too.

When Sasha and I had crashed, we'd crashed.

The door's knob turned, and its hinges made their sweeping sound before it clicked shut behind her. The thud of her shoes hitting the floor as she took them off carried through the house.

"I'm so sorry to come this late, Jax." Emery sniffled, emerging from the entryway. The second she spotted Sasha, her eyes widened. "Oh my God. I'm sorry. I'm interrupting. Again. Shit. I'll go. Forget I was ever here."

"Don't you fucking dare." Red coated my vision.

Because there was red on her face.

Red in the form of a welt. Red splashed across her cheek. Red that would likely turn to black and blue.

Sasha gasped. "Emery."

My best friend swallowed hard, dropping her gaze. "It's not what it looks like."

"Really?" My nostrils flared. "Because it looks like you got punched in the fucking face."

Her eyes swam with tears.

"That son of a bitch." I stalked for my phone, still on the kitchen island. "I'm calling the cops."

Emery ran for me, her socks slipping slightly on the hardwood floors. "Don't call Zak."

"He hit you." That motherfucker. Calvin deserved to rot in jail.

Was this the first time? Had this happened before, and she'd just hid it from me? My heart hammered as rage spread through my veins like wildfire.

"You can't." Emery sobbed, trying to wrestle the phone from my hands. "Stop."

But it wasn't her hand that made me stop. It wasn't her hand that stole the phone away. It was Sasha's. "Jax."

Her voice was steady and calm, her grip firm. Anchoring.

One touch and enough of the fury ebbed for me to slow down. And think. "You have to call this in. Maybe you don't end up pressing charges, but it needs to be on record."

Emery shook her head. "I can't."

"Emery."

"Jax, I—"

"Either the cops pay Calvin a visit. Or I do. Your choice."

She gulped but pulled her phone from her coat pocket. Her fingers were shaking as the tears streamed down her face. But she made the call.

"Zak? It's Emery."

The murmur of his voice was audible, though not loud enough to make out what he was saying. But Emery nodded and inched away, crying as she listened.

She didn't have to tell him what had happened. She just answered whatever questions he asked with a series of yeses and nos.

We all knew the way Calvin treated her, including Zak, the local sheriff.

"Fuck." I dragged a hand through my hair, my heart still hammering. "I should have done something. It shouldn't have come to this."

Sasha gave me a sad smile. "You gave her a place to come. That's all you could do."

I reached for her, hauling her into my chest. With my nose buried in her hair, I breathed in the sweet, fresh scent of her perfume.

Her arms snaked around my face as she pressed her nose to my heart. "I should go. Let you two talk."

"Don't even think about it." I held her tighter, waiting until Emery was off the phone.

"He's coming out here," she said.

"And Calvin?"

A new wave of tears shone in her eyes. "He's sending a deputy to the house."

Her asshole of a husband had better spend the night in a cell.

"I'm going to make some tea," Sasha said, loosening her hold.

She didn't know where I kept the tea bags. She didn't know where I kept my coffee mugs. She didn't know that the kettle was in the cupboard beside the glasses.

I would have followed her into the kitchen anyway, just to help, but the look that she gave me before walking away might as well have been a leash tugging me along in her wake.

Emery unzipped her coat and tossed it on a stool at the island. Then she wandered into the living room, plucking a throw blanket from the arm of the couch and wrapping it around her shoulders before curling into the oversize chair.

I rummaged around a cupboard for a couple of tea bags that were probably expired, but I couldn't find a date, so I set the water to boil anyway. As the flames on the stove's burner roared, I braced my hands on the counter beside Sasha.

"What do you like in your tea?" I asked her.

"I don't drink tea."

"Of course you don't." I shook my head, barking a dry laugh.

If she hadn't forced me into the kitchen, I'd be interrogating Emery. It was going to happen, but before that, I needed to calm down. Sasha knew it. She'd played me well.

So I pulled her into a hug, holding her tight, until the kettle began to steam and whistle.

"Emery, do you want tea?" I asked.

"Sure," she murmured.

I fixed her a mug, letting the bag steep, then Sasha and I joined her in the living room.

Emery's hands folded around the cup as she inhaled the steam.

Sasha sat close to me on the couch, her hand going to my knee. When I opened my mouth to talk, she squeezed my leg, her nails digging in hard.

"Fine," I mouthed. I'd be quiet and wait.

So we waited. And waited. And waited. We waited until headlights flashed outside. Until I greeted Zak at the door, shaking his hand as I invited him inside.

"Hey, Em." His voice was gentle as he took the empty chair. Zak nodded at Sasha, a wordless introduction, but settled into the silence seamlessly.

Once upon a time, he'd been in Emery's close circle. There was a reason she hadn't called 911, but his personal number instead. He was older by nearly a decade. He'd gone to high school with West. But once upon a time, we'd all hoped she'd see Calvin as the asshole he was.

And see the way Zak looked at her.

Other than the agony in his gaze, he kept his expression neutral. Years of training had taught him how best to approach victims, so if giving her a few minutes to sip that tea made it easier, so be it.

"It's not what you think," she finally said.

I opened my mouth to call bullshit.

Sasha's nails once more dug into my thigh. Damn, this woman had strong hands.

My nostrils flared, but I clamped my mouth shut.

"We were fighting," Emery said. "It's been . . . hard, lately."

"How often do you fight?"

She shrugged. "A few times a week. Usually, I come and crash out here."

Zak nodded, taking out a notepad and pen from his jeans pocket. He'd put on his sheriff's black button-down shirt, but I hadn't seen him in the full uniform since he'd been a deputy himself. "What was different about tonight?"

"He went out for drinks with Jonathan." Calvin worked as a carpenter for a local contractor in town. Jonathan was just as much of an asshole, probably why they got along so well. "He came home late. I was already in bed. He, um, wanted sex. I told him to go fuck himself in the shower."

Sasha let out a soft laugh.

Emery met her gaze, a faint smile on her lips that soon fell flat. "We started fighting. About money. About sex. About never going to see my parents in Tulsa. About the way his mom talks down to me. About everything. It's always like that. We just circle around these topics over and over and over again, and it's always the same. So I told him I was done."

Did she mean it? Did she really mean it this time? She'd told me she was done before, but Calvin would win her back with apologies and promises of change. Nothing ever changed.

"I packed a bag, and he followed me into the closet. He started accusing me of having an affair."

"With who?" Zak asked.

"Jax." Emery kept her eyes glued to Sasha, like she'd somehow become the safest person in this room. Maybe that was true.

Sasha just stared right back, like she'd gladly offer that security.

I could have kissed her for being here for my friend. I would kiss her for it later.

"I swear, there is *nothing* between me and Jax," Emery said. "Nothing. I know it's weird that my best friend is a man. It's probably strange for you to see me here a lot. I get it. I'll understand if it makes you uncomfortable and you need us to spend less time together."

"It doesn't bother me," Sasha said.

Her gaze was aimed straight. No flicker to the ceiling. A truth.

"Thanks." Emery sniffled, wiping beneath her eyes. When her fingers skimmed her red cheek, she winced. "I kissed him once. Jax. When we were thirteen. It was disgusting. Zero desire to repeat that experience."

Sasha smiled, and there was a bit of tension that faded from her shoulders. Like maybe she'd needed to hear it from Emery too.

"I told Calvin there was nothing going on with Jax. He didn't believe me. He kept yelling. We were still in the closet, and it just kept getting louder and louder."

My hands balled into fists, but I kept my mouth shut.

"I told him to get out of my face. He didn't. I pushed past him and almost made it to the garage door, but he grabbed my arm. I backed up against a wall, and he just kept yelling." Emery closed her eyes, her chin quivering. "I'm so tired of yelling."

Zak's jaw clenched as he scribbled a few things on the notepad. "Then what?"

"He started yelling in my face. His arms were straight, extended at the sides of my head. Sort of trapping me in place. When I told him I wanted a divorce, he pulled a hand back like he was going to punch the wall. I moved at the same time. His hand grazed off my cheek before it slammed into the drywall. There's a hole in it now."

"Do you believe he meant to strike you?" Zak asked.

"No, I don't. He wanted to scare me. The minute he realized what he'd done, he backed off. Started apologizing and crying. Promised it was an accident. He didn't try to stop me when I left."

It didn't matter if it was just an accident. Calvin never should have stopped her in the first place. Never should have tried to scare her.

"What's happening with him?" Emery asked Zak.

"A deputy went to the house and picked him up while I was driving out here. He'll be at the station when I get back to town."

She nodded, her gaze dropping to her mug. "I'm not pressing charges. It was an accident."

"What?" Venom dripped from my voice.

She finally met my gaze. "It's the truth, Jax. I'm still leaving him. I'm filing for divorce. But I'm not putting him in jail."

Zak's broad shoulders sagged. Either from relief. Or defeat.

What happened when Calvin apologized this time? What happened when he begged for another chance? If what she said was true and he hadn't meant to hit her, what happened during the next fight when he decided aiming at the wall wouldn't be enough?

"This is a good thing," Emery said.

"How the fuck is this good?" I seethed.

"I wouldn't have left otherwise," she whispered. "We both know I wouldn't have left."

"Sometimes, we need the worst to make us change," Sasha said.

The way she spoke made the hairs on the back of my neck stand on end. It sounded like she had experience with this. Like she'd survived the worst. She wasn't talking about the death of her parents, was she?

"I'll never go back. I swear." There was steel in Emery's voice.

I hadn't heard that sort of determination from her in a long time.

"Can I crash in your guest bedroom for a while?" she asked me. "Until this gets sorted?"

"Of course."

Emery turned to Zak, her eyes softening. "Thanks."

"Welcome." He stood, lifting a hand to wave. Then he walked out of the living room, about to disappear. Except he slowed behind Emery's chair. He lifted an arm, like he was about to reach for her. But then he dropped it at his side and walked to the entryway.

I followed, shaking his hand before he ducked outside. Then I collected Emery's bag that she'd dropped beside her shoes.

She'd folded the blanket and was putting the mug in the dishwasher when I returned.

I dropped her stuff on the island and went to the freezer, then took out the plastic quart bag full of corn syrup. It was a trick Grandma had taught me. The syrup got cold but not hard. It made a better ice pack than anything you could buy.

"Thanks," she said when I handed it to her. "I'm going to bed."

"Night."

She snagged her bag, about to disappear, but stopped and crashed into me for a hug. "Sorry."

"Don't apologize. You okay?"

"No, but ask me again tomorrow." She lowered her voice to a whisper. "I like Sasha."

"So do I."

"Keep her, all right?"

I glanced over Emery's head, finding Sasha's beautiful eyes waiting. "That's my plan."

Chapter 18
SASHA

Exhaustion weighed like a thousand pounds on my shoulders. My feet ached. My eyelids were heavy. My mouth stretched in a yawn. It took all my strength just to shift my car into park and push open the door.

I didn't care that it was only five thirty. I was scarfing whatever leftovers were in the fridge, then immediately going to bed.

With my work tote slung over my shoulder, I trudged to the door and stepped inside.

There was a person in my kitchen.

"Ah!" I screamed, the exhaustion gone in a blink.

There was a person in my kitchen. Why was there a person in my kitchen?

"Hi." Emery gave me an apologetic smile as she dried her hands on a towel. "Sorry. Didn't mean to scare you."

"Hi," I drawled, pressing a hand to my racing heart, then I glanced around the room to make sure I'd come to my house, not Jax's.

Yep, this was my house.

"You didn't notice my Jeep out front, did you?" she asked.

"Huh?" I turned to peer out the nearest window. Sure enough, there was her Jeep. "Oh."

Seriously, I needed to get to bed. If I'd missed an entire vehicle, I was a hazard to my own health.

Last night, after Emery had slipped away to the guest bedroom, Jax and I had gone to bed, too, but neither of us had been able to sleep. We'd tossed and turned for hours, until finally, I'd given up, and he'd walked me to the cabin so I could get ready for work.

"How was your day?" she asked.

"Fine." I kicked off my shoes and walked to the island, inhaling the scents of vanilla and sugar and chocolate. A cooling rack of cookies was on the counter. The sink was piled with mixing bowls and spatulas.

"Cookie?" Emery asked.

"What kind?" Wait. That was not the question I should be asking. "What are you doing in my house?"

She simply smiled and took out a plate for two warm chocolate chip cookies. "I hear congratulations are in order."

"Oh." Was that the reason for the cookies? "Yes."

"Jax told me earlier."

Emery was the second person to say congratulations today. Just like he'd warned last night, Indya had come into my office first thing this morning with a bouquet of roses.

The list of people who knew about the baby was growing, yet I hadn't told a soul. The only time I'd had to say "I'm pregnant" out loud had been to Jax and on my initial call to the doctor's office. Otherwise, for months, those words hadn't crossed my lips.

I should have felt guilty for letting Jax make the announcements. But I had to tell Eddie. That would be hard enough. If Jax wanted to tackle everyone on the resort, I'd let him.

"A girl?" Emery asked. "Jax said you are naming her Josephine."

I nodded. "After my mom."

"That's sweet." A flash of sadness crossed her expression, but she hid it quickly. Then she snatched her own cookie.

I popped a bite into my mouth, moaning as the chocolate melted on my tongue. Screw dinner. I'd have a handful of these, then pass out in a sugar coma. "These are so good."

"Thanks."

"How are you?"

"Meh." She lifted a shoulder. "Better than last night."

A bruise had bloomed on her pretty face. Jax feared she'd have a nasty black eye, but so far, the only evidence of last night was on her cheek.

"Have you talked to him?"

She nodded. "Jax drove me into town earlier to get some stuff from the house. I called him first and told him not to be there. He said hello. Then okay. That's it. Two words."

Was that a good thing? Or bad? Her voice was flat, so I couldn't tell from her tone.

"It's done." Emery gave me a sad smile. "I talked to a lawyer this morning."

"I'm sorry."

She shrugged again, just as the oven's timer dinged.

While she rushed to take out the next batch of cookies, I slipped down the hallway to my bedroom, more than ready to get out of the jeans I'd worn all day.

Despite the hair tie that was looped through the buttonhole and secured to the button to give the waistband a little slack, they were still snug. I'd just lifted my sweater, about to unwind the elastic, but the moment I stepped into the bedroom, I froze.

Emery's panicked voice called from the kitchen. "Sasha, wait."

I didn't wait. I walked into my closet.

The sweaters and blouses that I'd hung on hangers weeks ago were gone. The pants I'd folded on the shelves were missing. The shoes I'd lined up neatly in pairs had vanished.

"Shit." Emery flew through the doorway. "Jax is on his way. I was supposed to delay you."

"Delay me. From finding this?" I pointed to the empty closet. Well, not entirely empty. There were four unpacked suitcases on the floor.

She gave me another exaggerated frown. "I'm sorry. It was his idea."

"To relocate my stuff?" I spun in a slow circle, scanning the room.

My lip balm was gone from the nightstand along with my phone's charging cord. My pillow was not on the bed. At a quick glance into the bathroom, my toiletries and toothbrush on the vanity had been replaced with three bulging travel cases.

"Jax." I pinched the bridge of my nose. "Did he seriously move me out of this house?"

"Yes."

I stared at the bed, wishing I could climb beneath the warm quilt. I would. Soon. But first, I had a man to strangle.

"I've never seen him like this," Emery said. "He's always been the guy who didn't want a commitment. Even when he dated Robin when we were younger. I think he stayed with her for as long as he did because he knew it would be drama when they called it off, so he waited until they were in college and away from the bullshit here in town. He never acted like it was lasting. And with anyone since, he's been checked out. Until you."

"It's the baby," I said.

"It's not." She shook her head. "It's you."

Was that true? Did I want it to be true?

Yes, damn it. I wanted Jax for myself. I'd wanted him for longer than I was willing to admit. And after last night, there was no going back. There was no forgetting.

My stomach knotted.

What were we doing? I couldn't ask him to pretend it hadn't happened, not again. Not after last night. And I wouldn't be able to pretend either.

But if—when—my heart was broken, if we hurt each other, our baby girl would be caught in the middle.

Besides, I was moving. I wasn't made for Montana. The idea of another cold winter made my insides roil. Except how could I leave? How could I take a daughter from Jax?

I wouldn't ask him to leave this ranch. I wouldn't ask him to move away from his family. I sure as hell wasn't going to live without my Josephine.

Here I was, stuck. Totally stuck for the next eighteen years.

This was it, wasn't it? If I wasn't going to beg Jax to move, if I wasn't going to separate him from our daughter, then I was stuck here.

I lived in Montana.

Oh my God. I lived in Montana.

My heart sank slowly, like a feather floating to the ground. I lived in Montana.

Shouldn't I be more upset? I wasn't *not* upset. But I wasn't freaking out either. Maybe that freak-out would come after eight to ten hours of sleep.

Huh. Montana was the last place I'd ever expected to end up. What would Eddie say?

"Sasha?" Emery put her hand on my arm. "Are you okay?"

Was I okay? "I don't know."

"Sasha." Jax's voice called from the living room.

I swallowed hard, blinking the world into focus. Then I marched out of the room, leveling Jax with a glare.

"Before you rip my head off"—he held up his hands—"hear me out."

I stopped in front of him, crossing my arms over my chest. "I'm listening."

"This is just temporary. Emery and I will kill each other if we have to share a roof for more than a few days at a time. She's a slob."

"Hey," Emery scoffed, coming up behind me.

He jerked his chin toward the kitchen and the mess from her baking.

"Whatever," she muttered, snagging a cookie from the rack before retreating down the hall. Probably to unpack *her* stuff in *my* bedroom.

"What makes you think we can live together?" I asked.

"What makes you think we can't?"

"Don't answer my questions with questions." I fought a yawn and failed. "How do you know that we won't be at each other's throats?"

He bent low, his mouth hovering an inch over mine before it drifted across the line of my jaw, dropping to my neck. "I'm hoping we'll be at each other's throats."

His voice whispered across my skin, sending tingles down my spine. My breath hitched. *Damn it.*

"No, Jax. This is a bad idea."

"It's temporary."

Temporary. Like a sleepover. *Sleep.* I needed sleep. Tonight, I didn't care where I slept. I just needed a blanket and a pillow. Tomorrow, when I wasn't so exhausted, I'd argue with him about moving my stuff.

"Fine," I muttered.

A low chuckle rumbled in my ear before he dropped a kiss to my cheek, then stood tall, grabbing my hand and pulling me to the door. "Night, Em."

"Night!" she called from the bedroom.

"Did you really get all my things?" I asked as I stepped into my shoes and he put on his boots.

"Yep." He grinned as he opened the door. "Even the air mattress."

I rolled my eyes as we set off for his house.

"It only took me five trips. Walking, back and forth. You weren't kidding when you said you didn't have much."

"Nope. I travel light," I teased. I wasn't sure if I was a light traveler. I hadn't ever traveled. Moving from California to Montana was the longest trip I'd taken since high school. "It was easier to move here if I didn't have a lot to haul. And I don't need much."

I couldn't afford much.

California was expensive. My paychecks had been enough to cover my living expenses, but every month, there seemed to be less and less left over. My savings were nonexistent, and my parents hadn't been wealthy. What I'd inherited hadn't even covered the funeral costs.

Jax kept my hand as we walked, slowing his pace to match mine. "Be warned. I had a meeting with Indya and West today, and she's already planning a baby shower. She doesn't know how to throw a party that's not over the top. That includes gifts."

I groaned. "Isn't that going to be awkward? She's my boss."

"This baby is her niece. She'll spoil her without restraint."

For my daughter, I kind of liked that she'd be spoiled by her family.

My feet came to a halt.

"What?" Jax asked, his eyebrows coming together as he stopped too.

Family. She was going to have a family.

An aunt. Uncle. Cousins. Grandparents.

Two parents.

She was going to have everything that I'd missed for ten years. Everything truly important in this world.

Lucky girl. *My* girl.

We weren't alone. I wasn't alone. And we lived in Montana.

Tears surged, either from the hormones or the exhaustion or one too many life-altering realizations in a single day.

All this time, I'd been so focused on being pregnant. I'd spent countless hours learning about what to expect during each trimester. What changes my body would experience. What would happen when I went into labor.

The details were terrifying. I'd been so focused on everything that scared me, I hadn't looked far enough into the future.

I hadn't thought about everything *she'd* have.

And everything she'd give me.

"Hey." Jax's hands came to my face, sliding into my hair.

"Sorry," I blubbered, sniffling as he wiped beneath my eyes. "It's been a long day, and I'm emotional and tired, and I cry over everything right now."

"Cry it up, beautiful." He kissed my forehead, then hauled me into his chest.

Leaning on him was dangerous, but I did it anyway, burrowing into his shirt until the sting in my nose was gone. "Better."

He studied my face to make sure I wasn't lying, then he dropped his mouth to mine for a kiss. A kiss that said *hello* and *don't cry*.

It started slow and gentle, but with every heartbeat, the intensity spiked. Until the kiss was all-consuming, and the rest of the world faded to a blur.

Nothing about the way his lips and tongue moved was rushed. This kiss wasn't a prelude. This wasn't Jax rounding first base to chase toward second or third.

He kissed me like he was settling in to kiss me for the rest of my life.

It was a long, languid kiss. And it still ended too soon, just as the world flipped.

Jax gave me a soft, easy smile as he broke away. "Hungry?"

Such a simple question, like everything wasn't turning upside down and right side up for the thousandth time.

Maybe someday I'd get used to the flipping. Maybe I'd learn to enjoy it.

Maybe I was already, just a little.

"Can you do something for me?" I asked him.

"If you ask me to sleep on that air mattress tonight, it's a fuck no."

I laughed. "It's not that. Remember how you told me you'd make me fall in love with Montana?"

"Yeah."

"I need you to do that." Before the baby was born. Before October.

His smile widened as he took my hand, but instead of him leading me inside, we cut through the grass between the house and cabin.

The meadows beyond us were green and lush. The constant rain and drizzle from April had slowed as the days morphed into May. Every morning, dew sparkled on the grass. By noon, the sun had chased it away.

After a few minutes of walking, Jax stopped us, bending to pluck a white wildflower. Then he used the petals to tickle a line down my temple.

"Close your eyes."

"Okay." I obeyed. "Now what?"

"Breathe."

"That's it?" I popped an eye open. "*Breathe* is your master plan?"

"Close your damn eyes, woman."

They drifted shut, a smile on my mouth. Then I breathed.

In and out. Over and over. Each inhale was a long and lung-straining breath. Each exhale washed away the stress from last night and a busy day at work.

A bird whistled a tune as it flew overhead. In the distance, cattle bellowed. The wind rustled leaves in the grove of nearby trees.

My shoes sank deeper into the earth with every breath, like I was finding my center. A balance I hadn't felt in years.

Or maybe my feet were growing roots.

"Keep breathing, babe."

Babe. Baby. Honey. Beautiful. Sweetheart.

Jax didn't use a single endearment. He used them all. He seemed to tailor them to his mood. Babe, for the normal moments when we were just talking. Honey, when he wanted to be sweet. Baby, when we were in his bed.

"Smells nice, doesn't it?" he murmured.

"Yes." It smelled like spring.

It smelled like a fresh start.

The air was relaxing. The sunshine warmed my face. I yawned again, unable to stop myself.

The touch of his lips on my forehead made me open my eyes.

"Let's go inside," he said.

"Okay." I yawned again.

It should have been strange, walking into his house after he'd moved me in without my permission. It should have been awkward, given how little time I'd spent in his home. But it just . . . wasn't.

I did everything I'd planned to do at my own house. I found my clothes put away in his closet, so I changed out of my jeans and into my favorite sweats. I raided the fridge and found leftover lasagna, so I heated up a plate for us both.

With dinner scarfed, I went to Jax's en suite bathroom, where my toiletries were in the top drawer and my toothbrush was in the holder beside his.

I washed my face. I tied up my hair. I climbed into bed, knowing Jax would join me when he was ready. And as I drifted off to sleep, I tried not to panic that Jax had made sure to clarify this, not once, but twice.

Temporary.

This was only temporary.

~

Eddie,

I wish we hadn't moved. Everything changed when we moved. I was so desperate to start fresh, but it was a mistake. When did I start making all the wrong decisions? It seemed like such a good idea at the time. Except looking back, we should have stayed where we were. Even though we were fighting. Even though we were sick of each other. Even though every day was so hard. I wish we hadn't moved.

S

Chapter 19
SASHA

Jax was wearing his cowboy hat while driving his truck, one wrist dangling over the steering wheel. Sunshine streamed through the windshield, highlighting the chiseled corners of his jaw.

It wasn't at all like the dark winter night of the party, but I couldn't shake the sense of déjà vu as we drove through the ranch to the resort.

"What?" He glanced over and smirked.

"Nothing."

"Liar." He stretched a hand across the console, taking mine off my lap to hold between us. "Checking me out, Vaughn?"

"Maybe."

His grin widened. "Good."

I blushed, tearing my gaze away, and smiled out my own window. It wasn't normal to smile this much. Definitely not for me. But I couldn't stop.

Jax and I had settled into an easy routine over the past two weeks. Too easy, considering we were still getting to know each other. Yet easy was the only way to describe it.

I didn't trust easy. I didn't expect it to last.

But for now, I was enjoying it, just a little. Until it was gone.

Living with Jax wasn't as complicated as I'd thought it would be. Our routines had synced seamlessly. We showered together. We ate together. We slept together. And God, the sex. It was constant. I craved him to the point of distraction.

My gaze drifted back to his side of the truck, taking another long look as heat bloomed in my center.

"If you keep looking at me like that, we're going to be late."

"You shouldn't have worn the hat." I bit my lower lip as he shifted, adjusting his cock with his other hand.

"Later." He lifted our clasped hands and nipped at my wrist, his teeth grazing my skin. Then he growled, part lust, part frustration, as the lodge came into view. "Whose idea was this?"

"Yours." I laughed, wiggling my hand free from his grip so I could make sure the collar on my shirt was straight.

It had been when I'd gotten dressed, but then Jax had pulled it to the side to kiss my collarbone as he'd helped me into the truck.

I flipped down the visor, making sure the color in my cheeks looked like blush and not the orgasm Jax had given me before we'd left the house.

"Shit," I muttered.

"What?"

I pointed to the mirror. "I look like we just had sex."

"We did just have sex."

"I don't need to look like it before a work function."

He chuckled. "It's just the Saturday barbeque."

"With my boss, employees, and a slew of guests in attendance." I shot him a frown before smoothing my hair. "Everyone is going to know that we're . . . something."

What were we? A couple? A fling? It wasn't my style to have a relationship this obscure. But I was scared to ask.

This was either casual or serious. And both answers were terrifying. So I was embracing the unknown.

"Hate to break it to you, babe. But everyone already knows that we're *something*." He spoke that last word through gritted teeth, hinting that he wasn't thrilled with the obscurity either. "It's not a secret that you're pregnant. Or that we're living together."

"Temporarily living together, right?"

"Yeah. Temporarily."

My heart sank a bit every time I heard that word, even though we had no idea how long this temporary arrangement would last. Emery seemed content in the cabin, and Jax didn't want to rush her off the ranch.

She'd mostly stayed to herself these past two weeks. She drove into town for work each morning and returned to the cabin each night. She'd hired a lawyer for the divorce. And she'd started searching for a new place in town. But the search was slow, and it had only been two weeks.

No one was pushing her to make these big changes at once. And I wasn't complaining about sleeping in Jax's bed each night.

The parking lot was crowded at the lodge, forcing us to park at the end of a row. We climbed out, and I breathed in the June air, the sun warm on my face.

Ever since he'd taken me into the meadow behind the house, I found myself breathing in the air differently. Deeper. Fuller. I let it fill my lungs, holding it for a moment. Savoring it.

Montana air was fresh. Clean. Almost as addicting as Jax.

"Ready?" he asked as we set off for the lodge.

"It's not my first barbeque, you know."

"I know." He snagged my hand, holding it tight.

"Jax," I warned, trying to wiggle free. "Work function."

"Family function, Sasha," he corrected, his grip unmovable as his jaw flexed. "Saturdays are a family function. You want to pretend we're nothing Monday through Friday, fine. But Saturdays, we're going to be real."

Wait. Pretend we were nothing? Maybe I didn't know exactly how to define this relationship, but it wasn't nothing. "I don't pretend we're nothing."

"Then hold my fucking hand."

I laced our fingers together.

The irritation on his face faded as he stared down at me, shaking his head like he wanted to say something more. But he stayed quiet as we skirted the exterior of the lodge, passing the Beartooth cabin on the way to the rear patio.

Voices and laughter greeted us along with the scents of campfire smoke and grilled meat. People milled about the open space, visiting as they sipped cocktails or champagne or beer.

From the sheer number of bodies, it looked like most guests had come tonight.

West and Indya were talking to a couple from Texas who'd just arrived yesterday. When Indya spotted me, her smile widened, and she waved us over.

Only before we could join them, the twins came out of nowhere, slamming into Jax's legs and rocking him on his heels.

"Uncle Jax, you gotta see this." Kade grabbed Jax's free hand and began pulling with all his might.

Jax laughed. "What do I gotta see?"

"We went fishing today." Kohen was out of breath like he'd been running for an hour. He grabbed Jax's wrist, pulling with his brother. "And Reid is cooking our fish for dinner. You gotta see how big it is before he cuts it up."

"Okay. Let's see this fish." Jax winked at me, then let go of my hand.

They veered toward the firepit as I walked to Indya's side, greeting my boss and the guests.

Whether Jax thought so or not, tonight was a work function, so I wandered from group to group, ensuring everyone was having a nice time. The kitchen staff set up the cheeseburger bar while the waitstaff filtered through the patio with trays of light appetizers.

Jax was pulled from the twins by guests, and like the night of the party, his eyes were often waiting when I found him in the crush. We finally made our way back to each other just as a local musician began playing her guitar from the opposite end of the patio.

"Hungry?" he asked, handing me a glass of sparkling water.

"Yes." Most of the guests had already made it through the line.

"There's Dad." He jerked up his chin at Curtis as he emerged from the lodge's back doors.

"Evening, Son. Hi, Sasha." Curtis grinned as he walked over, hand outstretched for Jax. I expected a handshake, too, but before I knew what was happening, Curtis wrapped me into a hug.

"H-hi." My arms flailed for a moment, unsure of where to settle. They landed on his sides as I hugged him back.

Curtis hugged tight, tighter even than Jax. Before he let go, he gave a last squeeze around my shoulders.

It was familiar, even though I hadn't felt it in a decade. It was a dad's hug.

I'd forgotten how much I missed my dad's hugs.

The emotion, the memory, clawed at my throat. But I wasn't going to cry in front of guests, so I swallowed hard, and when Curtis let me go, I let Jax haul me into his side. I leaned on him until I caught my balance.

"Now that it's not a secret, guess I can finally say congratulations," Curtis said. "I've got a friend who does custom woodworking. I'd like to—" Whatever he was going to say was cut short the moment Lily appeared at his side.

Jax's entire frame stiffened.

I fought a lip curl.

And Curtis's eyes widened as he looked down at his ex-wife, clearly shocked she'd be this close.

"Uh, hi, Mom." West walked over with Indya, both of them sharing a look. "Didn't realize you were coming out tonight."

She shrugged. "Tara's meeting me out here later. I've got to get the scoop on her and Reid."

"We were just about to get a cheeseburger," Indya said. "Would you like to join us?"

She was clearly trying to get Lily away from Jax or Curtis. Maybe both.

Lily picked up on it, too, and a flash of pain crossed her expression before she nodded. "Sounds great."

West held out his arm, ready to escort his mother. But before she took it, she gave Jax a sad smile. "It's good to see you. And you, Sasha. How have you been feeling?"

"Fine, thanks." As much as I didn't like how she'd treated Jax, my mother would have rolled over in her grave if I were impolite.

"Good. That's wonderful." She looked between the two of us. "West says it's a girl?"

"Yes." I nodded as Jax's nostrils flared.

"Congratulations." She gave him another smile, then her gaze flicked to Curtis. "Hi, Curtis."

"Hi, Lily?" It sounded like a question. He blinked a few times, staring at her with his jaw slack, even as she took West's arm and walked away.

"What the fuck?" Jax muttered.

The color drained from Curtis's face. "She said that to me, right? She said hi to me?"

"Yes," I drawled. Why was that surprising?

"I need a drink." Curtis gulped, then breezed past us for the bar.

"Um, what was that about?" I asked Jax.

Jax's gaze tracked to where Lily was in line with Indya and West. "She hasn't spoken to him in over a decade. Not a single word."

"Seriously?"

"Seriously. How hungry are you?"

Starving. "Not very."

"Mind if we head home?"

"Not at all." I took his hand, and the two of us slipped into the lodge, disappearing without a goodbye.

He walked fast to the truck, fast even by my standards. But I kept up, and this time, it was me gripping his hand so he couldn't shake it loose.

Jax didn't say a word as we got in his truck and reversed out of the lot, heading away from the resort. He drove faster than normal, the truck bouncing and swaying on the rough road.

It wasn't until we were at the last grove of trees on the drive to the house that he finally took his foot off the gas. His shoulders slumped, and as he blew out a long breath, he slowed us to a crawl.

"Sorry. That was . . . weird," he said.

"It's all right."

Jax pressed the brake until we were stopped. We were in the middle of the road, but it was his road. If this was where he wanted to talk, then I'd listen. "I told you my mother left me here with Dad when I was a baby."

"I remember." Some of the details of his drunken rambling from the night I'd told him I was pregnant were fuzzy, but that story wasn't one I'd forget.

"Dad went to Vegas with some friends for the National Finals Rodeo. Got wasted and met her at a bar. They hooked up. I was the unexpected surprise."

It was the nice way of saying he was an accident. A mistake. I'd always hated it whenever parents called their children mistakes, now more than ever.

"Dad fucked up, but he owned it. Told Lily everything and begged for her forgiveness. She stayed with him. Even after my mother left me here a year later."

Yes, Lily had stayed. But that wasn't quite good enough, was it? Not when she'd hurt him too.

"You know the rest," he said. "When Lily and I got into that fight years ago, when I gave her that ultimatum, Dad was pissed when she didn't let the name thing go. I don't know the details, but I guess they got into a fight too. She hasn't spoken to him since."

"Until today."

He nodded. "Until today."

"Why?"

"No idea." He shrugged. "It was strange, right? She's been acting strange."

If I was being honest, Lily *was* acting nice. She was acting toward them the way she'd always acted toward me. But I didn't know her well enough to say if it was strange. She was clearly trying to mend the rift with Jax.

That's what I'd tell him if I was being honest.

But I didn't want to be honest, not yet. Not when I was still angry at her on his behalf.

Jax drummed his fingers on the steering wheel. "Did you know she hasn't set foot in Dad's house since the day she moved out? That was ages ago. Any time she'd come to visit West and me, we'd meet at the lodge. But she never went back to that house. Sometimes she'll get mail that's meant for him. Mostly it's junk that's addressed to them both and goes to her house, but she keeps it. Then she gives it to West to deliver to Dad."

"Why won't she go to the house?"

"I think because she loves him."

She loved him. But she didn't speak to him and had forced West to be their go-between. "Lily is a confusing person."

Jax barked a laugh. "Yes. That's for damn sure."

"I don't understand."

"Neither do I." He pulled his hat off and raked a hand through his hair. "Or, I didn't until West explained it. Lily loves Dad. She probably always will. She doesn't date. Neither does he. She won't forgive him for cheating, but she's still in love with him too. They live separate lives. They're divorced. But she loves him. And I think that's why she doesn't go to the house. It hurts all over again. And she's spent so long being hurt and angry, she can't stop now."

"Ah. So Lily isn't done punishing Curtis."

And maybe she had every right to inflict that punishment. Maybe the way he'd broken her trust and her heart deserved a lifetime of silence. Maybe, in her shoes, I would have done the same.

Except I couldn't rationalize how she'd treated Jax.

"I've been thinking about her a lot lately," Jax said, his voice quiet and guarded. "I get why she didn't want me to call her Mom. If I put myself in her shoes, I can understand. But in my shoes, it still hurts."

Damn you, Lily. I regretted being polite at the barbeque.

"Anyway." Jax drew in a long breath and took his foot off the brake, following the bend in the road. "Sorry about dinner."

"I'd rather it just be us anyway. I'll make—" My sentence was cut off when we emerged past the trees, and I spotted a large navy truck at the cabin. There was a man outside. "Who's—"

"Motherfucker." Jax shot us forward, sending me deep into the seat.

"Jax, who is that?" I asked, even though I had good hunch.

His hands strangled the wheel as we flew toward the cabin. "Calvin."

Chapter 20
SASHA

"Stay put," Jax ordered as we came to a sliding stop beside Emery's Jeep. The second the tires stopped, he was out the door.

I was definitely not *staying put*. With my seat belt unbuckled, I hopped out and slammed my door. No one even glanced toward the noise.

Emery was on the porch, arms wrapped around her middle, staring at the man whose knees were in the dirt. Tears streamed down her face.

They streamed down Calvin's too. "Please, baby. Don't do this."

Jax's hands balled into fists as I came to a stop at his side. He gave me a frown but otherwise kept his attention on Emery and Calvin.

"Em, you know I'd never hurt you. It was an accident. I swear. Shit has been bad with us lately, but we can fix it. Please, give me a chance to fix it."

She wiped at her cheeks, her gaze flickering to Jax and me. There wasn't much color in her ashen face, but the slight pink in her cheeks drained, and she ducked her chin like she wanted to hide.

We shouldn't be here. We shouldn't be watching this. I put my hand on Jax's arm, giving it a slight tug, but he was immovable.

Not a chance he'd leave Emery here alone.

"Calvin, get up," Emery said.

He shook his head. "No. Not until you give me another chance."

The man was the portrait of remorse. He clasped his hands together, more tears streaming down his face. There was no mistaking the desperation in his voice, and for a moment, my heart squeezed.

Then it hardened to stone.

He was manipulating her. He was playing the victim. He was laying on the guilt so thick it blanketed the ground like a gray, dismal fog.

Jax opened his mouth, like he was about to step in, but I dug my nails into the cotton of his shirt. He clamped his teeth shut with an audible click.

Emery had to recognize this. She had to be the one to send him away. Otherwise, he'd never stop. And this cycle of theirs would go on and on and on.

"Please," Calvin whispered. "I love you. You're my wife."

Fresh tears spilled down her cheeks. "I can't keep doing this."

"I'll change. I swear. We'll do that counseling stuff again. I'll cut back on hours at work. We can fix this."

She swallowed hard, shaking her head. "You said that last time we had a fight."

"I mean it this time."

She stared at him for a long moment. "You said that last time too."

Calvin gulped as Emery straightened, her shoulders squaring.

"I think you should leave," she said.

"Emery, I—"

"It's done, Calvin. We're done."

The air rushed from my lungs.

Jax's shoulders dropped as he blew out his own breath.

Before he could say another word, Emery turned and disappeared inside the cabin, slamming the door.

Calvin hung his head. If he wasn't already on the ground, he would have crumpled to the earth.

I took a step away, about to retreat to the truck, but Jax didn't budge.

He stared at Calvin, waiting as the minutes dragged on, until finally, the other man shifted and pushed to his feet.

Calvin stared at the cabin's front door for a long moment. "Fuck you, Haven. This is your fault."

Asshole.

"I'm not the one who hit her," Jax said.

"It was an accident." The look Calvin sent Jax was sheer malice. "Maybe if you hadn't been fucking my wife all year, she wouldn't have left me."

The sound Jax made was part laugh, part scoff. "Get the hell off my property. Don't come back."

Calvin only arched his eyebrows, a silent challenge for Jax to make him leave.

My heart climbed into my throat as my hands wrapped around Jax's forearm. "No, Jax."

Every muscle in his body seemed to tense, like a predator ready to strike. But the only move he made was to jerk his chin toward Calvin's truck.

"Fuck you." Calvin flipped us off, then stormed away.

The slam of his driver's side door made me jump. Then the engine roared to life, and he sped off down the road, dust flying in his wake.

Only when the sound of his truck was gone did I breathe. Then I rushed for the cabin, knocking as I opened the door. "Emery?"

She was standing at the window that overlooked the kitchen sink, staring out into the green meadow that stretched beyond the glass. "He's gone."

There was pain in that statement. Not gone, as in today. Gone, forever. Her husband, gone.

Maybe they hadn't been in a good marriage, but she loved Calvin, didn't she?

"I'm sorry." I went to stand at her side and put my arm around her shoulders.

"Me too." She leaned her head against mine. "That was the hardest thing I've ever done in my life."

"It's not easy to cut someone out of your life, especially when you know you're breaking their heart."

She closed her eyes. "Whose heart did you break?"

Eddie's. I broke Eddie. In every way imaginable. And I had to live with that for the rest of my life.

"Do you want some time alone?" I asked my own question instead of answering hers.

"Yeah," she murmured, standing tall to wipe at her eyes. "I think so."

"All right." I dropped my arm and, when I turned, found Jax's gaze waiting.

He wasn't focused on Emery. No, he was locked on me.

Which meant he'd heard Emery's question.

And he'd listened to me dodge it.

"You okay, Em?" he asked.

She shrugged. After a scene like that, a shrug was probably as good as anyone could hope for.

"I'll call you later," he said.

She nodded, her voice raw as she said, "'Kay."

He gave her a sad smile as I crossed the room, walking for the door. He followed me outside and into his truck.

"Sasha—"

"Please, don't ask." I dropped my chin. If he asked, I'd tell him. And I wasn't ready to tell him, not yet.

His disappointment filled the cab, but he stayed quiet as he took us to his house.

I slipped to the bedroom as he took off his boots. The lights were off, the evening sunset streaming in through the windows in pink and peach and golden rays. I slumped on the end of the bed and closed my eyes.

With every breath, I waited for the twist in my chest to loosen. For the weight to disappear. But it wouldn't. Not until Jax knew the truth. Not until I told Eddie about the baby.

Secrets were heavy, especially when you carried them alone.

My hand floated to my belly.

Once upon a time, I'd told my mother everything. She'd been my secret keeper. I wanted to be that for my daughter so she wouldn't have to carry her secrets alone.

"Tell me a truth." Jax's voice was a low murmur from the doorway.

I opened my eyes. Jax leaned against the threshold. "I'm scared of what this will be like when it ends."

That I'd go back to the cabin once Emery left, and we'd return to being . . . friends. That eventually, he'd find a woman who wasn't quite so closed off, quite so scared of being trampled, quite so messy and broken. That he'd realize I was just too much work.

"Why do you think it will end?"

"History." The good never lasted. It was either killed in a car crash. Or pummeled in a miserable fistfight.

Jax shoved off the door and crossed the room, kneeling in front of me. He looked like he was about to say something, but the sight of him on his knees reminded me too much of Calvin from earlier, so I reached for him, grabbing him by the shirt to pull him closer.

He rose up, his mouth capturing mine as I lay back on the bed, his shirt still balled in my fist. His weight settled beside mine on the mattress, his tongue sliding past my lips, and the moment it swirled against my own, everything beyond us faded to a blur.

The noise in my head quieted. The worries vanished.

A hum vibrated from my chest as I threaded my hands into his hair, tugging at the dark-blond strands.

Jax slanted his mouth, delving inside before he nipped at my bottom lip, leaning away. His Adam's apple bobbed as his blue eyes searched mine. "Baby, I promise—"

"Don't," I whispered, putting my finger over his lips before he could finish that sentence.

He frowned but stayed quiet.

We weren't at the point of making promises. We both knew that. There was too much uncertainty ahead of us, too many unknowns.

And if he made me a promise, I wasn't sure I'd survive if he couldn't keep it. Not that he wouldn't try. Jax Haven was the type of man who'd move mountains to keep a promise, even if it destroyed us both.

I ran my thumb over his lower lip, my hand sliding across his jaw. Then I leaned up and took his mouth.

Jax growled, the sound a dark rumble in his chest as he took control. Gone was the sweet, gentle touch. He devoured me, pouring every bit of his frustration into the kiss.

My breath hitched as his hand slid up my ribs, cupping my breast. I arched into his body as heat coursed through my veins. The throb in my core became a steady drumbeat.

He nipped at the corner of my lips, biting hard enough to sting. Then we became a frenzy, each sitting up to strip out of our clothes, all while our mouths fought to stay locked. He had me naked in seconds, my clothes landing in soft thumps on the floor.

I wasn't as quick and only managed to get his shirt off before I got distracted by the warmth of his skin against mine. My hands trailed through the dusting of coarse hair over his heart, dropping to those muscled abs. My fingertips whispered along the peaks and valleys as they trailed lower and lower and lower.

With a series of quick flicks, his belt buckle was loose, the metal cool on my bare hip. Then I tugged the button free, sliding the zipper just enough to dive inside and wrap my hand around his cock.

"Sasha." Jax tore his mouth free from mine and bent to take a nipple between his teeth.

My grip on his erection tightened. The harder I squeezed, the harder he sucked.

"Jax," I hissed as he kneaded my breast. "I need to feel you."

He growled, then stood and stripped out of his jeans. With every movement, his thighs bulged and his biceps flexed.

God, he was gorgeous. Hard work had honed Jax's body into rugged lines and ripped muscle. I craved him more and more each day.

There was no foreplay as he came back on the bed and settled into the cradle of my hips. We didn't need foreplay, not when I was already soaked. He positioned himself at my entrance and thrust deep.

"Yes." I stretched as he filled me, my nails digging into his shoulders as I adjusted to his size.

Easy. With our bodies connected, it was just so easy.

"You feel so damn perfect, baby." He latched his mouth onto my pulse and sucked as he eased out and drove inside.

His cock hit exactly the right spot as he set a steady rhythm with his hips. My legs trembled as I clung to him, holding on for the ride.

"Look how good you take me," he murmured, dropping his head to watch as he thrust inside my body.

"Jax." My voice became a breathy whisper as my inner walls began to flutter.

He sealed his mouth over mine, his tongue sweeping inside. He kissed me like he fucked me, hard and insistent. Like he was making a point.

Like he was making the promise I'd stopped earlier.

When I came, it was on a cry down his throat. My body writhed beneath him as white spots blanked my vision. Somehow, the orgasms stretched longer, hit harder. Every time we were together, it was better than the last.

My toes curled. My heart thundered. Pleasure rippled through every bone in my body.

Jax came on a groan that vibrated from his chest to mine. He poured inside me, his face twisted in beautiful ecstasy. And when he finally collapsed, breaking our connection as he rolled to the side, we twined ourselves together in a mess of tangled limbs.

His hand dived into my hair. Mine to his. His mouth was waiting when I found it for a quick kiss. As we relaxed into the pillows, his free hand shifted to my belly, splaying across the swell of our daughter.

The light was still bright outside. We both needed dinner. But as Jax's frame relaxed into the mattress, I curled tighter into his arms, snuggling close with my ear pressed to his heart.

I waited to slip free until his breathing evened out and he was sound asleep. Then I padded from the room and tugged on his shirt and a pair of my sweats from the closet before inching the door closed and retreating to the kitchen.

The tote that I took to the office every day was on the island. I slipped out a notebook, opened the spiral-bound cover, and flipped to a blank page.

Jax wanted to make promises.

Maybe someday soon, I'd let him.

But before that point, he needed to know the truth. About my past. About the real reason I'd come to Montana.

And before I told Jax, I needed to be honest with Eddie.

Except as my pen inked blue words on the paper, a confession wasn't the letter I wrote. Not yet.

There were other things to say first. Things I should have told him a long, long time ago.

~

Eddie,
You deserved better than me. I wish I could have been
what you needed. You deserved better.
      S

215

Chapter 21
JAX

My head felt two sizes too big. My nostrils were raw from so much nose blowing. Every time I swallowed, it felt like razor blades scraped along my throat, and damn it, this ringing in my ears was getting fucking old.

"Tell me a secret," I said as Sasha filled a water bottle from the sink.

I asked her for a secret every single day. Every single day, she told me something trivial. But I still kept asking.

"You're sick," she said.

"That's not a secret."

She smirked. "So you're admitting that you're sick?"

"I'm not sick," I muttered.

"Yes, you are, and you should stay home," Sasha said, screwing the lid on her bottle. "I have never met anyone so set on denying the obvious, but Jax, you're sick."

I didn't have time to be sick. Admitting it felt like defeat, so I refused. "I'm fine."

She rolled her eyes. "Go back to bed."

Bed was exactly where I wanted to spend my day. But . . .

"I can't." I sighed and grabbed my coffee cup.

Grandpa had called last night and asked if I could ride his new horse this morning. Apparently, when he'd gone out yesterday, his gelding had acted like a shithead, nearly bucking Grandpa off.

My grandmother had banned him from riding the horse again, but now we had to decide if we were going to keep the animal or sell him. West was swamped with haying all week. The resort was a goddamn madhouse with the summer rush, so I couldn't spare a guide to do it.

So I was going out there before my stubborn father jumped in to "help." He wasn't as young as he liked to think he still was, and the last thing we needed was a wreck where he got injured.

Besides that, I'd mostly avoided my grandparents for nearly two months. Ever since I'd told them about Sasha and the baby, our conversations had been limited. A phone call here and there to say hello. We'd crossed paths at the lodge a few weeks ago. I'd even stopped bringing Grandpa his weekly lotto tickets.

The last time I'd gone to their house had been the casserole night. It felt like yesterday, not over a month.

Time was moving too fast.

Sasha had been living with me since the end of May. Emery had texted me last night that she'd found a cute new place in town and was meeting with a real estate agent today to put in an offer. But even after she moved out of the cabin, Sasha was under my roof.

Indefinitely.

The baby was due in three months. Which meant I had three months to get her to sink into this thing between us. Three months to keep chipping away at those walls.

They were coming down, inch by inch, but this routine we'd fallen into lately felt precarious, like it was just a matter of time until something came along and fucked it up.

If that thing was a snide or rude comment from my grandparents, I'd lose my mind. Not that I expected them to be anything except polite to her, but I wasn't taking chances.

It was time to clear the air. Whether I felt like shit or not.

"Want to meet me for lunch?" I asked Sasha.

"No, I want you to do whatever it is that you have to do, then come home and sleep." She put her hand on my cheek, her thumb tracing the line of my jaw. "But since I don't think you'll listen to me, then yes, we can meet for lunch."

"I'll come to the lodge." I dropped a kiss to her forehead, then followed her to the garage.

She'd protested parking inside. It had taken me three nights of orgasms to convince her to hang the spare door opener on her visor. But I'd won out.

Sasha might be stubborn, but I had her beat.

"Take it easy today," she said as she opened her door.

"That's my line, sweetheart."

"I mean it, Jax. You're sick."

"I'm not sick," I lied.

She gave me another long, loud sigh. Then she went to her car and slid behind the wheel.

But I didn't go to my truck in the next bay. I walked outside, following the line of her tires until I was in the driveway.

The July morning air did wonders to clear my head. I inhaled, holding it in my lungs, as I tipped my face to the clear blue sky and let the sun warm my face.

On my next inhale, a cough erupted from my chest, sending me into a hacking fit that doubled me in half.

Fuck. I was sick.

I didn't have time to be sick. I didn't want Sasha to get sick, which was why I had a kink in my neck from sleeping in the guest bedroom for the past two nights.

My head was in a fog, but I shoved through the haze and got to work. I went to the stables first, giving all of the guides a wide berth because we couldn't afford to have this cold to run through the staff, not with fully booked excursions from dawn to dusk.

After ensuring everyone had their orders for the day, I retreated to my office for an hour of paperwork. When the summary sheets began to blur together, I loaded up my saddle and spurs, then drove to my grandparents' house.

They met me at the door before I had the chance to knock.

"Mornin'." Grandpa shook my hand.

Grandma narrowed her eyes at my face. "What's wrong?"

"Nothing."

"You sound sick."

I waved it off. "I'm fine."

She pursed her lips. "I'll make you soup."

"You don't need to. Sasha made chicken noodle last night." And not that I'd tell Grandma, but it was the best damn chicken noodle soup I'd ever tasted.

"So you two are . . ." Grandpa trailed off so I could finish his sentence.

"Living together. Having a baby. Still not getting married."

His frown pissed me right the fuck off.

"You know what? Get the hell over it," I barked. "I realize this isn't the traditional path to a family, but guess what? My origin story isn't exactly traditional either. Sasha is important to me. So figure out a way to support us both. Or you can forget about having much to do with your great-granddaughter."

It was the harshest I'd ever spoken to my grandparents—the head cold was to blame. I was not about to keep my child away from them, but if I had to make idle threats so they'd pull the sticks out of their asses, so be it.

They shared a look and, with it, one of their famous silent conversations. That many years married, living together, they could probably read each other's thoughts by now.

Grandma broke first, her eyes softening. "Can you bring Sasha over for dinner?"

"Yes." I nodded. "Dinner would be great. She likes cheeseburgers."

"*You* like cheeseburgers." She scoffed. "What does she actually like?"

"Anything but grilled cheese."

Sasha had eaten the sandwich I'd made her, but I suspected it was because she'd slathered it in strawberry jam.

"Okay. I'll make your favorite pot roast." Grandma elbowed my grandfather in the ribs.

"Oof." He grunted, but the frown disappeared. "Sorry. We'll be supportive."

"Appreciated." I pulled the leather gloves out of my jeans pocket. "So where is this horse?"

~

"We're keeping this horse," I told West, my phone pressed to my ear as I rode Grandpa's gelding through a meadow.

"Thought it was a shit."

"He's definitely got an iron will, but I like him." Not for Grandpa, but myself. And maybe, after he settled and matured a bit, after I'd spent countless hours riding him around the ranch, he'd be a good horse for Sasha.

His personality reminded me of her a bit. Strong. Stubborn. Graceful. Smart.

The sound of an engine hummed in the background on the other end of the line. West was probably in a swather somewhere, cutting hay.

It didn't matter to him that his wife was filthy rich. It didn't matter that he had hired hands who could do the bulk of the haying each summer. My brother wasn't the sort to sit idle when there was work to be done.

I guess we had that in common. "I'm going to ride him to the stables. Check in on everything. Then probably put him out with your horse, if that's okay."

"Fine by me," he said. "How busy are you today? I had an idea and wanted to get your take on it."

"About?"

"Running some yearlings. I've been looking at cattle prices, and we've got so much grass at the moment. It might make sense."

"I've got time to talk."

"Sounds great. I should be done here shortly. I'll meet you at the stables."

"See you in a few." I ended the call and shifted on my saddle, tucking the phone into a jeans pocket. Then I steered the black gelding toward the river so we could head to the stables.

West didn't need my input on the ranch. It was his to run and manage, and while I owned my own acreage, the bulk of the land was under his name.

But West included me in decisions anyway. He asked for my opinion, even though he had the final say.

It was a far cry from how the ranch had been run under Dad's charge. Dad hadn't been the type to take advice, at least not from his sons.

But that, along with so much else, had changed in the past seven years.

For the better. Thanks to Indya. Thanks to West.

And lately, thanks to Sasha.

Indya might have returned from her maternity leave, but she wasn't working full time. Not with the boys home for summer break and Grace so young. So while Indya was spending more time at home with her kids, Sasha ran the resort like it was her own.

Indya had done a hell of a job building out this business. But she'd also moved quickly. There'd been a frantic tempo for the past seven years, like everyone was racing from one task to the next. And Indya had been managing too much for too long.

Sasha had brought this cool, leveling energy. She was a calming force.

I don't think anyone even realized it had been missing until she showed up. Just like I hadn't realized how lonely I was until she came into my life.

The idea of going back to casual hookups and meaningless nights made my skin crawl.

I wanted Sasha's car parked next to mine in the garage. I wanted her shoes on the mat beside my boots. I wanted her shampoo on the shower shelf and to find stray hairs in my bathroom sink.

I was falling for her.

Hell, I'd already fallen.

It would have been the best feeling in the universe, except I had no idea if she was falling too.

Sasha was affectionate. She touched me as often as I touched her. The sex was out of this fucking world. But I kept replaying the conversation from last month.

I'm scared of what this will be like when it ends.

She was so sure it would end. Why? What the hell had happened in her past?

There was someone. She related too closely to Emery for there not to have been someone in her past.

Who'd hurt her? How many times would I have to beg for a secret until she actually told me the truth?

Three months. That's all we had left together. Then there'd be three of us. Then everything would be different.

Three months.

It wasn't going to be enough, was it? What if we needed more time?

My phone rang in my pocket, the noise causing the gelding to jerk. I dug it out, an unknown number on the screen. My thumb hovered over the red button, about to decline it, but then the horse spooked.

One moment I was in my saddle. The next I was flying through the air, landing on the ground so hard it knocked the air from my lungs.

The horse thundered off through the meadow, running like a grizzly bear was on his heels.

"What the fuck?" I hissed, sucking in a breath. Pain exploded through my shoulder as I shifted, and damn it, my arm wouldn't work right. It hung limp against my side, the ache so fierce it made my head spin.

Shit. This was bad. My shoulder was probably dislocated. All because of that fucking horse.

It kept running, getting smaller and smaller in the distance.

Gritting my teeth, I forced myself up to a seat.

The spinning got faster. Something wet dripped down my neck.

With my good arm, I reached to feel the back of my head. The last thing I saw before the world faded to black was my fingertips coated in blood.

Chapter 22
SASHA

"We're set for next October," I told the bride on the other end of the line, my office phone sandwiched between my shoulder and ear so my hands were free to scribble on a sticky note.

Hamilton wedding weekend October 29th

"I'll pass your information along to our event coordinator, but please feel free to call me if you have any questions."

When she ended the call, I put the phone away and shook my mouse, adding the wedding party to our reservation system. Then I kicked off an email to Marsha, the event coordinator, and crumpled up my neon-yellow note.

Next October, the bride would be getting married. And I'd have a one-year-old daughter. My hand splayed across my bump.

Even with the loose blouse I'd paired with jeans this morning, there was no hiding my belly. Not that I wanted to hide it.

I wasn't ready for this baby, but I was getting there. Slowly. Day by day, I was getting there.

Jax was a big part of that progress. He was the balancing force I'd been missing for so long. He was the place I could lean when the world flipped. He took everything in stride and nothing too seriously.

Maybe it was rubbing off because the past month or so together had been the best I'd had in, well . . . ever.

Even with my frantic work schedule, I was relaxed. He relaxed me.

There were five other sticky notes scattered across my desk, each from different phone calls I'd taken this morning. My inbox was swamped, and I had a few voicemail messages to return. But they'd have to wait.

My stomach growled. Where was Jax? Maybe he'd decided to take the day off like I'd suggested this morning. Maybe he'd finally admitted to himself that he was sick.

I picked up my phone, about to send him a text, when it buzzed in my hand.

Micah.

"Hi," I answered immediately, shifting out of my chair to cross the room and close my office door. "Thanks for calling me back."

"Hey, Sasha. No problem. Sorry it took me a few days."

"That's all right." It was always a few days from the time I left Micah a message to when he called me back. I was trying not to take it personally. "How is he?"

"He's good."

The air rushed from my lungs. That was the first time Micah had ever said something positive. "Can I talk to him?"

"Not yet."

My momentary relief and joy died a quick death. "You said after three to six months, we'd be able to talk. It's been over nine."

"Three to six is what typically happens, but every individual is different. Eddie needs more time. This is a long road he's walking. I'm not going to push him until he's ready."

Meaning, Eddie didn't want to talk yet. And I needed to stop pushing. "All right."

"Keep writing letters."

The letters. The stupid freaking letters. Micah always deflected to the letters.

Letters that never received a reply. Letters that were still too short. Letters that felt like chucking a piece of my soul into a void. But if that was what it took, then I'd keep writing.

"Okay." I sighed. "Thank you."

"Anytime. Take care." He hung up on me first.

I set my phone down and stared at the screen saver. It was a grainy black-and-white photo of the ultrasound pictures. It had been there for weeks, but I could still see the photo it had replaced. It was like the pictures were layered, and if I squinted enough, the photo of Eddie and me would peek through.

The screen saver used to be us together on a rare day when we'd both been happy. We'd snuck away to the beach and asked a stranger to take a picture. Our arms had been wrapped around each other. His cheek had rested on my hair. And we'd smiled. Real, happy smiles.

It was the last time I remembered us both smiling together.

It was nearly two years ago.

I opened my desk drawer and took out a piece of paper. Then I wrote a letter, tore off a piece of my heart, and sealed it in a plain white envelope.

The mail went out every day, but these letters weren't something I wanted mixed in with resort business, so I tucked it in my tote for the next time I drove into town.

My stomach growled, louder this time. So I pulled up Jax's name, about to text him when once again, the phone buzzed first.

West.

He'd never called me before. Not once. My stomach dropped, dread creeping down my spine.

"Hello?" I answered, already standing and picking up my tote.

"Hey, Sasha." There was a gentleness in his voice.

The gentleness that came with bad news.

"Is it Jax?"

"Yeah. It's Jax. He's okay. But my dad is coming to pick you up at the lodge."

I swallowed hard, my head starting to spin. "And bring me where?"

"The hospital."

~

"You weren't supposed to call her." Jax shot his brother a glare from his hospital bed.

I blinked. "I'm sorry. What did you say? You weren't going to call me?"

"I didn't want you to worry."

"You have a concussion and a dislocated shoulder." My nostrils flared as I tossed out a hand. "You're in the emergency room."

"They relocated the shoulder, and it's not my first concussion. I'll live. Be good as new in an hour. Don't get worked up about this, sweetheart."

"Do not"—I pointed at his face—"call me sweetheart right now."

He held up his free hand because the other was in a sling.

"You shouldn't have been out riding," I said. "You're sick."

"I'm—"

"Fine?" I finished for him, my voice cracking.

My heart was beating too fast. My head hadn't stopped spinning since the moment West had called to tell me he'd found Jax's horse without Jax. And when he'd tracked down Jax, he'd been sitting in the middle of a field, having just woken up after being knocked out.

Maybe another woman would have pandered to him. Would have peppered his face with kisses and cried tears of joy that he was okay.

When I'd arrived at the hospital, I'd calmly asked the doctor for a full rundown of Jax's injuries and a detailed explanation of his recovery plan. The moment the doctor had left the room, there'd been no kissing or crying. Not when the red haze of fury descended.

I was so mad I couldn't see straight.

"Sasha, I'm fine," Jax said. "I promise."

"Our location would suggest otherwise." I paced at the foot of his bed, wrapped my arms around myself to hide the shaking. The tremors had started in my fingers, then spread to my hands. They'd worked their way up my wrist and forearms, moving to my shoulders like they were taking me apart one inch at a time.

"You scared me." I swallowed past the lump in my throat. "You got hurt and didn't want me here."

"Babe, I'm okay. Come over here and sit down."

I shook my head, worrying my bottom lip between my teeth.

West and Jax shared a look, but I ignored it and kept pacing.

What if West hadn't found him? What if that phone call had been different? What if—

I squeezed my eyes shut to block out the what-ifs. I kept them closed so tight it made my head ache. It was pointless. Nothing could erase the sterile scent of the hospital. There was no shutting away the noise of nurses working beyond the closed curtain.

"Sasha, I think you'd better sit." West put his hand on my arm, steering me toward a chair.

"I just . . . need some air." Before he could stop me, I shrugged off his grip and ducked through the opening in the curtain.

"Shit. Get me the fuck out of here," Jax clipped.

"If you leave, it will take twice as long to get discharged. Stay put. I've got her." It was a woman's voice I heard, familiar, but I couldn't place it. Not over the sounds of machines beeping and people talking.

I didn't turn to see who was following me. I kept walking, past the red exit signs until I was outside, breathing summer air that smelled like fresh-cut grass. A lawn mower buzzed in the distance as I walked to a bench outside the emergency room's doors and sank into the seat.

Then I squeezed my eyes shut again, this time focusing on my breathing. In and out. Over and over. Until my head stopped spinning. Until the shaking ebbed. Until my heart climbed out of my throat.

The sunlight was blinding when I opened my eyes, so bright it took me a second to realize I wasn't alone.

Lily sat on the bench at my side with a brown paper bag in one hand. "Need to breathe in this?"

"No." I sucked in another deep breath. "I'm not good at this. When people I care about get hurt."

"Most aren't," she said. "But you did good. You kept it together until after you spoke to the doctor. Most fall apart before they even get to that point."

I sighed. "I didn't realize you were in there."

"Curtis called me. I was, um, hanging back."

Had that been her decision? Or Jax's?

"He shouldn't have been riding," I said. "I should have made him stay home."

"Nothing you could have done would have kept him home. Trust me. Jax hates being sick. He was always the kid who refused to admit he didn't feel good. He never wanted to miss out on anything."

That was a mother's observation.

"Why wouldn't you let him call you Mom?" The question flew out of my mouth before I could swallow it down. "Sorry. That's none of my business."

"It's okay." She gave me a sad smile, then stared into the distance. "If I could go back in time, I'd do a lot differently. Not wait so long before I owned my mistakes. That was a mistake."

Me too. If I could go back, I'd change so much.

"Have you ever had your heart broken?" she asked.

"Yes." Though probably not the way Curtis's affair had shattered hers.

"I love Jax. Very much." She patted my knee. "He'll make a wonderful father. And if you'll let me, I'd love to be part of this baby girl's life. I realized that if I don't make amends, if I don't fix this, I'll miss out on her."

Yes, she would. "That's Jax's decision, Lily."

"I know." She did her best to hide it with a smile, but there was defeat in her gaze. Like she expected to be as removed from my daughter's life as she was from Jax's.

And she knew the only person to blame was herself.

For the first time since Jax had told me about their history, my heart went out to Lily. It wasn't right how she'd treated Jax. But she knew that too.

Maybe it was too late to repair that much damage.

For my own sake, I hoped there was no such thing as *too late*.

"Are you okay?" she asked.

"Yes. Thanks for sitting with me."

"Anytime." She stood, the paper bag in her hand crinkling.

I shoved to my feet, about to head for the doors, when I turned and found Jax's blue eyes waiting.

"Discharged?" Lily asked, pretending like he hadn't been listening to our conversation. How much he'd overheard I'd have to find out later, but from the stony look on his face, it was plenty.

"Yeah," he told her. "Dad's going to drive us home. West is still inside."

"I'll, uh, go find him." Lily walked past him, slowing to put her hand on his arm.

The touch was brief, no more than a brush of her fingers on his skin, but Jax didn't jerk away.

"I'm sorry. I don't think I ever said that," she whispered. "I'm sorry, Jax."

Maybe that hope I was holding for myself would hold for them too.

He dipped his chin but otherwise didn't speak as she walked away, leaving us alone on the sidewalk.

He'd shoved a few folded papers into the back pocket of his jeans. With his good arm, he rubbed a hand over his jaw, then he blew out a long breath. "I have a concussion. I dislocated my shoulder. And I'm sick."

"No kidding," I muttered, closing the distance between us.

As soon as I was within reach, he hauled me into his chest.

I buried my nose in his shirt, breathing in his scent. "Sorry I freaked out."

"Sorry I scared you."

It wasn't the injury that had scared me. It was him.

I needed him.

I needed Jax more than I'd ever needed another person.

"Can I call you sweetheart now? Or are you still too mad at me?"

I shrugged. "Give it a try, and see what happens."

"I'm okay, sweetheart."

He was okay. We were okay. If there was a shred of anger left, it faded away.

I tilted my chin up, staring into his beautiful eyes. Then I rose up on my toes for a kiss. "Let's go home."

∼

Eddie,

I'm sorry. I should have told you I was sorry a long time ago. Micah called me today. He told me to keep writing these letters, but I don't know if I should anymore. Do you want me to just disappear from your life? Leave you to move on? If you do, before I stop, know that I'm sorry. For everything.

 S

Chapter 23
JAX

The rodeo emcee's voice blared through the speakers at the fairgrounds, mingling with laughter and conversation and the buzz from the crowd.

To my left, the stands were crammed with people watching the team roping event in the arena. To my right, concession stands were lined up in a row. And at my side, Sasha walked with her hand in mine. The evening sun shone in the distance, but it paled in comparison to the glow on her face.

It had been about two months since the day I'd landed myself in the ER after getting bucked off that horse. And somehow, Sasha became more beautiful each day. I'd known pregnant women before, but Sasha put them all to shame.

Her belly stretched the cotton of her black T-shirt dress. The long sleeves were pushed up her forearms, and she'd pulled her hair into a high ponytail earlier when she'd complained about being too hot. The weather in early September was still warm, but by the time the sun set later, there'd be a chill.

She had on tennis shoes. I'd had to tie the laces for her at home because she couldn't reach her feet anymore.

Her days of fast walking were on pause. She meandered, the slow stride either because she was busy soaking in the spectacle or because she was getting tired. Probably both.

Between the chaos at work and the energy zapped by the baby, she usually crashed each night around nine, after we ate dinner and I gave her an orgasm.

"Funnel cake or mini doughnuts?" I asked her. The scents of fried bread and sugar and cinnamon hung in the air as we passed the booth selling both.

"Doughnuts." She rubbed her side. "Or nothing. I'm hungry, but there isn't any more room."

"We'll get doughnuts. I'll eat whatever you don't."

"Okay." She leaned her head against my arm as she yawned.

"You want to cut out early? Go home?" For the first time in my life, I wouldn't object to leaving the Big Timber Rodeo early. Not if it meant we could be alone.

"No." She shook her head. "This is an experience. I like these adventures where you get me to fall in love with Montana."

That wasn't the only purpose of these adventures, as she called them. I needed her to fall in love with me too.

To catch up to the place where I'd been for a while. Maybe since the day I'd watched her battle Carla over that shopping cart.

We had just over a month left before the baby was born. Sasha hadn't moved out, even after Emery had left the cabin for her new house in town. I was taking that as a good sign.

But I still didn't know how Sasha felt. And I hadn't worked up the courage to tell her how I felt either.

It was there, on the tip of my tongue each night, but something was holding me back. Something I couldn't explain.

Maybe because I couldn't remember the last time I'd said those three words.

As a kid, I'd told Lily that I loved her. I think she'd probably said it back, but I couldn't remember. Dad was not the type of man who said *I love you* often, especially to his adult sons. West said it all the time to his wife and kids. To me? Nah. We were brothers, raised by the same man, and it wasn't something we told each other either.

Was it the lack of practice? Or was I just scared because I honestly didn't know if Sasha would say it back?

Self-preservation had won out, and at the moment, I was simply glad she'd hold my hand in public. That I could kiss her whenever she walked into a room.

We got in line for mini doughnuts, and I shifted to stand behind her, wrapping an arm around her chest so she could lean back against me.

"Are you okay?" she asked.

"Yeah."

"You seem quiet tonight."

"All good, honey." I kissed her hair.

"What's your favorite time of day?" she asked, her hands coming to my forearms.

"Sundown." I let my gaze wander past the fairgrounds and to the Crazy Mountains in the distance. Their jagged peaks were lit in gold as the sun skimmed their tips.

"Why sundown?"

"That's when all the pretty girls come out to play."

"Seriously?" She jabbed her elbow into my ribs. "Jax."

"I'm kidding." I chuckled. "I like the end of a long day. Maybe because I feel like I'm always rushing out the door in the mornings, always in a hurry to get the day started. But usually by sundown, there's nothing to do but stop and breathe. Take a moment to celebrate the victories, even if they're small. Enjoy those last few rays of magnificent sunlight."

Sasha craned her neck to meet my gaze. "I like that."

"What's your favorite time of day?"

She looked to the same place I had a moment ago, soaking in the orange and yellow and pink and blue of sunset. "It would be cliché to say sundown now, so I'll say midnight."

"When you're fast asleep."

"When all the boys come out to play." She giggled.

I laughed, too, bending to kiss her cheek as we shuffled forward to place our order.

We were good together. So fucking good. She felt that, right? She knew we had something special here that wasn't just because of the baby?

I'd want her whether she was pregnant or not.

Her hand dropped from my arm, her palm settling on my thigh. Even through my jeans, I felt the heat from her touch.

She felt it. She *had* to feel it.

"Jax." Sasha slipped out of my grip. "Are you sure you're okay?"

"All good," I lied, shoving worries aside and placing our order. Then, with a paper boat of cinnamon-and-sugar-coated mini doughnuts in hand, we settled back into our stroll, wandering toward the beer gardens.

West and Indya were somewhere in the fray. They'd left the kids at home tonight with Lily as their babysitter. Dad was probably in the gardens with them. My grandparents were sitting where we'd left them in the stands.

We'd gone to dinner at Grandma and Grandpa's place twice in the past two months. One look at Sasha's belly and they'd been on their best behavior. Grandpa had been working on a pair of custom leather booties for the baby. Grandma stopped by the lodge at least once a week with some sort of treat for Sasha, cookies or cake or pie.

My family had embraced her, exactly as I'd asked. They were hers, as much as they were mine.

All she had to do was let them in.

Not that they saw the guard she wouldn't drop. Sasha was nothing but polite and gracious. But I saw the distance she kept. She didn't willingly seek them out. They were . . . friends.

Even Indya.

But they weren't family. Not yet.

Maybe that was simply because Indya was her boss, and this was all so damn new. But I felt an underlying hesitancy. A fear that if she got too close, she'd lose them too.

Or maybe these were my own fears, and I was projecting. It was likely nerves about the baby, but I couldn't shake the feeling that something was coming. Something would fuck up the good we'd found over the past couple of months.

"Jax, do you want to leave?"

"What? No." Sort of.

"What's wrong?" she asked. "You've been . . . broody tonight."

"Broody." I arched an eyebrow. "You must have me confused with West."

"West isn't broody."

"You didn't know him before Indya."

She sighed. "Nice deflection."

"I'm fine." I brushed a bit of cinnamon and sugar from the corner of her mouth. "Guess I'm just tired too. It's been a long week."

We were still in the thick of the busy season even though the calendar had flipped to September. Rather than entertain families on summer vacations, we were hosting larger groups of adults.

A party of fifteen guys in their thirties had arrived yesterday for some sort of reunion to spend a week hiking, riding, and fishing. There were two more wedding parties later this month, and both had sold out the lodge.

Sasha hadn't slowed a bit, even with her October due date rapidly approaching. Indya would be covering the bulk of Sasha's workload while she was on maternity leave. Tara and the other managers would step in to help. But Sasha was doing everything possible to prepare for her absence. She worked so frantically it was like she was scared her job wouldn't be waiting.

It would be there. For her, it would always be there.

For her, I'd be there too. Always.

"Want to build the crib tomorrow?" I asked her.

"Oh, um, I was planning on working tomorrow."

Tomorrow was Saturday, but I wasn't going to point that out. "We'll do it when you're done."

"Okay." Except she sounded like she'd rather do anything else.

The nursery at the house was a mess of gift bags and boxes at the moment. Indya had thrown Sasha a baby shower last month, and the generosity of not only Indya but everyone at the resort had shocked even me. It wasn't just clothes and diapers. They'd even bought us some furniture.

The pile of presents in the middle of the nursery's floor was practically a mountain.

I'd assumed the reason Sasha hadn't started clearing the mess was because she'd been so tired. Or maybe it was overwhelming.

The disarray was beginning to grate on my nerves.

The nursery, along with the primary suite, was one of the bedrooms I'd added onto the house during the remodel. It had been a guest room, but I'd moved the actual bed and other furniture to storage.

Didn't Sasha want to decorate? Organize? Weren't pregnant women supposed to go through a nesting phase? If anything, she seemed to be avoiding that room. Why?

"Why don't you want to build—" Before I could ask what she was thinking, a commotion at the beer gardens stole my attention.

Calvin came stumbling out of the entrance backward, like someone had shoved him through the gap in the fenced area.

"Hell," I muttered.

Sasha stopped, her hand tightening in mine.

I shifted and angled my body in front of hers as Calvin regained his balance. Well, sort of.

He swayed on his feet as he shuffled away from the gardens, lifting a hand to flip off someone inside. "Fuck off."

Someone hollered back the same.

He sneered but walked away, two steps, then three. The moment he faced forward and looked up, he spotted us and stopped. Calvin's lip curled. His eyes were glassy. His face red.

"Shit. He's drunk."

I gripped Sasha's hand, about to leave because the last damn thing I needed with my pregnant girlfriend—*was she my girlfriend?*—was drunk-asshole drama.

But before we could turn around, Calvin barked my name. "Haven. Figured you'd be here. Surprised you're not with my wife."

"Ex-wife." Or soon to be. Emery had filed the papers, and now they were just waiting for the divorce to be finalized.

Calvin came closer, near enough I could smell the beer on his breath. He glared at me, then shifted his eyes to Sasha and her belly. "You don't care that he's been fucking Emery on the sly for years?"

"Enough, Calvin," I snapped. "There's nothing with Emery. Never has been."

"Maybe not now that you knocked up this bitch."

My reaction was instant. I dropped Sasha's hand and the mini doughnuts. I moved so fast the motherfucker didn't have time to blink before my fist connected with his nose and blood sprayed.

Sasha gasped.

"Fuck!" Calvin's hands flew to his nose as he doubled over, lost his balanced, and dropped to his ass. "You broke my fucking nose!"

"Never speak about her again." My chest heaved as the adrenaline and rage surged.

People streamed out of the beer gardens to see what was happening. West and Dad were with them, both hurrying to my side, likely to stop a full-fledged brawl once Calvin found his feet.

The intervention was unnecessary. I held up both hands and stepped back. "I'm done."

A woman I recognized from around town rushed to Calvin's side. "Baby, oh my God."

Baby? Clearly, he was really hung up about Emery if he'd already moved on. Or maybe he'd been cheating on Emery for years, deflecting his own mistakes onto her. Whatever. Not my problem anymore.

"Good?" West asked.

"Yeah." Damn it. I shook out my knuckles.

The woman helped Calvin to his feet, hoisting him up by an arm.

He shot me a glare, his nose still bleeding, but for once in his life, he made the right decision and let the woman help him toward the bathrooms.

"What was that?" Dad asked.

"He called Sasha a bitch. It pissed me off."

"Well, that makes sense." West glanced around. "Where is she?"

"Right—" *Here.* She'd been right beside me. "Sasha?"

I searched the area but couldn't find her in the crowd. "Sasha," I called.

No answer.

"I gotta go," I told West and Dad, already walking away, shaking out my knuckles again as I scanned the line of concession stands.

Where'd she gone? I looked over my shoulder, about to head the other way, but a swish of dark hair streaming through the exit caught my eye.

"Sasha!"

She kept walking. Fast.

"Damn it." I broke out into a jog, weaving past people as I ran to catch up.

She was halfway through the parking lot when I fell into step beside her.

"Babe—"

"I want to go home, Jax. Now." Her voice was as cold as ice.

I sighed. "All right."

We walked in silence to my truck, and even when I opened the door to help her inside, she shied away from my touch.

"I'm sorry," I said when I climbed behind the wheel. "I shouldn't have hit him."

She swallowed hard, then shifted to stare out her window.

Son of a bitch. As much as I wanted to blame this on the pain in my ass that was Calvin Hill, this was on me.

"Sasha." I waited until she looked at me. "I'm sorry."

All she gave me was a nod. Then she stared out her window again, and with every mile of the drive home, she didn't so much as move.

The moment I was parked in the garage, she was out the door.

I caught up to her in the mudroom, reaching out a hand to steady her while she toed off her shoes. But the moment my fingertips grazed her elbow, she stepped away.

Then she left me alone with two discarded white Nikes.

And knuckles that needed to be iced.

Chapter 24
SASHA

"Jax." My voice was barely louder than a breath across the pillow.

He didn't stir. His mouth was parted as he slept on the other side of the bed, and though there was only a foot of space between us, it might as well have been a mile.

We hadn't spoken after the rodeo. I couldn't speak to him, not yet. I'd needed time to wrestle with bad memories first. Of fists flying. Of a nose crunching. Of blood gushing.

So when we'd made it home, I'd retreated to the bedroom and changed into one of his T-shirts. I'd taken to sleeping in them, since none of my own pajamas fit. Then I'd climbed into bed, feigning sleep when he'd eventually joined me.

For the first time in months, he hadn't held me close.

It was cold without him. Too cold.

Careful to keep my movements as gentle as possible, I slipped from beneath the sheets and padded across the dark room, easing into the closet, and felt along the hangers for one of his flannels. I shrugged it on, the hem skimming the middle of my thighs, then pushed up the sleeves as I inched out of the room, silently closing the door once I reached the hall.

I waited, ear pressed to the wood, listening for any sound. Only when I was certain he was still asleep did I tiptoe across the hallway to the nursery.

There was a lamp with a pink shade in the pile of gifts on the floor. I carried it toward a wall, plugged it into an outlet, and cast the room with soft light.

When Indya had asked if she could throw me a shower, she'd told me I had to register. I'd never registered for anything before and didn't want to just pick random items, so I'd spent countless hours browsing nursery ideas.

I'd found a photo of a room with dove gray walls and a white crib framed with a pale-pink canopy. The designer had decorated one wall, floor to ceiling, with butterflies. I loved butterflies, so I'd registered for butterflies and a pink canopy and a white crib with a matching changing table.

The furniture I'd planned to buy myself, but Indya had surprised me. It was a gift from her and West.

Nearly everything on my list had been purchased, along with countless other items I hadn't even known we needed. I still wasn't sure what was so magical about a Diaper Genie, but the canister was in the nursery's corner beside the unopened box with the crib.

I sat down on the white faux-fur rug that the housekeepers had given us and crossed my legs. Then I ran my hand along its smooth fibers.

It was all here, the makings of a beautiful nursery for my baby girl, but I hadn't been able to set it up. Every day for the past month, I'd walked past this room, stealing glances at the gift bags full of clothes and blankets that needed to be washed and folded. Except I always found an excuse to stay out of the room.

Didn't expectant moms love this stuff? What was wrong with me that I had zero desire to decorate a nursery?

The nearest bag was just inches away from my knee. There was a pair of lavender pajamas inside, the cotton adorned with silver stars. But

I couldn't make myself reach for it. I couldn't take it out of that bag and start making piles of laundry.

So I just sat there with the light from that pink lamp to keep me company until a tall, muscled body appeared in the doorway.

Jax was only wearing a pair of tight black boxer briefs. He studied me for a moment, like he was assessing whether it was safe to cross the threshold. But then he came inside and sat behind me, his long legs stretched beside mine as he pulled my back against his chest, like he was my personal chair.

I relaxed against him, soaking in the heat from his naked chest as the silence wrapped around us.

"Why don't you want to set up the nursery?"

"Because I'm scared I'll love it," I whispered. "And have to leave it behind."

Jax buried his face in my neck, breathing deep. "Get it out of your head that you're leaving."

"You said this was temporary."

"It's never been temporary, baby. I only said that to get you under this roof. But make no mistake, you're not going anywhere."

I leaned away as he straightened, his gaze locking with mine. There were promises in his blue eyes. Words I wanted to hear, but was I ready for them?

"This is our house," he said.

God, I wanted that. A home. A life.

"Tell me you hear me, Sasha. Say it. Out loud. This is our house."

He might as well have asked me to jump off a cliff. To free-fall and trust that he'd be at the bottom to catch me.

Maybe it was finally time to trust. To say fuck it and just fly.

Tears swam in my eyes, like something in me was breaking apart. Walls. Chains. The duct tape that had kept me together for a decade. "This is our house."

"I've got you, babe." He folded his strong body around mine, enveloping me in his arms. "I've got you."

I heard him. But what if I believed him too?

I burrowed into his embrace, breathing in his comforting scent.

Jax shifted to splay his hand on my belly just as the baby kicked. He'd felt her move before, and like the other times, a laugh of pure wonder filled the room. "Think she's telling us to set up her room?"

"Yeah."

But neither of us moved. Not until my legs were asleep and the pinch in my lower back forced me off the floor.

"You sit." Jax pointed to the gray velvet rocking chair in the corner, a gift from Curtis. "Read me instructions as I build this crib."

I went over and sank into the plush cushion, gently gliding as he started opening the box.

It was time, wasn't it? If this was our home, if we were building furniture, sharing a life, it was time to start telling secrets. Real secrets.

Jax deserved to know my truths. Before he made promises, before those words, he should know what he was getting into.

"Jax?"

"Yeah, darlin'."

"Tell me to tell you a secret."

He stilled, standing tall. "Tell me a secret."

"You know what I love most about working at the resort? Everyone thinks I have my life together. That I'm organized and in control. It's my big secret. I'm actually a hot mess. I have next to nothing to show for my life. You moved everything into this house in five trips. Walking. I'm broke and paying off a mountain of debt from school. I don't have many friends. No family to come visit me in the hospital when the baby is born. At work, I portray the woman I might have become if my parents hadn't died. But it's a lie. You ask me to tell you my lies. *I'm* the lie."

It was a confession months in the making. It came out in a rush, but it clawed at my throat, like I was breathing fire. Like every instinct was screaming, "Fake it!" so I had to keep faking it.

But what if I stopped? What if I was just . . . me?

Jax's eyes were soft as he stared. Too soft. I'd cry if he looked at me with pity, so I dropped my gaze to my lap and the swell of my stomach.

Wasn't it supposed to feel better when you bared your soul? Wasn't it supposed to be a relief?

I wanted to pull it all back inside. I wanted to rewind time and keep pretending. Keep faking.

Except that was not the example I wanted to set for my daughter. If I wanted to be her secret keeper, then I'd have to teach her how to tell them. I'd have to show her how to be vulnerable.

So I closed my eyes and let the walls come crashing down.

"What if I mess her up?" I whispered.

"You won't." Jax crossed the room, kneeling in front of me. Then he took my hands, bringing my knuckles to his mouth. "What did I tell you earlier?"

"A lot."

"I said I've got you. I do, Sasha. I've got you."

But I heard something else entirely.

I've got you.

I love you.

The tears were instant. "I'm sorry about earlier."

"It's my fault."

I shook my head, pulling my hands free to wipe my eyes dry. "No, it's not you. Something happened a while ago. Tonight just brought back some bad memories."

"What?" His entire body went taut.

I couldn't sit still and tell this story, so I inched forward, bracing my hands on the chair's arms to shove myself up. But it wasn't easy to climb out of the chair, so Jax stood and pulled me to my feet.

He shifted to the side, watching as I bent to pick up a gift bag, the present with the lavender pajamas.

I took them out, running a hand over the soft fabric as he took the chair, elbows braced on his knees as he waited.

We were almost there. We were almost through the worst of my past. It was almost time to talk about Eddie.

I opened my mouth, about to say his name, but stopped short.

Not yet. Not quite yet. Eddie needed to know first. About Jax. About the baby. After all we'd been through, he deserved to know first.

So Jax would get that last secret.

Later.

For now, I'd start by explaining the fight.

"About a year ago, I came home from work one night and went to get a bowl of cold cereal, but I was out of milk. I decided just to run to the convenience store two blocks over from my place and get a gallon. The neighborhood wasn't the best, but it wasn't the worst in Sacramento either. I walked fast. It took less than five minutes to get there. I grabbed my milk and left. I was about halfway home when I heard a strange noise."

All this time had passed, but that noise still echoed in my mind, as real as if I was still standing on that dark street corner. Maybe it was normal not to forget the sound of pain and violence.

"I saw these two men fighting. Well, it wasn't really a fight. One was on the ground while the other kept punching and kicking him, over and over. I dropped the milk, and when it hit the sidewalk, it sounded like a ball bouncing before the lid flew off and it splattered. It's weird how you remember sounds, isn't it? How they stick with you?"

That was what had sent me racing away from Jax at the rodeo tonight. Not the blood. Not the speed with which he'd moved, as fast as a lightning strike. I'd run away from the sound of flesh striking flesh.

"I tried to break up the fight. I tried to stop the guy who was pummeling the man on the ground."

Jax's jaw clenched, his hands fisting as the muscles on his arms flexed.

"Not the smartest move," I said, picking up another gift bag, this one full of ointments and lotions, none of which I knew how or when to use.

"In the fray of it all, I was shoved away, and I tripped over the curb. I fell backward and hit my head. I blacked out. Woke up to sirens as the cops drove up."

"Sasha." Jax hung his head. "Is that why you freaked when I got bucked off that horse?"

"Part of it." I walked to the changing table, a white piece that matched the crib, and began unloading the bag of baby products into the top drawer. "It was a drug deal gone wrong. I hate drugs."

"Me too."

I folded the bag once it was empty, starting a pile for them on the table.

"I shouldn't have hit Calvin." Jax stood. "I'm sorry."

"You already said sorry."

"I own my mistakes."

"I know." It was what I loved about him.

He was honest and good down to the marrow of his bones.

Had he heard Lily say basically the same thing about mistakes at the hospital months ago? Maybe they had more in common than he wanted to admit. Maybe, despite her mistakes, she'd taught him the right things.

He walked over, pushing my hair off my temple. "It won't happen again."

I leaned into his touch and drew in a long breath. And there it was, the relief I'd expected earlier.

There was more to that story. More he needed to know.

Later.

After I sent one last letter.

Then Jax could have all my secrets. All my lies. All my truths.

"Do you still want to build the crib?" I asked.

"Not especially." He bent with fluid grace and swept me into the cradle of his arms.

"Jax, I'm too heavy."

"*Pfft.*" He walked to the door, turning sideways to whisk me out of the nursery and across the hall. Then he carried me to bed, laying me down as he hovered above me.

It was like a slow dance, the way he removed the clothes from my body. I'd told him all those months ago I didn't want to dance, but he'd found a way to do it anyway.

When we were both naked, skin against skin, he knelt between my legs, drawing my hips up his muscled thighs. Then he thrust inside, driving deep. Our hands were threaded at my sides as he rolled his hips, bringing us together in a slow rhythm.

His eyes stayed locked on mine as he fucked me thoroughly. Beautifully. My orgasm came over me like an ocean current, tugging me under until I was riding a wave that rolled through every bone, every cell.

When Jax came, his body was tense and trembling, his head thrown back.

"Sasha." My name was a groan and a prayer. Another sound I'd never forget.

When we were both spent, he collapsed beside me, hauling me close, my back to his front. He laid his hand on my belly and kissed my hair, murmuring something as I drifted to sleep.

Murmuring the something I wasn't ready to hear. Not yet.

Not until I wrote another letter.

A goodbye letter.

~

Dear Eddie,
You were wrong to hurt that man. You were wrong to sell those drugs. I know you don't want to hear that, but you were wrong. We have to start owning our mistakes. Mine was not holding you to yours.

I wanted to tell you in person or at least over the phone, but I have some news. I'm pregnant. I'm having a baby girl next month. We're going to name her Josephine.

I love you. I'll always love you. But this is my last letter for a while. I hope we find a way back to each other someday. Maybe this time, we could be friends. I'll be here. I'll always be here for you. Even if it hurts. I'll be here.

Sasha

Chapter 25
JAX

The clank of metal on metal greeted me as I crossed Dad's driveway.

"Damn it." His voice carried from the open garage door. "You miserable piece of shit."

"Hello to you too, Dad."

His head whipped up from under the hood of his riding lawn mower, squinting into the afternoon light. "Jax?"

I strode into the garage and out of the bright sun. "Hey."

"Hi. Sorry. Didn't hear you pull up."

"That's all right." I pointed to the mower's exposed engine. "What's wrong?"

"Hell if I know. I think it's the carburetor. The engine keeps stalling. But whoever designed this setup was a sadistic bastard. I had to practically dismantle the whole thing to get it cleaned. And now that I've put it back together, I can't get it to start."

The fact that this machine had lasted this long was actually a credit to the sadistic bastard who'd designed it. It was the same mower I'd ridden around when I was a kid, earning three dollars from Dad every time I cut the lawn.

I toed the front tire with my boot. "You do remember that you're a millionaire, right? You can afford a new mower. I bet the dealership in town would bring one out tomorrow."

"Why would I buy a new one when I can fix this one?"

"Can you fix this one though?" I teased.

Dad frowned. "Well, I guess that remains to be seen. But I've been at it for three hours already. I'm not a quitter."

I chuckled. "Want some help?"

He handed over the wrench. "Have at it."

We spent the next thirty minutes hunched over the engine, both tinkering and guessing at the problem. Until finally, when we turned the key, the ignition caught, and the motor hummed to life.

"I'll be damned." Dad laughed over the noise that filled the garage. He let it run for a moment, then shut it off. "Thanks."

"No problem."

"You're not working today?" he asked, like he'd just now realized it was a Thursday and normally I'd be at the resort during this time of day.

"I'm working. West needed some help moving cows in the east meadow. Saw your garage open as I was driving back and thought I'd say hi."

"Glad you did." Dad started putting tools away in the chests against the far wall. "How's it going?"

"Busy." The past two weeks had been hectic, not only at work but at home.

Sasha had jumped into nesting with both feet. Every night when we'd get home, I'd help her with whatever she wanted to do in the nursery, and after two weeks, it was ready to go. There were butterflies everywhere and more pink than I'd ever thought I'd have beneath my roof.

That nursery was my favorite room in the house.

Now that it was done, maybe she'd slow down, though considering her hours at work were as long as ever, I wasn't holding my breath. The lodge and cabins were still teeming with guests.

"How are you?" I asked.

"Can't complain." He opened a drawer on his tool cabinet, putting the wrench in the designated space. They were all arranged by size.

How many hours had I spent in this garage, working on a project with Dad, watching as he put away his tools? There was a reason I knew how to build and rebuild engines. He'd taught me everything he knew about mechanics. About fixing a leaky sink or changing a light fixture. About riding horses and raising cattle.

He was a good dad, despite the disagreements we'd had years ago after he'd sold the ranch. Curtis Haven had made plenty of mistakes in his life, but he was a good dad.

"Can I ask you something?" I asked.

"Shoot." He turned, leaning against the workbench.

"When Indya bought the ranch, did you know she had a history with West?" It was a question I'd been curious about for years, just hadn't bothered to ask.

Originally, Indya had planned to stay here for only a year after the sale. She'd wanted to turn the resort and its financial problems around, then move on to other ventures. She'd made a deal with Dad to ensure that when she left, West would be in charge. She'd basically forced Dad into retirement.

I'd always wondered if he'd agreed because it was the best option. Or if he'd known that if Indya lived in Montana for a year, maybe she and West would rekindle an old flame.

"Had a hunch," he said. "The weeks she'd come visit with her family when they were younger, he'd disappear completely. But I was never sure. Why?"

"Always wondered." I shrugged. "Is that hunch why you sold the ranch to her?"

He sighed. "I wish I was that romantic. I sold it because we needed the money. I had us in a damn fine hole. She was a way out."

I hummed, reaching for a rag on the mower's seat to wipe my hands. "Did my mother ever contact you?"

Another curiosity. But the reason I hadn't asked wasn't because it just never came up. This was a question I'd been wanting to ask for years, but I hadn't worked up the courage. Probably because I already knew the answer.

Dad blinked, like he'd gotten whiplash from the change in topic.

"I've never asked you that before." I tossed the rag, streaked with black, aside. "It's been on my mind lately."

Sharing secrets and lies with Sasha had brought the skeletons out of the closet. They'd been shoved away for too long, and I wasn't going to shove them back.

"I get it. You're about to be a father. Makes a man think." His eyes softened. "I wish I could say yes. I wish I could say that she called me to check on you."

But he couldn't. We both knew that.

I hadn't needed her. Not with Dad. Not with Grandma and Grandpa. Even Lily. But I'd always wondered if she'd looked back.

Now I could put it away. For good.

Focus on Sasha. Focus on our daughter.

"Thanks, Dad. I'd better get back to work," I said. Except before I could leave the garage for my truck, the crunch of tires on gravel carried from outside.

Dad and I made our way to the driveway just as an SUV parked beside my truck.

"Is that . . ." His jaw dropped.

Lily opened her door and stepped out.

"She talked to me at the barbeque?" he murmured.

Was that a statement? Or was it a question because, even months later, he still couldn't believe it had happened?

Dad cleared his throat, smoothing down the front of his shirt as Lily moved to the back door of her car, taking out a box wrapped in pink striped paper.

When she turned and looked at the house, she paused, her gaze raking the porch to the roof to the dormer windows. She hadn't seen this house in ages. Why now? I doubted that gift was for Dad.

She squared her shoulders and walked over, giving us both a nervous smile. "Hi."

Dad opened his mouth, but no words came out.

"Hey." I came to his rescue. "What's up?"

"I, um, was looking for you. I stopped by the stables and didn't see you in your office. And no one was at your house. So I, uh, thought I'd check here." Her gaze darted to Dad, then away again. "This is for you and Sasha."

Lily thrust the pink box into my arms, then stepped back, once more barely glancing at Dad before she looked to the ground. "I'm sorry to bother you."

That was an apology to Dad, not me.

What the hell was happening right now? Not only had she actually addressed his existence, but she was here, on his property. Voluntarily. She could have just left this box on my desk with a note.

"It's no bother, Lily." Dad stared at her like she was a dream. "You're welcome here anytime."

Part of me wished he had said the opposite. That he had sent her packing. Tell her that she'd missed her chance while she'd been so busy holding on to her resentment and heartache.

But the other part of me, the part that would always look at Lily like a mother, the part that knew Dad would love her until the day he died, was glad the icy silence between them was beginning to thaw. For his sake.

"That's a baby blanket." She pointed to the box in my hands. "I've been making it for a while. I've never made a blanket before, so it's not the best."

"Thank you." *Well, fuck.* That was thoughtful. And kind. And any fool could see she was trying. Hard.

"I wrote a letter." She forced a wider smile, but it wobbled, like she was about to cry. "That's for you."

"Okay." I slipped the envelope from the pink ribbon.

"Please don't read it right now." She held out her hands. "It's, um . . . an apology. For a lot of stuff. Mostly for the fight and how I acted. I thought it would be easier to get it all out on paper, but now that I think about it, I probably didn't word it right. It'll just make everything worse. Let me—"

I shifted to the side when she reached for the envelope, trying to take it back. "I'd like to read it."

Lily looked seconds from tears. How hard had it been for her to come here? To write the letter she didn't want me to read?

"I heard you at the hospital," I said. "When you told Sasha you wanted to be a part of my daughter's life. Did you mean it?"

"Yes." She swallowed hard. "I love you, Jax. I've done a pitiful job of saying it. And showing it. I'd like a chance to do better."

Damn. I rocked on my heels like she'd punched me square in the heart.

Lily sniffled, dabbing at the corners of her eyes. Then she gave Dad a sad smile.

She didn't have to tell him she loved him. She'd always love him.

Love had never been the problem. But until she was ready to forgive him, they'd linger in this limbo.

Lily, hating Dad for a mistake nearly thirty years old.

Dad, hating himself for the same.

They'd be trapped with it, the anger and hate, until they could let it go.

Was that my problem too? Was I stuck in this limbo with them?

"I'm not going to call you Lily," I said. "I'm not going to call you Mom either. How about Nana?"

This time, she couldn't stop the tears before they spilled over her cheeks. "I'd like Nana. Very much."

With a nod, I left them in the driveway, taking the gift and letter to my truck.

They were still standing in the same place, staring at each other, as I drove away.

A small laugh escaped as I rolled down the road.

That was not how I'd expected today to go. I drove past the stables when I made it to the lodge, parking in the empty spot three spaces down from Sasha's car.

She was at her desk when I strode into her office, Lily's letter tucked in my pocket.

But the note was forgotten the moment I saw her face.

She was white. Her hands were shaking as she clutched a piece of paper.

"What's wrong?" I ran across the room to her side, my heart leaping into my throat. "Sasha, is it the baby? Are you hur—"

She flew out of her chair and dropped the paper like it was on fire. Then she raced for the door. It was the fastest she'd walked in months.

I was about to chase after her, but the page she'd dropped snagged my attention.

FUCK YOU

There were letters scattered across her desk. There had to be a dozen or more. Some were longer than others. Each page had Sasha's neat, clean handwriting.

And scrawled on top of her script in angry, vicious red ink were words I couldn't unsee.

FUCK YOU
FUCK YOUR BABY
YOU LEFT ME
I HATE YOU
I FUCKING HATE YOU

My jaw clenched.

Who the fuck was Eddie?

Chapter 26
SASHA

I felt Jax behind me. I had for the past ten minutes. But I kept walking. And he kept following.

He'd probably seen the letters. He'd probably taken one look at the ugly red words scribbled over my notes and thought the worst. Maybe he believed Eddie's words.

That I'd left him. That he hated me.

It was strange that for months I'd been this weepy, sniffling, hormonal mess. But on a day like this, with my heart broken and aching, my eyes were dry.

I couldn't cry.

So I kept walking. Down the road that led away from the lodge. Past the cabins that we rented to guests. Toward the grove of trees and the bend in the road where I'd gotten my car stuck in the snow this winter.

Step after step after step.

FUCK YOU

YOU LEFT ME

I HATE YOU

It hurt. It hurt so much I could barely breathe. But I did because I had to breathe. I drew in the air, holding it in my lungs as the tennis shoes Jax had helped me tie this morning crunched on the gravel beneath their soles.

In and out. Breath after breath. I held in the clean, crisp fall air the way Jax had told me to breathe months ago when he'd walked me into the meadow behind the house.

It smelled like grass and earth and last night's rain.

I'd been at the Haven River Ranch for nearly a year. I'd experienced every Montana season. And I could say now that autumn was my favorite.

The trees around us were a riot of color from gold to green to orange.

"When I was a kid, I used to make place mats." The moment I spoke, Jax walked up to my side, matching my pace.

It wasn't fast. I was too tired, my heart too heavy, to walk fast anymore.

"Place mats?" he asked.

"Yeah, out of leaves. Did you ever do that? Go on a nature walk and pick up pretty leaves. Then smash them between two pieces of wax paper with a bunch of crayon shavings. My mom would iron it all together, and we'd have place mats."

"I think we did that in school once for an art project."

I slowed and veered to the side of the road where the leaves lay undisturbed on the rocky shoulder. It wasn't easy to bend to the ground, but I managed to pick up a perfect, spade-shaped yellow leaf. Pain shot through my side that made me wince, but it eased as I stood tall.

"Did you see the letters?" My gaze stayed on the leaf as I twisted the stem between my fingers.

"Yes."

The air rushed from my lungs. Maybe it would be easier this way. Like having Jax tell everyone I was pregnant, those letters would be the introduction to Eddie.

Not a great first impression.

All this time, nearly a year, and I'd wanted to talk to him. I'd waited and waited and waited for any scrap of attention he'd throw my way. How many times had I called Micah?

Did Micah know about this? Had he condoned such a ruthless, soul-crushing reply?

Eddie hadn't just written me a letter. He'd taken all of mine, every single one that I'd written, and thrown them in my face. He hadn't even bothered to find his own paper.

FUCK YOUR BABY

If he'd left that one out, maybe I'd be crying right now. But he'd gone too far. He'd crossed a line.

So Eddie wasn't going to get my tears. Not today.

"Sasha." Jax plucked the leaf from my fingers. "Talk to me, babe."

There was worry etched on his face. The last time someone had looked so worried about me was years ago. Before the accident. Before Mom and Dad were gone. They'd worried about me. But since then?

No one. Not really.

Not until Jax.

I loved him because he worried about me. I loved him for a lot more than that, but the worrying was important.

I worried about him too.

I loved him.

So I took a deep breath of the cool Montana air and told him the last secret.

"Eddie." It hurt to say his name. "He's my little brother."

Jax blinked, like the world had flipped on him. "You have a brother?"

"I have a brother." I nodded. "He's eleven years younger than me. My parents hadn't wanted other kids, but he was an accident."

Not a mistake. I'd never heard Mom or Dad say the word *mistake*.

"They used that word sometimes when he was around. It was always teasing or in jest. They'd say things like 'our accident baby' or tell people he hadn't been planned. I don't think they realized he'd remember it. They probably figured he'd forget."

Eddie had never forgotten. *Accident* wasn't exactly a word you wanted associated with your entire being.

If anyone could understand, it was Jax.

"Maybe if they hadn't died, if they'd been around for longer than the first seven years of his life, he would have learned to laugh about it too. He would have realized it was just an expression that adults really shouldn't say. But . . . they died. And of all the things he remembers about Mom and Dad, I really wish that wasn't one of them."

Understanding crossed Jax's expression. "That's why you told me we'd never call Josephine an accident."

"Yeah." I gave him a sad smile. "Not ever."

He took my hand. "Not ever."

"Can we . . ." I turned, pointing to the lodge.

I'd already walked too far. Another step in the wrong direction and he'd have to carry me home.

Jax would do it. He'd sweep me off my feet and hold me in his arms for miles. So we needed to turn back before he decided on my behalf that I'd walked too far.

"Yeah." He took my hand as we headed down the road, one slow step at a time.

"Eddie was so little when Mom and Dad died. He was in second grade. We didn't have any grandparents. My mom had a sister, but they hadn't spoken in a long time. I guess my aunt didn't like Dad, so I decided I didn't like her. Dad was the youngest in his family, and my two uncles lived with their families on the East Coast. After the accident, Dad's oldest brother offered to take Eddie, but he didn't know them. *I* didn't know them. And Eddie was my brother. I couldn't imagine not having him around."

I'd been enrolled in college when Mom and Dad died, but I hadn't started school yet. I hadn't moved out. I'd never lived anywhere else but our house. And after the funeral, I just couldn't leave.

"So you took custody," Jax said.

"Yeah."

"You were eighteen."

"Yeah," I repeated, my voice quieter this time.

"Fuck, Sasha. That's . . ."

Too much.

I'd been too young to be Eddie's parent. We'd both gotten lost in our grief. The responsibilities I'd shouldered hadn't helped.

"I should have let him go to my uncle. Maybe. I don't know. I've second-guessed that decision so many times I've lost count. My uncle offered, but he didn't act like he really wanted Eddie. The last time I talked to him was the day I told him I was going to petition the court for custody. He didn't contest it."

"And everyone else?" Jax asked.

"No. No one objected. The last time I spoke to anyone in my family was at Mom and Dad's funeral."

They'd all disappeared from my life. Not that we'd really had them before, either, but they'd left us to grow up alone.

Jax's jaw ticked, but he stayed quiet.

Maybe sending Eddie with our uncle would have been worse. He might have ended up exactly where he was today. But I'd always wondered if that was the first wrong decision in a long line of wrong decisions.

"I worked as hard as I could. Mom and Dad didn't have much money. They were the type who'd rather take us on a trip than squirrel away cash for a rainy day. So I got a job at a hotel, cleaning rooms. I took classes at night to get my degree. I was gone a lot. Eddie was mostly on his own. He'd hang out at friends' houses. I enrolled him in every after-school program I could find. On days when I needed help, I'd beg the neighbor to let him hang out. But that was mostly when he was younger. Once he got a little older, he was alone most of the time. He was alone too much."

It had been easier to ignore the grief. I'd made sure I was so busy I didn't have time to face it. To feel it.

Meanwhile, Eddie had been a little kid, left with nothing to do but miss our parents.

"I tried so hard to manage it all. When I say it out loud, I sound like a deadbeat mother. Leaving a little kid to his own devices. But I swear, I was trying so hard."

It was important that Jax knew how hard I'd tried. How hard I would always try for our daughter. I'd burn myself to the ground trying not to fail her the way I'd failed Eddie.

"Hey." His hand tightened in mine. "I know."

I didn't deserve his faith in me.

"So you stayed in your parents' house?" he asked.

"Yeah. For about six years. The bills began to stack up. I got credit cards and used them to keep afloat, only paying the minimum amount every month. I couldn't afford the mortgage and insurance and taxes. And it was so hard, Jax."

I still felt the weight of those years on my shoulders. "Living in that house, hearing their voices, going into the kitchen expecting to see Mom and finding a stack of dirty dishes instead. Seeing Dad's golf clubs in the garage collecting dust. We were living with their ghosts, and one day, I just . . . I couldn't do it anymore. I needed a change."

I regretted that decision to move. But at the same time, I didn't.

Eddie had been thirteen when we moved. Could I have lived in that house for another five years until he turned eighteen? Financially, maybe. It would have been hard and grueling. But emotionally? Never. Those walls had been suffocating me, little by little, each day.

"I found an affordable apartment. I sold most of Mom and Dad's stuff to pay off my credit cards. The important stuff, I kept. Dad's clubs. Mom's favorite books."

"Where are they?" Jax asked, probably because he hadn't moved golf clubs.

"Storage. I really should get rid of the locker, but it's cheap, and I wasn't sure where I'd go after Montana."

Jax stopped walking. "*After* Montana? You were going to leave?"

"Yes."

"Not anymore." His grip on my hand tightened.

"Not anymore." I leaned into his arm, drawing from his strength, stealing the surety that had lured me in from that first day in the grocery store's parking lot.

"What happened after you moved?" he asked.

"Trouble." That was the only way to describe it. Eddie had spiraled into trouble.

Looking back, it had all been him lashing out because I'd taken us from the house and his school and his friends.

"His grades started slipping until he was barely passing. Once he got into high school, he made friends with the worst possible kids. He was getting into fights. They were accused of vandalizing a car, though the school couldn't prove it. And when he was at home, which was rare, we fought all the time."

I'd ask him to do his laundry; he'd call me a bitch. If I told him he had to do his homework before seeing his friends, he'd tell me to fuck off and storm out the door. Whenever I'd asked him to talk, he'd blown me off. And he'd started referring to himself as the accident. The mistake.

For Mom and Dad.

For me.

"Everything just spun out of control. Until it got so bad . . . we landed here."

"We?" Jax asked. "Your brother is here?"

"He's in Montana. That fight I told you about? It was Eddie. He got into drugs. Mostly weed, but some painkillers too. He got into that fight because the guy that Eddie went to buy pills from tried to steal his cash. So Eddie beat him up."

"Eddie was the guy who knocked you down when you tried to break up the fight?" Jax's nostrils flared. "That's how you got the concussion."

"It was an accident." How many excuses had I made for Eddie's behavior? Even now, when he'd been guilty, I was still defending him.

It wasn't black and white. Maybe that's why I could empathize with Emery. It wasn't an easy task to cut out a person you loved from your life.

"That was about a year ago. He was sixteen. Angry. Strong. He got arrested. So did the dealer. The judge took pity on Eddie, mostly because of his age. Rather than send him to juvenile detention, we were able to get Eddie into a camp for troubled teens."

"A camp? What kind of camp?"

"I didn't even know they existed until then. But it's a camp and a school. It's here, in Montana, about four hours away."

Eddie had tutors who'd help him catch up on school. It was an alternative to high school in a controlled setting. There, he'd have peers who shared a lot of his feelings. Friends, I hoped, he could relate to.

"It focuses heavily on wilderness therapy. It's secluded, and the kids live on the property. They spend some time living in the school itself, but other times, they go into the woods and camp with counselors."

Every morning, the kids would pack up camp, then set out on a hike. Once they found their next stopping point, they'd build camp for the night, cook meals, and talk. Then they'd go to sleep, and the next morning, do it all over again. For weeks and weeks.

"It's supposed to help them reset. Shut away the world and give them a chance to feel."

Maybe I needed a wilderness camp.

Actually, I guess I'd found one. The Haven River Ranch.

"Sometimes kids stay for six months before they go back to live with their families. Other times, they stay longer. Micah, that's Eddie's therapist and my liaison with the school, told me he thinks Eddie should stay even longer. They don't have the typical school year calendar, but he's had some behavior problems, and he still isn't doing well academically."

So he'd stay until either Micah gave the go-ahead for him to leave. Or until Eddie turned eighteen and he could leave without anyone's permission.

"I haven't talked to Eddie since the day I dropped him off. I've called and spoken to Micah, but he doesn't think Eddie is ready to talk to me yet. Instead, he asked that I write letters. Today was the first time I've heard back."

Jax blew out a long breath, then let go of my hand to throw an arm around my shoulders. "I'm sorry, honey."

"Me too."

All these months I'd been questioning Micah's choice to keep us separated. But given what had shown up through the resort's mail today, clearly, I hadn't been giving Micah enough credit. The distance he'd imposed between us must have been more necessary than I'd realized. Eddie was angrier than I'd realized.

Was this part of the therapy? Letting Eddie send whatever he wanted in reply? Or had those letters been sent without Micah's knowledge?

"He's so mad at me, Jax." My heart cracked, thinking back to the seven-year-old boy who'd clung to me at Mom and Dad's funeral. The boy who used to jump off the bus and run into my arms whenever I had a day off and was waiting for him at home.

We'd had good days. There'd been plenty of good days. But somewhere along the way, I'd failed him.

"The camp is a private facility. It feels like a last resort. It's not exactly cheap either. But if it keeps him out of jail, then I'll pay."

"Is that why you were sleeping on an air mattress?"

Yes. "I didn't mind."

"Sasha." Jax let me go to drag a hand over his face. "Why didn't you tell me any of this?"

"I failed Eddie. I was his parent. And I failed. What if I fail with her too?"

What if I wasn't capable of being a mother?

"You won't." Jax hauled me into his arms, holding me on the side of the road. "It's not the same, Sasha."

"I'm the same."

"Yes, you are. You'll be the best mother in the world. You have sacrificed everything to give your brother the best possible chance. You haven't failed him. Not in the slightest."

God, I wanted to believe it.

He took my face in his hands, tilting it up until our gazes locked. "I've got you. When it comes to the baby and life and all things. I've got you. Do you have me?"

The emotion I hadn't been able to find earlier came rushing forward, and my eyes flooded. "I've got you."

"Together." He stroked his thumb across my cheek, catching a tear. "We do this together."

"Okay," I whispered, collapsing into his chest.

"Come on, sweetheart. Let's go home. Want me to carry you?"

"No, I can walk."

So we set off on the gravel lane, slowly, thanks to the flash of pain in my side.

A pain I ignored because it dulled compared to the pain in my heart.

Chapter 27
JAX

Sasha's whimper woke me from a dead sleep. "Jax."

"What?" I pushed up on an elbow, instantly awake. She was sitting up in bed, bent over her stomach. My hands flew to hers, pressed on the sides of her belly.

"Something isn't right." She sucked in a sharp breath. "It hurts."

"We're going to the hospital." I was out of bed in a second and racing for the closet. I got dressed faster than I'd ever gotten dressed in my life, then grabbed clothes for Sasha.

She'd shifted to the edge of her bed, her face twisted in agony.

My heart and stomach dropped in free fall. "It's going to be okay."

She nodded, but tears glistened in her eyes as I pulled a hoodie over her head, helping get it over the T-shirt of mine she'd worn for bed. Then, leg by leg, I helped her into my sweats, rolling up the ankles twice before helping her stand.

One step and she hissed, curling forward.

Before she could object, I swept her into my arms and carried her out of the bedroom and through the dark house.

I didn't bother finding her shoes. I'd carry her into the hospital too. So I took her to the truck, setting her in the passenger seat before I ran inside for my own tennis shoes and the overnight bag she'd packed last night after we'd gotten home from that walk.

It was the walk, wasn't it? I'd let her walk too far. Or maybe it was the stress of those fucking letters from her brother.

Dr. Green had told Sasha at her last appointment that he wanted to monitor her blood pressure. It wasn't a major risk yet, nothing to indicate preeclampsia. But it had elevated over the past few weeks, and he'd made a note that it was something to keep an eye on.

She'd been working too hard. I'd let her work too hard. Even when we came home from the lodge, she went straight to work on the nursery. Then those letters had arrived, and it was too much stress.

Green had told us to cut back on stress. To slow down.

Why the fuck hadn't we listened?

I threw Sasha's bag into the back seat, then climbed in, reversing out of the garage the second the door was open. We flew down the road, the truck's engine revving as I hit the gas.

"Jax." Sasha clutched the center console. "Not too—"

She winced again before she could tell me to slow down.

I drove faster, flying through the ranch in the dead of night, guided only by my headlights and the moon. The instant we hit the highway, I floored it, blowing past every speed limit as I hauled ass to town.

With one hand, I kept a firm grip on the wheel. With the other, Sasha's hand clutched mine, squeezing tight every time it hurt.

"It's too early for contractions." Her other hand was in constant motion as she rubbed circles across her belly.

That's what they were, though, weren't they? These were contractions.

We still had three weeks. We were supposed to have three more weeks.

We were supposed to go to Bozeman so she could have the baby at a big hospital, with lots of doctors and equipment in case of the worst.

Was this the worst? I shoved that thought out of my head, focusing on the road.

"It'll be okay." I brought her hand to my lips, kissing her knuckles. Then I kept my eyes on the road, wholly alert because the last fucking thing we needed tonight was to hit a deer.

"It's too early," she whispered.

It was too early.

My phone. Shit. I'd forgotten my phone. Why hadn't I grabbed the damn thing? I should call the hospital first. Let them know we were on our way. But in my rush to leave, I'd forgotten it on the charger beside our bed. Sasha hadn't brought hers either.

So I drove and said more silent prayers in thirty minutes than I had in a year.

As the lights of town came into view, twinkling beneath the midnight sky, I loosened a breath. But I didn't let up on the gas. Not until we were in the hospital's lot.

I parked outside the emergency room, then ran around the truck to carry Sasha inside.

Lily was at the desk in the emergency room. The moment I strode through the doors, she shot out of her chair and jogged across the small lobby. "What's wrong?"

"She's having pain. I think it's contractions."

"It's too early." Sasha's eyes were wide, and she wiggled for me to set her down, but I kept her cradled close.

"Let's get you into a room." Lily waved for us to follow her through the entrance and into the ER.

The beds were empty, every curtain open. Lily walked past the quiet nurse's station and around a corner. Through another doorway, I recognized the hallway that led to the doctors' offices where we normally went for Sasha's checkups, but everything was in reverse, like we'd come through a back entrance. I hadn't spent enough time in the hospital to memorize the layout.

Lily took us to a large room in a corner. The lights flickered on the moment she crossed the threshold. There were machines against the wall I didn't recognize. The bed in the center of the room was covered in a simple white sheet and blanket.

"This is our delivery room," Lily said. "I'm going to get ahold of the doctor on call."

Sasha nodded as I set her on the bed.

"How often are you having the contractions?" Lily asked.

"Every two minutes," I answered. I'd kept track on the drive.

"How long do they last?"

"Two minutes," Sasha said. "Give or take. I had some pain earlier today, but it wasn't consistent, so I didn't worry about it. It felt more like a bad side ache. But then it got bad and woke me up."

"Okay." Lily gave me a small smile, then walked to a supply closet against the wall. "We'll get the doctor here to help, okay? Hang tight."

"My truck is in the loop," I told her. "I need to move it."

"I'll take care of it." She took a folded, faded green gown from the closet and brought it over for Sasha. "Go ahead and get changed."

"Okay." Sasha stood on bare feet.

"Keys." Lily held out her hand, waiting until I set them in her palm. "I'll be back soon."

As she swept out of the room, closing the door as she left, I helped Sasha change out of the sweats and into the gown. Then, after another contraction, my breath lodged in my throat until it passed, I helped her into bed and under the thin white blanket just as a knock came at the door.

Lily entered, Sasha's bag in hand along with my keys. "Doctor will be here in ten minutes."

Lily had worked in the ER for years. She made more money on the night shift, and though she'd told West she was ready to retire, our small town was usually fairly quiet. They ran on a skeleton staff this late, calling in doctors and nurses as needed.

At least it wouldn't take long for Dr. Green to get here. We could make it ten minutes. The air rushed from my lungs. "Okay."

"Your nurse will be in shortly too. She was just finishing up with another patient."

"Wait. You're not our nurse? Why can't you do it?"

Differences aside, tonight, I needed a mom.

"I'll be here too." She took my hand and squeezed. "I'm not going anywhere. But the other nurse has more experience with deliveries. I want you to have the best."

"Okay. Thank you. I'm glad you're here tonight."

"Me too." She gave my hand one last squeeze, then slipped out of the room.

"What do you need?" I asked Sasha. "Water? Are you thirsty? Are you warm enough?"

She shivered, from terror, not the cold room. The fluorescent overhead lights brought out every bit of fear on her face. They sucked the color from her already pale skin. "It's too early."

I sat on the edge of the bed, clasping her freezing hands between mine. "She'll be okay."

Please, let her be okay. Both of them.

"Ouch." Sasha gritted her teeth as the next contraction hit, this one coming even closer on the heels of the last.

Where the fuck was the doctor? It had to have been ten minutes, right?

"Breathe, baby. Just breathe."

Sasha endured two more contractions before the door finally opened.

Except it wasn't Dr. Green who stepped inside. It was Robin.

For fuck's sake. This was not what we needed tonight.

"Hi, Sasha." Robin came right to the bedside, sitting on the edge opposite mine. "I hear you're having contractions. We're going to get you hooked up to a monitor and see what's happening, okay?"

"All right." Sasha nodded, her hand clutching mine.

I pushed a lock of hair off her temple, feeling the sweat dampening her skin.

Robin gave her a kind smile, then stood to wash her hands. She was a flurry of movement, working fast and efficiently.

Where was that other nurse? Who was going to help Robin?

Maybe I should have driven Sasha to Bozeman. Maybe we should have raced for a city. But it was too late now. By the time Robin had Sasha hooked up to a monitor that showed the contractions, they were coming less than a minute apart.

"You're having this baby tonight," Robin said. "I'm going to go get a few things ready. Call button is on the bed's remote if you need anything."

"It's too early." The panic in Sasha's face was like a knife to my heart. "It's three weeks early."

"It is early, but you're on the cusp of full term," Robin said. "And your labor is progressing very quickly. Give me a few, all right? I'll be back soon."

Robin left the room in a hurry. She wasn't panicking, but she was moving damn fast. Was she a good enough doctor for this?

When I looked to Sasha, she had the same question in her beautiful eyes.

"It's too early, Jax." Fat, heavy tears streamed down her cheeks.

"She'll be okay." I bent, dropping my forehead to hers. "We're okay."

Sasha sniffled. "It was the walk. I shouldn't have—"

"Don't, darlin'. Don't second-guess. This stuff happens. It's not that early. All the checkups have been good. The timing on contractions are normal. It's going to be okay."

My voice sounded more confident than I actually felt, but thank fuck I'd read all of those pregnancy books. Otherwise, I'd be coming apart at the seams.

There were still plenty of risks. Complications. Preeclampsia. It was early, but it wasn't too early. We'd be okay. We had to be okay.

"I'm scared." Her chin quivered as her voice cracked.

"I got you." It was a fucking lie.

I was about to come out of my own damn skin, but for Sasha, I kept it together and rubbed her lower back as another contraction ripped through her body.

But she didn't scream. She didn't yell. She gritted her teeth through every second of the pain, her hands fisting the scratchy sheets, and endured it all.

When Robin returned, it was with three other nurses, each dressed in a shade of blue scrubs. *Fucking finally.* They brought a flurry of activity into the room, moving with practiced efficiency.

"Have you delivered a baby before?" I asked Robin.

"One hundred and twenty-three," she said, rolling a stool to the end of the bed before taking a pair of latex gloves from the rack on the wall. She kept talking as she had Sasha pull up her knees so she could do an exam. "I delivered a lot of babies during my residency. This is my first since I've come home. But we've got all the equipment necessary, and if needed, I can perform a C-section."

Sasha's eyes widened. She didn't want to have a C-section. She'd told me that at least five times.

"I don't think we'll need to," Robin said, reading the panic on her face. "The baby is in the perfect position. Her heart rate is normal. You're almost there. She's almost here."

Our daughter. Our baby girl.

"It's too early," Sasha whispered.

"We're ready." I clasped her hand in mine, leaning in to kiss her forehead.

"It hurts." She sniffled, wiping at her face as more tears fell. "Distract me. Tell me a secret."

"I love you."

The words came out in a rush. It was effortless. As automatic as breathing.

It was the easiest thing I'd ever said in my life.

Machines beeped. The nurse in the corner was saying something to Robin—who rolled her stool away.

But they all faded to a blur as I took Sasha's face in mine. "I love you. I think I loved you the moment you tried to steal that shopping cart."

"Jax." Sasha's eyes searched mine.

She didn't have to say it back. If she wasn't ready, that was okay. *I* was ready.

After everything she'd told me today with her parents, with her brother, maybe what Sasha needed most was the chance to live easy for a change. The chance to fall.

And know that I'd be here to catch her.

She opened her mouth, about to speak, when another contraction hit. It came with a whimper of agony, the first sign she was losing control.

"No one will care if you're loud. Let it out," I said as the pain faded and she collapsed onto the bed.

"I don't want her to hear me scream."

"Robin?" I hooked my thumb to where she was talking with a nurse. "Who fucking cares?"

"No." Sasha gave me a sad smile, her gaze dropping to her belly.

Josephine.

She didn't want to have the baby hear her scream.

Because she remembered sounds. And she didn't want that sound in this room.

I fucking *loved* this woman.

I kissed her, hard and fast, then backed away so she could rest before the next contraction. "Tell me a lie."

"I hate Montana."

A grin tugged at my mouth. "Mission accomplished."

"Now a secret," she murmured, still breathing hard. "Tell me to tell you a secret."

"Tell me a secret."

"I love you."

Three words and I could breathe. For the first time in what felt like my whole life, I could breathe.

I needed nothing else. Not money. Not fame. Not power or influence. Just Sasha.

Tears mingled with our lips as I kissed her, soft this time. But like the last, it was interrupted by another contraction. And another. And another. Like dominoes, falling faster and faster, until Robin had donned a cap and covered her scrubs with a teal long-sleeved gown and was positioned at Sasha's feet.

"Hold her leg, Jax," she ordered. "Sasha, when I tell you, you're going to push. Ready?"

Sasha locked her eyes with mine.

I locked my arm beneath her knee. "I've got you."

She gave me a sure nod. "Ready."

The room seemed to go silent. Robin kept talking. Sasha was panting. The nurses gave her encouraging words with every push. The blood roaring in my ears drowned out every bit of the noise.

Until a sound cut through the haze.

A screaming baby girl.

My Josephine.

Chapter 28
SASHA

There was magic in a hot shower. My hands were in my hair, lathering shampoo as I tilted my head back beneath the spray and let the water wash away the fog from a sleepless night.

A lifetime ago, I'd been washing my hair in a shitty rental, and the water had shut off. A smile tugged at my mouth as I rinsed my hair clean.

I wished I could go back to that day. To reassure my past self that it would all be okay. That soon, the man of her dreams would flip her world upside down. That the lonely years were over.

The smile was still on my face as I got out of the shower and wrapped a towel around myself. It lingered as I stared in the mirror at the dark circles under my eyes.

God, I was exhausted. Blissfully exhausted.

It was October nineteenth. My due date.

Josephine was three weeks old, and I'd forgotten what it felt like to sleep for more than two hours at a time.

We'd spent some time at the hospital. More time than I'd wanted. But when Robin had assured us Josephine was healthy and could come home, we'd brought her to the ranch.

Jax had driven us home, on a Tuesday at sundown, to the Haven River Ranch.

Josephine was healthy and growing. She was tiny and loud. She was the light of my life.

And so was her father.

After combing my hair, I left it to air-dry, then padded to the closet. My clothes stretched along one half, opposite Jax's on the other. The hamper was overflowing with his things and mine. The bed was unmade, the sheets rumpled and our pillows piled in the middle where we slept, curled around each other every night.

Dressed in a pair of loose pajama bottoms and a tank top, I snagged one of his flannels to wear, then walked out of the bedroom, expecting to hear the TV. When I'd gone to take a shower, Jax had been in the living room watching football while Josephine had been in her swing.

But I didn't hear a sound from the living room. The only noise was the steady whir from the sound machine in the nursery.

I peered inside, finding Jax in the rocking chair with our daughter in his arms.

My heart swelled, so big I pressed a hand over my chest.

She was asleep, her perfect face serene and her hands curled into tiny fists. He was asleep, too, his head resting on the back of the chair, his mouth slightly parted.

On our final night at the hospital, Josephine had been fussy. Jax had taken her from the plastic bassinet and held her in the uncomfortable, too-small recliner he'd slept in for days. They'd both fallen asleep, just like they were now. A nurse had come in and scolded us about not sleeping with the baby in a chair.

But I'd waved her off.

He'd never drop her. Asleep or awake, he wouldn't let her fall.

He wouldn't let *us* fall.

I eased the door closed, careful not to make a sound, then walked to the living room, surveying the mess.

In the corner was a box, the lid propped open to reveal a pair of caramel cowboy boots. *My* cowboy boots. Curtis had brought them over last night along with dinner from the lodge so we wouldn't have to cook. Somehow, he'd learned that I didn't have boots, and any daughter of his needed boots.

I'd cried, and Josephine had chosen that moment to cry too. There was a lot of crying at the moment.

Josephine's swing and bouncer bracketed the coffee table. On the rug beside the couch was a changing mat and a few stray diapers spilling out of their package. The Kindle that Emery had bought me last week so I could read during the sleepless nights was on an end table. Jax's coffee mug from breakfast was beside it on a coaster.

Every room was the same. His things. My things. The baby's things.

The house wasn't cramped or cluttered, but it was full of life.

Except there was still a piece missing. *Eddie.*

I walked to the island and pulled out a stool.

The diamond ring on my left hand glinted as I reached for the tote I'd left on the counter.

Jax had proposed three days ago over breakfast for dinner. He'd put the ring on top of my pancakes.

The minute he'd slid it onto my finger, I'd felt this rush of certainty that I was exactly where I'd always been meant to be. Those roots I'd felt growing months ago had finally taken hold. All of the hard days I'd endured had been for a reason: to get me to Montana.

To bring me to Jax.

Someday, I hoped Eddie could meet him.

I fished out my laptop from the tote, moving it to the side as I pulled out a stack of letters. My letters that Eddie had sent back.

If Jax had his way, these letters would be kindling for the fire he built every night in the hearth.

Maybe my relationship with Eddie would never recover from the day I'd left him at the camp. Maybe we'd grown apart a long time ago. Maybe what he needed was time.

But I was going to keep writing. I'd thought it would be best to take a break, but he hadn't told me to stop writing. He'd accused me of leaving him.

So I wasn't going to give up. Not until he told me to stop. Maybe not even then.

Fishing out a notepad and a pen, I didn't let myself overthink the words as they flowed onto the paper.

Dear Eddie,

You have a niece. You're an uncle. Her name is Josephine, for Mom. And her middle name is Bryan, for Dad. Not exactly a typical middle name for a girl, but it was Jax's idea. Someday, I hope you meet them both. She's got my dark hair and his blue eyes. She rarely sleeps and cries a lot, but she's perfect. Baby poop is this weird yellow color, it's so gross. She loves to be swaddled really tight so she can't move her arms or legs, like a baby burrito. And she has the best eyelashes.

I love you. Even when you're mad at me, even when I'm mad at you, I love you. And I miss you. Every day, I miss you.

Sasha

I'd just signed my name on the bottom when my phone rang. I slid off the stool, searching through the mess to find it on the charger beside the fireplace.

My stomach knotted at the name on the screen.

Micah.

The one and only time he'd called me in the past year that wasn't in reply to a message of mine was to tell me that Eddie had gotten into a fight with another student. That both students had been reprimanded and sequestered for a week.

Was this another fight? Or something worse? My heart climbed into my throat as I answered. "Hey, Micah."

"Sasha?"

That voice. I knew that voice. My heart skipped. "Eddie?"

"Yeah, it's me."

My hand came to my mouth.

"Are you there?"

"Yeah." I cleared my throat as tears filled my eyes. "I'm here."

"Micah said I could call you."

"I'm so glad." I wiped at my eyes, trying to stop the tears that just kept falling, but at least he couldn't see me cry. "How are you? Are you okay?"

"I guess. I was out in the mountains for a few weeks. It snowed up there already."

"Oh. It hasn't snowed here yet."

"You're still at that ranch or whatever?"

"Yes, I'm at the ranch. At home."

"That's good." His voice was deeper than I remembered. Rougher.

How much had he changed this past year? What did he look like now? More like Dad? Or had his features matured into his own?

Oh God. We were talking. He'd called me. I covered my mouth again so he wouldn't hear me cry.

"I, um, wanted to say sorry. About those letters. I was having a bad day. Got mad and wrote . . . you know."

Yes, I knew. I'd memorized every word.

"I didn't mean it, Sasha. I wanted to write you and say sorry, but then Micah sent me on a wilderness outing because I was being a dick. He didn't know I sent those letters back to you. He was out sick one day, and I lied to one of the other counselors that I needed to send my sister letters and that Micah had already reviewed them. I told him about it today in our session, and he's, uh, pretty pissed off at me."

"That's why you're calling."

"Yeah. I really am sorry."

I swallowed the lump in my throat. "Thanks."

"Are you, um, okay? Did you have a baby?"

"I did. I actually just wrote you a letter telling you all about her."

The line went silent for a few heartbeats. "You wrote me? Again?"

"I'll always write you, Eddie. No matter what."

He sniffled, like I wasn't the only one crying. "I miss you. A lot. I want to come home."

"Home looks a lot different than it did. I'm not going back to California."

"I don't care. I just want to be wherever you are."

I sucked in a breath, fighting to keep the wobble from my voice. "I think you'd really like the ranch. Maybe you could come visit whenever Micah says it's okay."

"He thinks I should stay here. Finish out school. Did he talk to you about that?"

"Yes. I think maybe that's a good idea."

"Yeah. I have pretty decent grades."

"I'm not surprised." It was never a matter of intelligence with Eddie. He was incredibly smart. But he'd just stopped doing the work. "What do you want to do? Stay?"

He'd already stayed longer than the court-mandated period.

"Yeah, kinda. I have some friends who are staying too."

"All right. I'll visit with Micah, and we can finalize a plan."

"'Kay." He sighed. "Maybe I can call you again."

"I'd really like that."

"Me too." He went quiet again. "Sasha?"

"Yeah?"

"Can you read me your letter? So I don't have to wait for it?"

I nodded and walked to the island, returning to the stool as I read him the note.

"Josephine Bryan," he murmured. "That's a cool name."

"I think so too."

"I better go. It's almost lunch. Talk to you later?"

"I'm here. I'm always here. Bye."

The minute I ended the call, a fresh wave of tears flowed. I took a minute to breathe, to dry my face, then I stood from the stool.

Jax was leaning against the wall in the hallway, Josephine still asleep in the cradle of his arm. He shoved off the wall and walked over, holding out his open arm. I fell into his side, burying my face in his chest.

"You heard?"

"Yeah, sweetheart." Jax kissed my damp hair. "I heard."

I wrapped my arms around his narrow waist, holding tight. "Tell me a lie."

"I'm not tired."

I laughed. "Tell me a secret."

"I love you."

That wasn't a secret. We didn't have secrets from each other, not anymore.

So for the rest of my life, whenever he wanted a secret, I'd say the same.

"I love you too."

Epilogue
JAX

Nine months later . . .

Josephine's hand smacked me in the cheek as she babbled. "Aye-aye-aye. Baaaah."

"Da-da." I snatched her fingers, pretending to bite them as she giggled. "Where's Mommy?"

Sasha was supposed to meet us in the lobby at the lodge fifteen minutes ago. It wasn't like her to be late or not reply to my texts. She wasn't in her office or the dining room or kitchen, and when I'd gone to the event space to see if she was still setting up for the rehearsal dinner, the only people who'd been there were Lily and Dad.

They'd volunteered to help our wedding coordinator with any last-minute decorations so that Sasha and I could just enjoy the party tonight.

Over the past nine months, Dad and Lily had settled into a friend-ship of sorts. A truce. They didn't talk often, but they talked. And for the first time in a long damn time, my family seemed at peace.

"Mamamama." Josephine's string of *mm*s and *ah*s wasn't a clearly enunciated Mama, but it was close. Too close.

Josephine hadn't said Mama or Dada perfectly yet. It was still just garbled baby talk. But it wouldn't be long until she figured it out.

Sasha and I had a bet going which she'd say first. The winner got to pick sexual positions for a month, and I had some ideas.

"Da-da," I told my daughter. "Da-da."

She stuck a finger in her mouth.

"Come on, butterfly. Let's see if we can track Mommy down." I kissed her cheek, then headed for the door.

The moment we stepped onto the porch, Sasha came rushing up the stairs.

"Hey, you."

"Hi." She sighed. "Sorry."

"That's okay." I held out my free arm and tucked her into my side. "Everything all right?"

"Yes?" She looked toward the old barn, where we'd spent most of the past week decorating for the wedding tomorrow. "Just slightly traumatized."

"Say what?"

She reached for Josephine, taking her from my arms to hold. Then she motioned for me to follow her to the side of the porch, away from the door and any guests walking by.

"I was in the storage room looking for one more vase. I thought it would be nice to have a small bouquet at the cake table. There was a box tucked away in the back corner behind the shelves, so I was digging around for something. Emery and Zak came in, and before I could tell them I was in there, they, uh . . ." She shuddered as she trailed off.

My jaw hit the boards beneath my boots. "They hooked up?"

"Yep." She popped the *p*. "And from everything I had to hear, no matter how hard I plugged my ears, it wasn't the first time."

"Holy shit."

"Yeah. I've been stuck in that room for thirty minutes. I didn't dare take my phone out to text you. I should have said something, but I thought they were just kissing and then . . . boom. Not just kissing."

So she'd huddled in a corner, eyes squeezed tight and fingers in her ears, sitting still and quiet so our friends could fuck.

A laugh escaped my mouth.

"It's not funny, Jax." Sasha poked me in the gut. "There are things I did not need to know about Emery."

I grimaced. "Keep those details to yourself, babe."

Sasha groaned. "Literally the most awkward moment of my life."

"Did they see you?"

"No. I waited until they left, then snuck out and came over here. Before we see them at the rehearsal, I need a few minutes."

She wasn't going to get it. From past her shoulder, Emery and Zak came walking over, taking the porch stairs.

"Hey, guys." Emery smiled wider than I'd seen in years. Probably because she'd just gotten laid.

I grimaced again.

"What?" She gave me a sideways glance.

"Nothing," I lied and waved to Zak. "Glad you guys could make it tonight."

"Wouldn't miss it." He glanced at Emery.

She was trying her hardest to look anywhere else as a flush crept into her cheeks.

Gross.

It was about damn time these two got together, but I really didn't need the visual of them screwing.

Poor Sasha.

"Is there anything we can help with?" Emery asked.

"I think we're all set," Sasha said, brushing a lock of Josephine's dark hair out of her eyes. "West and Indya should be at the meadow with the pastor. We all need to meet there in an hour."

"We'll make our way over. See if there's anything we can do," Zak said. "Want to ride together, Em?"

"Sure." She shrugged, a smile toying at her mouth. "I guess."

They were definitely going to fuck in the back seat of his truck. I gagged.

Luckily, neither Emery nor Zak saw it. They were both too busy trying not to look at each other or walk too close as they headed for the parking lot.

Emery and Calvin's divorce had been finalized for months. He was still around town, acting like an asshole, but he wasn't Emery's asshole anymore.

I hadn't realized she'd been spending time with Zak lately, but damn if I didn't hope it would last. They were good for each other.

"Well, at least that was a distraction." Sasha blew out a shaky breath, then took her phone from her pocket. "He should be here soon."

Eddie was on his way to the Haven River Ranch for the first time.

He was coming to be here for our wedding.

West was my best man. Indya was Sasha's matron of honor. The ceremony would be small and intimate at a meadow about a mile from here. But the reception would be a riot. Every person on the resort was coming. Friends and family too.

Finally, Sasha was going to be my wife.

It would have been easier to get married in the winter or spring, before the chaotic summer season at the resort, but Eddie hadn't been finished with his time at the camp.

So we'd waited until June.

Until he'd finished school, had his diploma, and could start on the next chapter of his life.

It had taken me some time to come around where Eddie was concerned. Early on, after those letters he'd sent Sasha, I'd been hesitant about their relationship. I did not want her hurt again.

But a lot had changed in the past nine months.

Mostly, Eddie seemed to have changed.

They talked daily. Every evening, they'd have a video chat so he could see Josephine. Sasha still wrote him letters, and occasionally, he'd write a reply.

He hadn't had any behavioral issues at the camp in months, and Micah had all the confidence in the world that Eddie was ready to move on.

Starting today.

So he'd packed up his things and, this morning, left the camp after almost two years. This summer, he was going to live in the cabin next door. He'd spend a few months reconnecting with Sasha. Getting to know Josephine. Figuring out where he'd go next.

Eddie had mentioned college. He'd also talked about getting a job and working to pay Sasha back for his camp fees. Whatever he decided, that kid was lucky. He'd have his sister's unwavering support.

"You okay?" I asked Sasha. Was this too much for one day? An emotional reunion with her brother. A rehearsal dinner for our wedding tomorrow.

"You got me, right?"

"I got you."

She leaned into my side. "Then I'm okay."

Josephine yawned and rested her head on Sasha's shoulder. There'd been so much happening today, she hadn't gotten a nap. Either she'd conk out despite the crowds and excitement. Or she'd turn into a little monster. If—*when*—that happened, Lily was going to steal her away and take her to the house.

Lily and I were in about the same place as she was with Curtis. It would take more than nine months to repair our relationship, but it was getting better and better every day. Mostly because she loved my baby girl. And the feeling was mutual.

There was a good chance Josephine wouldn't say Mama or Dada first. She'd probably say Nana.

A car appeared in the distance, and Sasha stood taller, watching as it pulled into the lot. "Do you think that's them?"

Normally, we would have gone to pick up Eddie, but Micah had offered to drive him here. He'd be spending the weekend at the lodge, either to act as a crutch for Eddie or because Sasha had told them enough about the resort that both were curious. So we'd invited him to the wedding.

The car parked, and when the passenger door opened and a tall, lanky young man stepped out, Sasha sucked in a sharp inhale.

Eddie.

He scanned the area, face blank. But the moment he spotted his sister, he smiled so bright it rivaled the afternoon sun. He tore away from the car, running toward the lodge.

I slipped Josephine out of Sasha's hold as Eddie bounded up the porch stairs two at a time and practically tackled his sister in a hug.

"Hi." He laughed, picking her up off her feet.

"Hi." She laughed, too, even as tears filled her eyes.

Her makeup case was in the truck with Josephine's diaper bag so she could touch it up before the rehearsal.

"I missed you," Eddie said.

"I missed you too."

I let out the breath I'd been holding since dawn. I'd expected this to go fine, given how often they talked. But there was always the chance that it would be awkward or tense.

Eddie let her go and gave her a smile as she wiped at her cheeks. Then his gaze, the same brown as Sasha's, landed on Josephine. "Hi, Jojo."

Jojo had been their dad's nickname for their mom.

Josephine hid her face in my shoulder.

"She's shy at first. But it won't last," Sasha told him.

"That's okay." Eddie touched her elbow, then held out a hand to me. "Hi, Jax. I'm Eddie Vaughn."

Spoken like a man, not an eighteen-year-old kid.

"Nice to meet you, Eddie." I shook his hand. "Glad you could be here."

"Me too."

Eddie was tall, close to my six-three. Something I hadn't noticed through the video calls. He was a good-looking kid with similar features to Sasha's. There was no disputing they were siblings. He hadn't filled out his broad frame yet, but he would in time.

He glanced to the parking lot, where Micah stood beside his car. The older man had a proud grin on his face. "I'd better go get my stuff out of Micah's car."

"I'll give you a hand," I said. "We'll load it into my truck."

"Thanks." Eddie turned to Sasha again, smiling. Then he gave her another quick hug before he rushed down the stairs, rejoining Micah.

The moment he was gone, Sasha exhaled.

An exhale nearly two years in the making.

"He's different," she said quietly. "He's like the kid I remembered from before."

From before their parents died.

"I'll help him with his stuff." I handed her Josephine, knowing that holding our daughter for a few minutes would help her relax. Then I kissed her hair before striding across the porch.

When I glanced back, Sasha was swaying with Josephine in her arms. My heart swelled, like it always did when I watched them together.

All those months she'd been so scared about becoming a mother. She was an incredible mother. Our daughter was a lucky girl.

I was a lucky man.

It didn't take long to meet Micah and move Eddie's stuff to the truck. Then we all set off for the meadow, gathering with everyone for the rehearsal.

Once we'd practiced walking down the aisle, standing at the altar West and I had built, we all congregated at the barn for dinner. I was at the bar getting a beer when a hand clapped my shoulder.

Eddie smiled as he stood beside me, ordering a Coke from the bartender. "Thanks for letting me stay here."

"Of course." Effective tomorrow, he was my brother too. We'd do whatever we could to help him keep his feet.

"Sasha said she told you everything. About me." He swallowed hard. "Just want you to know I'm not that guy. I won't get into trouble."

"Appreciate that. I'd be lying if I said it hadn't crossed my mind."

"That's fair." He nodded. "I was angry for a long time. Micah's helped me see that I aimed it at Sasha instead of dealing with my emotions. She saved my life, sending me to that camp. I'll spend the rest of my life making that up to her."

I believed every word. "Glad you're here, Eddie."

"Me too," he said. "You don't have to say yes, but do you think you could teach me to ride?"

"Absolutely."

"Cool." He grinned, then filtered into the crowd mingling before dinner.

He'd mostly hung close to Micah during the rehearsal, but I'd seen him talking to West and my grandparents too.

Sasha was sitting at the table, holding a sleeping Josephine in her arms as she talked to Indya. Kade rushed over, whispering something in Indya's ear that made her eyes bulge and her body fly out of her chair. Then they both streaked out of the room, probably to find Kohen and whatever trouble the twins had found.

I took Indya's vacated chair, inching closer to Sasha as I threw a hand over the back of her chair. "Tell me a lie."

"This is the worst night of my life." She kissed me, then Josephine's forehead.

The baby girl in her arms who'd brought us together. Who'd made us a family.

Not an accident. Not a mistake. Our miracle.

"Tell me a secret," I said.

I expected her to say I love you, just like she always did these days when I asked for a secret. Instead, the corner of her delicious mouth turned up.

And she whispered into my ear.

"I'm pregnant."

Acknowledgments

Thank you for reading *Sunlight*! The Haven family has stolen my heart, and I hope you loved reading this book as much as I loved writing it!

Thanks to Maria Gomez and the team at Montlake! Thanks to Elizabeth Nover. To Georgana Grinstead. Thanks to Nicole Resciniti. To Vicki Valente and Logan Chisholm. And to my friends and family. I am so grateful for you all and unbelievably blessed to have you at my side.

About the Author

Photo © 2019 Lauren Perry

Devney Perry is a #1 Amazon, *Wall Street Journal*, and *USA Today* bestselling author of over forty romance novels. After working in the technology industry for a decade, she abandoned conference calls and project schedules to pursue her passion for writing. She was born and raised in Montana and now lives in Washington with her husband and two sons.

Don't miss out on Devney's latest book news. Subscribe to her newsletter!

www.devneyperry.com